When I Wasn't Looking

A Big Prairie Romance
Jennifer Rodewald

Rooted Publishing

Rooted Publishing

McCook, NE 69001

Email: jen@authorjenrodewald.com

https://authorjenrodewald.com/

CONTENTS

PROLOGUE

JUNE 1957

My Dearest Clara,

I feel like the stars are within reach. These hills lift me up, and anything is possible. The night sky above me dances with starlight. There is energy and beauty here, so different from our dusty plains. So much promise. Though I hated your tears, I know now that this was the right choice for me. Adventure is my insatiable need, and the success I know I am capable of fuels me onward. I cannot deny it any more than I could deny breath to my body.

But you are still my desire.

When I close my eyes, I see yours. So green and full of mischief and set aflame with passion. For me, I hope. Still, always, for me. Say you feel it too, my darling. Tell me it will always be so.

Miles cannot douse this passion we share, nor can time tame it.

I will make something of myself. If the Duke from Iowa can, so can I. And after, I will send for you. You will love the life I will make for us.

Wait for me, my beautiful one. We will be together again.

—H

CHAPTER ONE

HE DID NOT WANT to go.

As Grant Hillman jogged the wide dirt path, the image of that pesky invitation refused to be smudged from his mind. With it, the RSVP card. Today was the deadline. Grant did not like saving things for the last minute. He also did not like feeling like he must do something he did not want to do. And he strongly did *not* want to go to Craig and Brenna's wedding.

Why would they have included him on the guest list, anyway?

A dumb question. A rhetorical one, as Big Prairie was a small town. If they didn't invite him, everyone would talk. If he did not show up, people would talk.

If he did show up, no plus-one at his side, people would still talk. And shoot him not-so-surreptitious looks of pity. He did not like pity any more than he liked last-minute action. Or messes. Or things that slipped outside his control.

Grant pushed his strides into the incline of the running path, his mind moving at least double the pace of his feet.

Life was strange. This jogging thing he'd taken up, for example. He'd never been a runner. Not until he'd started dating Big Prairie's most celebrated runner. Brenna had been a high school distance state champion, a runner in college, and should have been a contender for the US Olympic team. Should have been, if Craig Erikson hadn't wrecked her entire world and left her brokenhearted in the middle of a crisis.

Grant's high school and college résumé basically read *quiet, rarely noticed, straight-A, average non-athlete*. Nothing at all like the home-town-hero-turned-famous-college-running-back that Craig had been. Grant never could compare to Craig, but Brenna had dated Grant anyway. It had been heady and sweet and mystifying—and that had been both good and bad.

Not that any of that mattered now.

Craig Erikson had come home again. At that point reality had become clear: Brenna was never going to be over Craig. Craig, and Craig alone, had her whole heart—it was never going to be Grant's.

Now the pair, who had been Big Prairie's *it* couple back in high school, were finally meeting at the end of an aisle, ready to pledge a lifetime together.

Good for them.

Honestly, Grant was happy for them. Happy for Brenna because she had her smile back. The one that was easy, lit her eyes, and spoke of peace rather than the wish for it. He wanted that for her.

That did not mean he wanted to play witness to the wedding. Was that wrong? After all, for a time he had sort of thought he would be the groom in that scene.

Would Craig and Brenna even notice if Grant attended?

Surely not.

The incline flattened, and Grant eased the strain of his strides as the trail led him into a stretch of birch and ash trees. He rolled his shoulders to work the tension out of his tight muscles as he settled into an easier pace. In front of him, the pathway stretched about the length of a football field, and then a gentle curve would take him to the river's edge for a quarter mile. Perhaps he would stop at the water, let his heart rate slow, and take in the shimmering green canopy of trees that tunneled over the river.

Next to the water, as the gentle current rippled silvery white in the late-May morning sun, he could fix his mind toward prayer, toward surrender, as he caught his breath. Perhaps then he would be ready to fill out that RSVP card: attending, one. He would then go online and purchase a gift, and after that, write out a card wishing the happy couple all the best and God's blessings on their life.

He would mean it too. Despite the sting in his chest.

God still saw him. Surely He did. Surely there was good ahead for Grant Hillman—even if he was an odd duck.

Mind made up, Grant slowed to a walk as he approached the shoreline. Once at the threshold of water, he lowered to sit on the damp silt. Later, he would regret the choice. He did not like messes, and without a doubt the black earth would cling to his sweaty running shorts. Sometimes, however, Grant deviated from his need for cleanliness and structure.

Sometimes.

His chest heaved and collapsed as his breath puffed, the rhythm slowing as he sat. Arms locked over his knees, Grant gripped one wrist in the other hand and stared over the sparkling water. His thoughts returned to where they'd just been, and he shifted them into prayer.

You see me, right? You'll bring good from this?

There was already good. Brenna was happy—that was good.

But I'm still here . . .

Emotion squeezed his chest, and he pinched his eyes shut. The prayer was not a new one. Grant could remember whispering such words ever since he was a teen. Since he realized he was really different from the other kids and his uniqueness had a way of isolating him.

When every other boy in his world was throwing balls and getting grass stains and smelling like the pungent mess only a male teen could muster, Grant was learning spreadsheets because he liked organization. He was practicing the cello because music spoke a language his soul understood. He was reading classical literature because they used precise language, unlike modern young adult books, and Grant preferred accuracy and specifics. He was lurking in his bedroom or at the tire swing in the gully by his house because he preferred quiet to the commotion of baseball games or group activities. And that way he could generally avoid his dad's inquiries about doing normal things, like football.

What kid grew up in Nebraska and did not love football?

It wasn't that Grant did not like football. As a game of strategy and strength, both mental and physical, he appreciated it, along with many other sports. It was the team togetherness that bothered him. Full locker rooms. Team huddles. Sweaty bodies in tight spaces.

No thank you.

Grant was a loner, and usually that was okay. Except when it made him feel . . . like an outsider. Big Prairie was like that old sitcom *Cheers*, a place where everyone knew your name. There was nothing worse when one lived in a small town like Big Prairie than to feel like an outsider.

Perhaps there was one thing worse—to feel like the outsider in your own home.

Grant was an odd duck. He had always been an odd duck. He did not do well in crowds or in most social settings, yet, though it seemed a contradiction, he battled loneliness. He owned an ever-present longing to be seen. To be accepted, even in his oddities.

To be loved.

Though fully recovered from his jog, Grant's heart rate surged. It always happened that way, when he allowed his thoughts to linger on the thing he felt was most out of reach.

But You see me, right? He put his thoughts toward what he knew in his heart. *You know when I sit and when I rise. You perceive my thoughts from afar.* Straight from the Word. God knew him.

He shut his eyes and returned to prayer.

You love me...

Sometimes that was a statement. A reminder and a reassurance. Sometimes, however, it was more of a question. Perhaps more often than Grant liked to admit. Specifically, when a wound to his heart had not yet fully closed.

Brenna Blaum was such a wound, and that silent prayer was a query, not a confidence.

Grant squeezed his fist against the surge of disappointment and then lifted his eyes to gaze across the river at the opposite shore. The small bank ran into a miniature escarpment—a wall of earth full of exposed roots and a smattering of determined vegetation. A narrow path—likely a game trail—climbed its way up twelve feet, leading to the level land above. Trees and shrubs filled his vision as he traced the land to his right. Among them, nearly hidden in the shadows cast by the canopy, stood the outline of a weather-beaten two-story farm home.

Old Man Teller's place.

A house of secrets and speculation. Old Man Teller was, like Grant, a loner. To the point he had rarely been seen in town. Unlike Grant, Mr. Teller was also named an angry hermit. It was the latter, rather than the former, that had truly isolated the man. Stories in town held that the man had lost his wife and son years before—long before Grant had been born—to his cold personality.

And if whispers were to be believed, he'd lived a lifetime of bitter regret.

A few people in Big Prairie had tried to reach out to the aging man. Most had failed.

The only person Grant knew who had made it through the front door was Miss Jane. No one knew exactly how the elderly lady managed it, and she would not say. Miss Jane was as tight-lipped about Harold Teller as the government was about Area 51. Grant suspected her cherry preserves might have had something to do with her feat. That, and her tough-as-nails determination.

Grant liked Miss Jane. Even if Miss Jane seemed not to care much for him—not after he'd started dating Brenna.

And there he was again, full circle. Back to Brenna Blaum.

Grant ran both hands over his face and into his hair and sighed. Or more accurately, growled. It was done. He and Brenna had been done for months, and Grant had done the breaking up. He had been okay. Truly, he had been. Right up until that blasted wedding invitation had been delivered. Good grief, that had been fast. Six months, give or take?

Why did that rub him so wrong?

In the place he had hoped an answer would be forthcoming, instead throbbed a vacant ache. Not for her, but for . . .

He did not know what.

Sitting there on a dirty log letting his thoughts dive into empty spaces was not helping. Grant stood, stretched his arms one way and then the other, and pivoted to return to the running path. As he stepped away from the water's edge, however, a splash made him stop dead. Spinning, Grant searched the river while panic surged in his veins.

The river was not deep. There were a few spots of ten-to-fifteen-foot pools, but in general the water only ran between two and four feet deep above the flat rocks that made up the bed. That splash had not been small. Not a sound made by a falling stone or branch. It had to have been—

A body broke the surface. Grant's heart stalled, and he did not even think before he charged into the water.

· · · · ● · ● · · ·

Great mother of pearl!

Sage's eyes flew open when a pair of arms hauled her up, dragging her from the gloriously chilled water beneath her back. Self-preservation kicked in full-fight mode, and she pushed at the muscled chest that she was locked against.

"Do not fight me," a deep rumble above her ear snapped. "I have got you, and I'm a decent swimmer, but you cannot fight."

"The heck I won't!" With the heel of her palm, Sage jabbed upward, intending to place a blow against this violator's nose. Her aim, blurred by the water dripping from her eyelashes, was off. She smashed his jaw instead.

"Ouch!" The arms that imprisoned her gripped tighter. "Woman, you are making this hard!"

"There's no way in the hottest part of Texas that I would make this easy for you, jerkwad."

The person holding her stilled. "What?"

He'd swam past the deep hole in the river that Sage had claimed as her swimming hole, and he had braced his stance against the sandy shale of the shallower riverbed.

"Let me go, villain! This body wasn't made to satisfy your lusts." Had she just spouted that in all seriousness? Pretty sure that was a line she'd narrated not too long ago. She might need to have a real conversation every now and then.

"My—" The arms that had been iron bars clasped around her dropped, and this stranger let Sage splash back into the water.

With a gasp, Sage plunged beneath the deeper water, and she kicked with all her muscles away from her assailant before she broke the surface again. While shoving her long, drenched hair out of the way, she spun around to gauge the evil man's position.

He stood on the solid base of the shallows, staring at her as if she'd lost her mind. "My lusts?" Dark brows drew inward, his mouth agape.

"Yes, *lusts*." Sage stayed in character—she didn't know why. Maybe out of habit? Perhaps because this guy seriously scared the bejeezus out of her . . . Or maybe, somewhere deep inside, buried beneath the very real fear the man had triggered, something in her latched on to the possibility that this could be entertaining.

Was she that nuts? Crazy did run in the family . . . Grandma Clara had been in memory care for years before she'd passed. Anger and dementia were a bad combination, by the way.

Sage pushed that thought toward the floor of her mind.

"That's what it's called, pervert. But you won't find me weak or willing. I will fight you at every moment. You won't walk away unscathed." Wow. She wished she was wearing her mic. This could be epic.

His brows folded downward farther. "Did you hit your head?"

"I beg your pardon?"

"Are you okay?"

"No! I'm not okay. I've been attacked." And also, she might be slightly damaged by a wee bit too much fiction combined with way too much time spent on her own, with imaginary people as her only companions.

"Do you know where you are?"

"What do you mean by such stupid questions?" Sage swam to the opposite edge and scrambled her way to the shore. "I did *not* hit my head. I'm not imagining anything, and I am completely in my right mind." *Maybe.* "I know exactly where I am. I know who I am. What I don't know, and I don't care to know, is who *you* are. You're a creeper. A villain. A lowlife man who sneaks up on unsuspecting young women to have his way with them."

Take that, jerkwad. Sage thrust her chin forward and crossed her arms over her chilly chest.

Mouth unhinged, the man began looking around them. To her side of the shore. Then his. Into the trees that surrounded them. Up toward Grandfather's ramshackle house.

Sage's heart rate throbbed with panic as her attacker silently assessed their surroundings. Suddenly reality overtook her easily triggered and abundant imagination. This could actually be a *very* serious situation. Not fictional. Not scripted.

Like, completely for real.

She could be in a whole lot of danger.

CHAPTER TWO

WHAT COULD SHE DO?

Sage's long, soaked broom skirt stuck to her wet legs, serving as a handicap to what she already knew would be a pathetically slow run—and that would be up the steep trail. Once there, where could she go? Gramps's place was hardly a fortress, and the frail old man she'd only met two weeks before would hardly serve as any protection. And even if he did, he was more bark than bite.

She was trapped. In trouble. Alone in a place she barely knew, facing a man who could overpower her despite her dramatic and feisty spirit.

"God, help," she muttered. A strange thing for her. She didn't actually believe in a god who cared one way or another about the doings of people on earth. Worth a shot, though? Perhaps it was just what all people cried in crisis. Like sneezing when you stepped into the sun—an uncontrollable and involuntary reaction.

"Is this a joke?"

Her attention ripped back to her foe. "What?"

"Like one of those ridiculous *gotcha* videos?" He scowled, his fingers rolling into fists at his side. "Is that what this is? You are making fun of me?"

He seemed . . . insulted. Deeply. Not angry, like his despicable plot had been thwarted. But *offended*, like she'd impugned his character. Still clutching her skirts, ready to raise them should she need to run, Sage's tense body eased a fraction. "This is no joke, sir."

"Why are you speaking this way?"

"What?"

"Like this is a scene from a novel. Why are you talking like this?"

"I am not." Sage nearly snorted at her own lie.

"You sound scripted." He looked around again.

For cameras? Did he seriously think she was punking him?

Okay, so she *had* gone into her dramatic zone. Could he blame a girl? After all, he'd attacked her. Could he seriously expect her to have a calm, rational, contemporary conversation about it?

"You attacked me."

"I did not."

"Are you calling me a liar?"

He rubbed his jawline, which dripped with river water. "I am thinking that you hit your head when you fell."

"Fell?" Sage snorted. "I didn't fall."

"You did. From up there." He pointed toward the overlook that was the edge of Grandfather's backyard.

"I'm telling you, I did *not* fall. I jumped."

Dropping his hand, he shot a fierce and disapproving scowled at her. "That was foolish. This river isn't deep."

"As you can now attest, mister, the river right here"—Sage pointed to her swimming hole— "is perfectly safe. At least ten feet deep. I've jumped more than once."

"You could have missed. You could have hit your head."

"I've already told you I didn't."

"I had no way of knowing that five minutes ago. All I knew was that there was a splash, and then your body, fully clothed, floated to the surface."

After glancing down at herself, Sage released her grip on her wet skirt entirely. "Do you mean to say you were *saving* me?"

Perhaps jumping into a river with a skirt on was strange. Not really for her—she was hot and wanted cooled off, that was all—but for others.

He crossed his arms over his chest, offense still carved into his frown. "You looked dead."

A hero? Oh, Sage loved a decent hero! That changed everything about this encounter. A tiny grin poked against one corner of her mouth. "That's not a very complimentary thing to say to a woman you've never met."

Lips parting once again, he gaped at her in stunned silence.

Deciding that he was, in fact, entirely harmless and telling the truth, Sage let her smile bloom full. Keeping to the shallows that ringed her swimming hole, she splashed her way toward him.

He backed away until the water receded from his hips to his lower calves. Gaze never leaving her face, his dark-brown eyes screamed wariness as she approached. Like he thought she might be one of those man-eating mermaids from *Pirates of the Caribbean*, out to drag him into the depths of her lair and have *her* way with *him*.

Oh, the delicious irony!

That nearly provoked an out-loud giggle. What a lovely plot she'd fallen into! Sage kept the laugh inside though, not wanting to startle away this already-stunned man.

She slowed her splashing steps and edged nearer as if she were approaching a frightened stray dog. This was a stark turn of events for the space of only three minutes. Cautiously, so as not to spook the clearly wary man, she slipped a hand toward him.

"I'm Sage," she said softly.

The man continued to stare at her. Bewildered. "Sage?"

"Yeah. That's me." She gestured to herself. "Sage." It felt like a scene from the early American colonies. She the English, he the wary Native.

Oh how she wanted to giggle!

He inspected her, his penetrating look moving from her eyes to scan her forehead, then both sides of her face.

"I promise I didn't hit my head. And I'm only a little crazy." Sage winked. "Just enough to be fun."

The skepticism didn't vacate his expression, though he did unfold his tightly crossed arms and reached to accept her offered hand. Silence was all that came from his pressed lips.

He was stern. Serious. Entirely too much so. Not someone Sage would usually bother with, because life had considerable heaviness all by itself. Sage wasn't looking to add such weighty people to the load.

But there was something about him. Something with depth and possibilities—both of which went beyond the obvious fact that he was well-built and possessed an easy-on-the-eyes profile.

Book-speak for *the man was handsome*.

And those dark eyes, they held . . . intrigue?

Likely her flourishing imagination. Even so, Sage's insatiable thirst for a good tale held her curiosity directly on this villain who turned out to be more heroic (at least in attempt) than evil.

She smiled wide. "This is the part of the scene where you give me your name."

"It is?"

"Yes. You do have one, right?"

"One . . ." The confusion molding his brow struck Sage as mildly adorable.

"A name," she said. "Or shall I refer to you as the attempted hero?"

"That is . . ." The confusion slid into full disbelief. "That is not necessary."

Sage tilted her head and employed her best teasing voice. "Perhaps it's ridiculous."

Joy of the day! The man smiled. It was timid, still baffled, and yet glorious.

"Yes. That title would be ridiculous." He shook his head as his grip on her hand firmed. "Grant."

"Grant?"

"Yes. I am Grant Hillman."

Sage pumped his hand once and then slid her fingers from his. "Well, Grant Hillman, you have the distinguished honor to be my first real acquaintance in Big Prairie. Aside from my grandfather and the woman who delivers his groceries. Aren't you lucky?"

"Not on a regular basis."

Sage raised an eyebrow. "Once again, not complimentary, Grant."

An adorable touch of crimson crept up his neck and threatened to spill over his face. Grant looked away and rubbed his jaw.

Sage kicked a light spray of water toward him. "You're forgiven. For now."

Glancing back at her, Grant's expression folded back into uncertainty. "Forgiven?"

"For all of it. Scaring me silly. Manhandling me. Not being gentlemanly. The whole lot. Only because we've just met, mind you. I'll have higher expectations in the future."

His silent stare felt both unnerving and thrilling. Sage wasn't sure what that meant. She hoped the beginning of a new and delightfully interesting friendship. Given that Gramps was both hard and failing and that her mother was not thrilled Sage was with him at all, she could do with something delightful, and she never tired of anything interesting.

When Grant failed to speak again, Sage spoke again. "We will have a future, won't we, Grant Hillman? After all, you owe me."

"Owe you? I thought you were hurt. Or dead."

"We already covered that."

His mouth moved twice before his voice worked. "Oo . . . oh."

"So we're agreed?"

"About what?"

"The future. That you'll do better in the future to meet my expectations."

"I do not . . . I mean . . . what . . ." Grant stopped trying to talk as perplexity left his mouth gaping yet again.

Sage laughed from her belly. Full force. She then settled a sincere smile on him and waited. Hoping . . .

Ah. There it was again. His timid-but-worth-all-the-effort grin. "You are teasing me."

"I am."

"I see."

She bit her lip, though her grin would not be tamed.

"Do you always tease?"

"As often as possible. Are you always serious?"

"More than most."

"Then our friendship will be an adventure—a collision of opposites." She stepped near enough to nudge him with her arm and relished a tickle of delight when his grin warmed into a full smile, certainly without his conscious permission.

"I think I should tell you I am uncompromisingly boring," he said. "You can ask anybody in town."

Sage shook her head.

"And I do not lie."

"I believe you." Sage stepped away, splashing toward her side of the river as she went and letting her semi-damp skirt trail along the water's surface. "But I do love a good adventure, Grant Hillman. And opposite characters make the most interesting stories."

When she reached the damp black earth of the shore, she looked back at him. He hadn't shifted an inch, and his gaze remained trained intently on her. All bewildered and serious and intrigued.

And handsome.

Sage couldn't help but thrill at that combination.

"I do look forward to beginning ours. Saturday afternoon, I think. Here." She pointed up to her grandfather's property.

He didn't respond. Sage didn't wait. She climbed her way up the trail, leaving him standing in the river.

Likely that was the first and only time she'd see Grant Hillman. Given that she'd just been her best weird self, leaving him gaping and statuesque. Once he broke through the trance, he'd be gone, never to be seen again.

But she hoped not.

Chapter Three

Sage. Sage . . . what? He had not even had enough wherewithal to ask for her last name. And yet the woman—quite possibly a made-up person created by his excessively lonely and stressed mind—remained firmly wedged in his head.

And the shocking part? Grant was grateful for it. With Sage, the possibly-not-real mystery woman taking up all the space in his thoughts, there was no room left for Brenna Blaum.

Ah yes. There she was again. Brenna. Soon to no longer be Blaum. The wedding . . . that was where Grant had left off. He needed to respond to the wedding invitation.

Freshly showered and dirty clothes that had smelled of sweat, earth, and—thanks to the mysterious Sage woman—river, now dutifully spending time in the wash cycle, Grant padded his bare feet across the clean wood floor of his kitchen, aiming for the low desk he kept in front of the back window. On the clean surface was his laptop—shut down, closed, and precisely positioned with an inch margin of desk at the top and to the left. His planner was top center, also closed and with the black gel Sharpie pen capped securely and lying exactly parallel to the planner, an inch of desk separating the two.

On the right-hand side, the desk lamp sat ready for duty, not a speck of dust littering its stand or globe shade. Positioned beneath the lamp was the rectangular wire basket in which he kept important papers. Bills waiting to be filed the night after the automatic payments went through. The reminder of the class coming up that would fulfill the last of the continuing education requirements to renew his child therapy license. And atop all those, that invitation. The one he had wanted to throw away but his compulsive need to do things properly would not allow. The one waiting for him to attend to, as was correct.

Posture straight, Grant lowered onto the chair, retrieved the invitation from the basket, and uncapped the Sharpie pen. With one quick swipe, he checked the box next to *attending* and then slid his hand over to fill in the number of guests.

One.

Yes, he would spell it out, not simply use the numeric value. Except, he didn't write it. Instead, his pen hovered over the blank, and the woman—Sage—rebloomed in his mind. Oddly, the distraction made him smile. Again.

And he let her steal his attention. A very un-Grant Hillman thing to do.

She was quirky with her dramatic speeches and flourishing movements. Not to mention the fact that she had jumped from a height of twelve feet into a river known mostly as shallow. More, that she was apparently staying at Old Man Teller's house—and how had Grant not thought to ask why?

And she expected a friendship between them. Should that alarm Grant?

Yes. Yes it should. As should the fact that he found such a free-spirited woman interesting to the point of absurd distraction.

But it did not. He felt keenly something entirely *not* alarm.

Perhaps because Sage was quirky. Or maybe because he did not actually think she was real?

No, that *would* alarm him.

Sage was real. He'd felt her weight and flesh in his arms. Heard her lilting voice. Enjoyed the brightness of her smile, once she had decided he would not harm her.

And, ah . . . that smile. A lovely smile on a beautiful face, with a pair of doe-brown eyes that shimmered with invitation.

Come into my world. There is laughter and fun here.

Grant sat back—slouching—and held the open pen aloft while he enjoyed the memory of Sage's smile. Of her dancing eyes, set off by the shining wet ringlets of fiery red hair. Her face had been oval and smattered with a rich constellation of freckles—none of which Sage had tried to hide, as Grant had not detected one bit of makeup on her creamy skin.

Sage was fresh and lovely and wild and . . . and captivating.

Grant might have lost his mind.

At the moment, he didn't miss it. He sat forward, fixing his posture as it ought to be and focusing his mind on the task. *Attending: one.*

Though his mind instructed that, his hand went rogue. When he pulled the tip of the pen from the RSVP card, he read instead *Attending: two.*

The ink dried. The deed was done.

Something twisted in Grant's chest. Painful and breathtaking, like panic.

Or maybe not. Perhaps the sharp twist was not panic at all. Maybe it was something else utterly. This was not normal—not like him at all.

Grant smiled as thrilling adrenaline raced through his veins.

· · · • · • · · · ·

The swordplay had been excellent.

At least, what had taken place within her imagination had been. Propelled by clever dialogue and perfectly timed action, the words on her tablet had sent her on a voyage to another time, another place. There, she was Captainess Everly Roark battling against her nemesis, the no-good pirate Wilder Hawk.

Removing the noise-canceling headphones and swiping her best mic away from her mouth, Sage wandered from her closet-turned-studio into the tiny upstairs bedroom she'd claimed and dropped onto her Moon Pod in a gloriously spent heap.

There had been a heart-stopping moment between Captainess Everly and Wilder Hawk. Eyes locked, breath panting, his gaze had grown dark and penetrating and ever so captivating! Oh, this story was so good. More than one plot twist ahead.

Sage hoped with every stitch of her creative self that she'd done the scene justice. Such vivid and captivating storytelling deserved her best. And as every committed narrator knew, the voice behind the narration could make or break a book. It was a heavy responsibility. She hoped the author would be thrilled with her work.

As she nestled into the beanbag chair, her heart rate settled back toward a resting rhythm. Twirling a corkscrew curl around her right index finger, Sage laid her head back, shut her eyes, and smiled.

Every good romance must have a sword fight. And a pirate who was more than a dirty rotten scoundrel.

Triggered by that, her thoughts shifted out of the world of fiction and directly to the man who had played the part of villain-to-more in her own little world.

She chuckled.

Grant had not exactly been a pirate, with his confused looks, stumbling retorts, and oh-so-clean-cut appearance. But he had been memorable. Over the two days since he'd "rescued" her, Sage had wondered about the man. Why had he been out this way, when in the two weeks since she'd been at Gramps's, she'd seen exactly one person dare to come that close to the farmhouse? No one bothered Old Man Teller, it seemed.

Crochety old duffer that he was, she didn't wonder why. While Sage had found that the rumors of his constant drunkenness had been greatly exaggerated, his crankiness was shockingly uniform.

No one dared to visit—that was, except Miss Jane. Sage had met her on the third day of her stay when the older woman had marched herself straight up to the front door, no fear in sight, not knowing Sage was even there.

"Don't take in no company, girl," Grandfather had grouched sternly, but Sage had opened the door anyway.

She found a lovely old lady with bright twinkling eyes and a firm determination concealed cleverly by a friendly smile. They exchanged a brief interlude of niceties, and then the woman thrust a box of canned goods into Sage's hands.

"Oh, thank you, Mrs. . . . uh, I didn't catch your name. I'm sorry."

"Miss Jane, my girl. That's what everyone in Big Prairie calls me." The woman leaned in and peered around the door, raising her voice a touch. "And Harold Teller does not scare me one bit. He's all bark and no bite. And even when he does try to bite, he's a terrible shot."

She paused with a wink. "No—on second thought, I rather think he's a brilliant shot. Not everyone can narrowly miss every single time." Then the woman, who certainly must be about the same age as Gramps, smirked, a knowing depth shining in her blue eyes.

"How many times has Gramps shot at you?" Sage had asked, though not horrified, as one might expect. Rather, she enjoyed this fun little twist in Gramps's lonely existence.

"Me?" Miss Jane snorted. "Not once. He knows I know his bluff, so he doesn't waste the ammo. There are a few men from town, however . . ." At that, Miss Jane laughed. She passed a basket of fresh biscuits and homemade cherry preserves from her arm to Sage's, then turned to go her way. "I'm in town on Main Street most days, if you need me, Sage

Greene. And"—she again lifted her voice—"that goes for you too, Harold. As always, you'd be welcome."

Gramps growled.

Miss Jane turned to go, lifting a hand in a backward wave as she continued toward the blue truck parked at the end of Grandfather's drive. Miss Jane hadn't come alone, as there was a blond woman in the driver's seat. Interesting that the younger of the pair had kept to the truck, engine running, and stayed at the *far* end of the drive.

Something intriguing in this otherwise dusty and cluttered isolated life Gramps lived. Sage yearned to imagine what sort of story there might be between crusty old Gramps and the lively Miss Jane.

And so had gone Sage's only encounter with anyone in Big Prairie. Right up until Grant Hillman had hauled her out of the river.

What another captivating little episode that had been. Hopefully with another scene to unfold.

Would Grant dare to come out to the old Teller place, as Sage had commanded?

Opening her eyes and craning her neck forward, she looked at her smartwatch—1:52. The whole morning had gone by, and Grant Hillman hadn't made an appearance.

It was Saturday, wasn't it?

She checked her smartwatch again. Yep. Saturday.

Had she given him a time?

Of course she hadn't. Sage didn't operate on *time.* She woke when she felt like it. Began narrating when her voice was good and warm and ready. Stopped when the strain in her throat told her that was enough. Read ahead for clarity. Ate when her stomach said she should. Planned a garden for the backyard, hoping for fresh produce this summer—if she stayed that long. And swam when the air conditioner–less house pushed her out the door and toward the river.

Time was an overrated convention. And Sage Greene had never been one for conventions.

She was, however, one for the completion of a fascinating narrative. Which meant that she *willed* Grant Hillman's appearance.

It would be such a disappointment otherwise.

CHAPTER FOUR

GRANT WALKED THE FAMILIAR path, though he took in the scenery as if it were new. Apparently, things looked different at a walk rather than a jog. Squirrels came into focus, and they chided him thoroughly for intruding on their wooded premises, interrupting their gathering of early food. The trees overhead became less of a Monet of green, blue, and brown and more of a crisp photograph of fresh spring leaves bursting open against a clear-blue sky.

It was a lovely day. One perfect for a jog. But Grant wasn't out for a jog—if he had been, he would have done so long before late afternoon. Before the flighty spring weather of Nebraska dialed up to summer-like temperatures.

He had skipped his morning jog though. Not much like himself at all. But the trail of his thoughts—not to mention the odd twists of his usually measured emotions—had not been typical either.

How could one strange encounter with an odd woman flip his personality like this? Grant Hillman was a master at self-control. Why then could he not take in hand his wandering mind? He knew no more than her name—Sage—and yet the little red-haired fairy that he might well have imagined had taken possession of his thoughts.

Who was she?

Where did she come from?

Why was she in Big Prairie at Old Man Teller's?

What sort of a woman flung herself, fully clothed, off a ledge into a river twelve feet below?

Why on earth could he not stop thinking of her?

Compulsive behavior was part of his ... personality. Grant knew enough about himself, clinically speaking, to come up with that analytical fact in answer to that last question. He did not like things left undone. He *could not* leave them undone. All dishes must be washed, dried, and put away before he could leave the kitchen. His bed must be neat and tidy even before he could allow himself to dress for the morning. The scant items left on his desk must be aligned perfectly before he could leave them. All clocks within his home and on his person must be perfectly in sync.

Things needed to be just so. Otherwise life felt like chaos.

And as to mysteries—problems to be solved? He would work them forward and backward, top to bottom, relentlessly chewing on them until the solution surfaced—no matter how stubborn it may be.

Grant did not like things left askew, undone, or unresolved. It had been one of the reasons he had pushed Brenna until she'd become angry enough to confront Craig. Unfinished business had a way of surfacing. If not dealt with intentionally, that surfacing often revealed itself in the most intrusive ways.

Like at a race, when her defenses were down and what lay buried in her heart had sneaked past her carefully erected barriers. All of Grant's suspicions had been confirmed in that moment—watching Brenna fly into Craig's arms, seeing the silent exchange in their collision. Craig had never stopped loving her—and that had not been what Grant had wondered. Craig Erikson's refusal to come home for seven years had all but screamed that truth.

No, the thing that had gnawed at Grant, the question he had needed answered, had revealed itself in that moment: Brenna's heart was still Craig's—angry and broken as it had been. She still loved him.

So then Grant had found his answer: let her go. And he had.

Mystery unraveled. Solution found. He could move on. And he was.

But what of this Sage woman?

Perhaps Grant simply needed to discover the answers to his list of curiosities about her. Then he could regain his mind from her playful fingers, shut his eyes without envisioning the sparkle in hers. Drift to sleep without the startling music of her laughter making him wonder . . .

Who is this woman? And why were his compulsive tendencies clamped on her?

The path he normally ran curved gently right. He followed it as a man drawn by something invisible but demanding. It straightened, and Grant felt a keen sense of déjà vu. He strode down the slight dip as the trail drew him closer to the river's edge. At the spot where the path came the nearest to the water, Grant stopped. There he stood still, studying the gentle current as it lazily moved east. Shadows and light played on the surface, creating a show of shimmering water and cloaked mystery.

Seemed fitting.

Grant lifted his gaze, taking in the layers of dirt and the tangle of recently exposed roots that climbed the sharp rise until his view settled on the house sitting up and away from that small cliff. It had been white at some point in the past. A charming white two story farmhouse overlooking the river. Someone's dream at one time.

Now it looked . . . haunted. If one didn't know that Old Man Teller resided within those chipped and filthy clapboard walls, one would assume it was abandoned. The aged green roof sagged, the broken shingles in desperate need of replacement. The back enclosed porch leaned off to the side, the window screens a shredded tangle of gray film now stirring in the breeze.

Why would anyone live there? Let alone a lovely girl of possibly twenty-five, alone with an old man known for his temper as much as for his desire to be left to himself?

As Grant examined the creepy property, he saw clear evidence of Sage's hands on the place. A woven hammock swaying between two large cottonwood trees, mostly hidden by the screen of lilac bushes currently in bloom. And peeking from the far corner of the house, the edge of a small round table. Perhaps there was a chair beside it? Maybe even two—one for Sage and one for the old man?

What *was* she doing there with him?

Aside from my grandfather . . .

Her grandfather! Old Man Teller was her grandfather?

There had been rumors throughout the years. Stories that Teller had had a wife and child at one time. But the many variations of the tale made it easy to brush it off as entirely fictitious. That, and Old Man Teller's cantankerous reputation. Who would have married a man such as that?

But Sage had mentioned her *grandfather*.

"What have you decided?"

Grant started and sucked in a quick breath, ripping his gaze toward the sound of her teasing voice.

There on a log, chin propped against one palm and an elbow jammed onto one knee, grinning with amusement, sat Sage.

She is real. Grant was not sure why he needed to silently confirm that to himself.

"Have you been watching me this whole time?"

"Of course. You make a good subject of study."

Heat feathered up his neck. He was not sure what that meant exactly, but her tone was flirty and somehow endearing. Shoving his hands into his pockets, Grant pivoted to face her. "Why are you on this side of the river?"

She shrugged. "I figured you wouldn't come to the front door."

"Why would I not?"

"Gramps is a beast. Isn't that what everyone thinks?"

"I have not met him, so I have no opinion."

Her brows dipped in as she examined him—or rather, that statement. "I think that's not true."

"I have not had an opportunity to meet—"

"No, the part about you not having an opinion. Certainly, if you know about him at all—even by rumors—you have an opinion. Also, you wore confusion and concern on your face, as plain as that sunshine in the sky, while you were looking at his house. I'll wager you think I should not be staying there with him. And that, Grant Hillman, would indicate that you have an opinion."

Tilting his head to one side, Grant stepped toward her. "I was wondering why you are staying there, yes. But perhaps that has more to do with the obvious state of the house rather than what your grandfather is or is not."

Sage sat up, letting her hand fall to her lap, and pinned her lips together. Her expression became a mild challenge. "You pay no attention to rumors, then?"

"I hear them. But I prefer to let people tell their own story, if they wish."

That earned him a wide, triumphant smile. Sage stood, dusted off her wide-legged pants, and marched her way to Grant's side. When she looped her arm through his, his heart did an odd little kick.

Likely simple shock at her instant trust and familiarity. That was not how Grant operated, and it was strange that anyone would. But he'd learned early on that people were different. Everyone had their unique quirks.

His just happened to be on the stiff and boring side.

"Shall I tell you my story?" Sage tugged him along the cool earth toward the river.

Grant looked at her as they stopped, her bare toes sinking into the water. She gazed back at him with those fun-filled eyes, her expression so open that it almost seemed . . . forced. Like a mask.

Most people had one or two of those as well.

Grant nodded. "If you would like to. Perhaps start with your whole name. These past two days I have only thought of you as *that Sage woman.*"

"That won't do, since we are going to be the closest of friends."

He snorted, remembering her penchant for dramatic speech. "We will see on that."

"You don't agree?"

"I will not give a promise if I don't know that I can keep it."

"Hmm." Sage nodded, then kicked a stream of water toward the river's middle. "Honorable. I like that."

"Since you called me a villain before, I take that as a promising step. Now, do you have a last name?"

"Greene." She looked back at him, wrinkling her nose. "Isn't that just the worst?"

"No. Green is a good color."

With a dramatic backward throw of her head and shoulders, Sage let out a long "Ugh!" Then she squinted at him. "Not that. Sage Greene. That is my name." She stood up straight again, lifting her brow with firm disapproval. "My mother thought it was clever, and now I'm stuck with it."

Normally serious and prone to taking others' distress as valid, even if it seemed a small thing, Grant was surprised to feel a tickle of a grin against the corners of his mouth. "Perhaps you would have preferred Olive?"

Sage stilled. Stared at him. And then . . . laughed. It sounded like sunshine and vanilla wafers. He didn't know how that was possible, but he did know he loved sunshine and vanilla wafers.

And Sage Greene's laugh.

"No, certainly I wouldn't want to be called Olive Greene."

"Hunter?" Look at him—*teasing*!

"That's not even a girl's name."

"These things are fluid. How about Kelly?"

Sage waved off the suggestion with her free hand. "That would have never worked for my mother—it isn't nearly obvious enough."

"That's true. How about Jade?"

She stilled, molding a serious expression. "Oh, I do actually like that one. Jade Greene."

Grant twisted his mouth and tipped his face upward in thought. "No." He shook his head and refocused on her face. He liked the smattering of freckles and found that he wondered if that smooth skin would feel like silk beneath his fingertips, if he dared.

He did *not* dare, and where on earth had that come from? He returned his thoughts back to the name. "I like Sage."

Ahem. The name.

And perhaps the woman. Time would tell.

Her grin spread in triumph. "I like you too, Grant. See, well on the way to closest of friends." She stepped forward, tugging his arm as she did.

He pulled her back. "What are you doing?"

"Taking you to meet Gramps."

"Through the river?"

"The highway bridge is three miles that way." She pointed west, behind Grant.

"I know, but . . ."

"You've already proven you're not afraid of water, and you won't even have to swim. We'll go around the deep pool."

"I think not."

"You think not?" Laughter sputtered from her nose.

"I have blisters from the last time I walked back in wet shoes."

"Then remove them." She tugged again.

He stepped backward. "Rain check."

She looked up to the cloudless blue sky, holding out a hand palm up. "No rain."

"Not today."

Sage's posture sagged, and she popped her hand on her hip. "Hmm. Stubborn. I don't know how I feel about that."

Grant swallowed, nearly caving to the inkling to give in. He didn't want to cross the river though. And he didn't want to meet Old Man Teller this way—like a foundling she'd dragged in from the forest.

What kind of impression would that leave? And aside from that, he did not want to be anyone's *foundling*. He had spent way too much of his life drowning in the sense that he was an outcast. He had no intention of going voluntarily back to it.

"Would you forgive the stubbornness if I met him in two weeks?"

Sage brightened. "Two weeks? What happens in two weeks?"

Hmm, this was . . . not planned. Awkward. He had scripted the request. *Ms. Sage, I wondered if you might give me the pleasure of your company on Saturday, two weeks from now. You see, I need a date for a wedding.*

Formal. Not too needy. And hopefully, such a speech would satisfy her obvious delight in dramatics.

"Hello? Grant? What are we doing in two weeks?"

He swallowed. "Going to a wedding?" Did his voice just crack? Like he was fourteen? Oh, this was a humiliating disaster!

"A wedding!" Sage laughed. "Who's wedding?"

"A friend's." He felt his insides wilt. Every part of this idea was stupid.

"What sort of friend?"

"A . . . close friend." It sounded more like a question than an answer.

One brow slipped upward on Sage's lovely face. "Are we friends of the bride or friends of the groom?"

Oh, the sun was growing warm. How late in the afternoon was it? Grant rubbed the back of his neck. "Of . . . both. I went to school with them. High school."

"Huh." Sage leaned away, her hand only loosely draped on his forearm now, and she gave him a hard study. Then she smirked. "Okay, Grant Hillman. I'll be your cheesy date to a wedding. But then you'll owe me a favor."

A blast of relief wafted through him, followed quickly by a hint of dread. "What favor?"

"To be determined." Sage lifted to her toes and leaned toward him. When she planted a kiss on his jaw, Grant nearly stumbled backward. She patted his arm and gave him another mesmerizing smile. "But it's gonna be a good one."

Grant waited for that hint of dread to balloon into full panic as he watched her splash across the river and then climb the soft dirt path with her bare-naked feet.

It didn't.

· · · ● · ● · · · ·

"Gramps, do you know a man named Grant Hillman?" Later that evening, hours after the sun had set, Sage stretched leisurely on the musty old sofa, her Harlequin novel drifting toward her belly until it rested there.

Sitting across the small room, dozing in his ancient recliner, a grizzly sound came from the silver-haired man. For a moment, that was all.

Typical. Conversation with her gramps was a thing of great effort. Most days it would be easier for her to dig up a full-grown tree and transplant it than to have an effortless chat with him. Gramps clearly didn't want her there, in his home. His life.

Mother's reprimand came sharply to mind. *We owe that man nothing.* *So what if he's decided to leave us the house? It'll be there after he's dead.*

Such deep resentment! Seemed over the top, especially considering that Mother had only met her grandfather once, at Great-Grandma Clara's funeral. That had been eons ago—Sage had only been a girl of eleven and remembered almost nothing about it. Only that Mom had fumed that the man had dared to show up.

Since arriving in Big Prairie to stay with him, more often than Sage wanted to admit, it seemed Mom had been right about many things concerning Harold Teller, Sage's great-grandfather. He was insufferable—at least nearly so. And he didn't want Sage infringing on his isolated and angry life.

But something in Sage demanded she stay with him. The man had spent an entire lifetime alone. Over eighty years locked up in this crumbling house with only ghosts of a splintered past for company. That was too sad to bear.

And the property? It hadn't borne nearly as much flood damage as those just a few miles to the west, upstream. "A mild consolation," Mom had said when Sage had called to report her safe arrival. "Not having to deal with flood damage will make it easier to sell once he's dead."

Such a cold, heartless response. Sage couldn't bear that, so she'd stayed. Defied her mother's disapproval and moved into her great-grandfather's dilapidated home.

Clearly she was the only one who thought this was a remotely good idea. And she didn't even think that. She simply didn't want to live out her life not having tried to make peace with a nearly century-long family drama. She knew Mother's side of the story—passed on by Great-Grandma Clara, who, to be honest, sounded like she had been as grizzly as Gramps.

But she didn't know Harold's.

Maybe it was as simple as Grandma Clara had claimed—he was a worthless man who had turned her and his child away, leaving her heartbroken, their son fatherless, and the pair of them struggling to make something out of life on their own—not to mention propelling their family into a downward cycle of fatherless homes. The beginning of the family curse.

Likely, that had been the simple truth of it.

But why would he leave his property to her mother—his granddaughter—if he had rejected his own child?

Atonement perhaps?

Sage didn't know. But she was driven to find out.

"Gramps." She sat up, speaking his name more sharply this time.

Another growl elicited from his side of the room, followed by a deep and gravelly, "What do you want, girl?"

"For you to answer me."

"About what?"

Why did you reject Grandma Clara? Why are you such a beast of a man? How is it possible that you have lived this long when you are so deeply poisoned with selfishness and bitterness?

Why are you leaving my mother an inheritance?

Sage left those questions for later and instead refocused on her initial query. "Do you know Grant Hillman?"

"No."

"You've never heard of him?"

"Of course I have. Boy grew up here."

"Then you know him."

"No. Never met him."

Sage sighed in exasperation. "Fine. What have you *heard* of him?"

"Quiet. Odd boy, growing up."

"What made him odd?"

"Didn't like football. Liked the cello."

A snort-laugh blew from Sage's nose. "Not liking football makes one odd?"

He didn't respond.

"Gramps, do not ignore me."

"He was just different. So said the town. That's all I know."

"Why did he stay in Big Prairie?"

"Why would I know?"

Sage let her own frustration out in a growl. "What does he do now?"

"I dunno. Something with kids, at the school."

Sagging back against the flimsy cushion at her shoulders, Sage sighed. "You've been very helpful—thank you."

"Don't know why you would ask me about people."

She lifted her book back to her face to read again. "Me either. It was a lapse in judgment."

Sage felt his eyes fall on her and hold. After several breaths, the sensation did not go away. She lowered the novel and looked across the room.

A firm stare met her gaze. "Why do you ask about him?"

"I met him the other day. He pulled me out of the river."

A new set of wrinkles folded on Gramps' brow. "Why did he do that?"

"He thought I was hurt, I guess."

Those furrow lines deepened. "Were you?"

"No."

"But he thought so?"

"Yes."

Gramps held his quiet, scowling study for several minutes. Then he tipped his head back, as if ready to resume his nap. "You shouldn't jump from the ledge. It's not safe."

"I wasn't hurt."

Another guttural sound came from his chest. Then, "Don't do it anymore."

"Gramps."

"I don't want you hurt, so don't." His tone was demanding and final.

And it only added to the mystery of Great-Grandfather Harold. Because apparently he cared.

CHAPTER FIVE

GRANT CHECKED HIS WATCH before reaching for his office landline: 12:28. Four minutes until the lunch bell would ring—and hopefully Trenton would show up this time.

The young man was still hit and miss on their lunch appointments. Craig had said he'd see that Trent kept them, but Grant had discouraged Craig from doing that—especially at this point in the school year, with only a week left before summer break.

"He can come if he wants to talk. I do not wish for this to be something you and he wrestle over." Truly, Grant didn't. The waters between Craig and the Fulton boys had smoothed considerably, and now that the adoption process was in full forward motion, Grant felt good about backing out of the situation a little bit at a time.

Craig needed to have the full reins.

Even so, he enjoyed the times when Trent brought his hot lunch tray into his office and talked. It was fulfilling to see Trent crawling out of the brokenness that his young life had been. Craig and Brenna were good for him and for his younger brother, Ashton.

Grant was thankful. Even when there was a pinch of . . . of being left on the fringes of something that mattered to him. Even when it stung to watch the little family form, reminding him that he was not part of one himself.

You still see me, right? Grant swallowed against the ball in his throat and reached for the phone as it rang for the fifth time.

"Hello." He employed his professional voice—which was not very much unlike his conversational voice. "This is Grant Hillman."

"Oh good. I was hoping you answered your own calls. What would I tell a secretary or whatever? I would say, 'May I speak to Grant?' And they might say, 'Who is calling, and what can I tell him it's about?' And then . . ."

"Sage?" That was not at all his professional voice. It was the one that seemed to be solely for this woman of the river, as she continually set him off guard.

Her rambling stopped abruptly, then she laughed. "You do remember me. What a relief."

"Umm. Yes. Quite well, Sage Greene." Warmth spread through his chest. Remember her? He would never be able to forget her, even if he decided he wanted to.

He had not decided anything of the sort. "I believe we have a date."

"Yes. About that."

His heart plummeted, causing his shoulders to sag as he slumped against the desk. Grant never slumped. Bad posture was an indication of laziness.

But he couldn't support a straight spine beneath this crush of disappointment. "Oh."

"Two weeks is too far away."

Grant barely caught his breath as his heart revived before she rambled on.

"Plus, I didn't even get your number. So I had to look you up, and all that gave me was the school's number. That is so awkward, Grant. You really shouldn't leave a girl in that sort of limbo. How am I to know that you're not going to stand me up?"

Grant had to shut his gaping mouth before he could form a reply. "I would never stand a woman up."

"Hmm." Her smile carried in that hum, making his own mouth smooth. "I believe you on that."

"Good."

A pause dropped between them. Uncomfortable and long. Certainly she was waiting for him to say something. Surely he should—and he would like to, but he wasn't sure what had just happened. What was she asking for, exactly?

His . . . number?

"Six eight seven—"

"Are you counting? You mixed up a couple of numbers."

"What? No." The top of his right ear itched. Or burned. Grant rubbed it. "I was giving you my number."

"Oh! Yay! Hold on." The sound of papers rustling around came from the background. "Okay, go."

Heart hammering, Grant had to swallow before his voice would work again. "Six eight seven. Five five two three."

Sage read the numbers back to him.

"That is correct."

"Fabulous. And you'll answer when I call?"

Every. Single. Time. Likely with the current grin that felt a little silly and yet somehow delightful. "Of course."

"Good. Now, let's talk about this two-week dilemma, shall we?"

"Umm . . . okay?" She thoroughly rattled him—proof being that Grant never spoke like that.

"Okay? No, it's not okay. I don't like it."

"You don't like . . . you do not want to go to the wedding with me?"

"No. That's not what I said. I said two weeks was too far away. If we are to be the closest of friends, as I have already decided we should be, we must get to know each other sooner."

"Oh."

"You don't agree?"

"Yes." Grant tried to steady the churn of confusion Sage provoked. She was a . . . a whirlwind. Knocking him off balance, causing him to stumble. Even so, that silly little smile still played on his lips, its unfamiliarity a delightful sensation.

Grant rubbed his jawline. Yes. That was his face he felt, and certainly he was not in some odd but pleasant dream.

"Good. I'm free tonight. Actually, I'm pretty much free every night of the week, because, as I've already told you, I know all of two people besides you in this little town."

"Oo-oh."

Another silence broke into her free-fall of words. In it, Grant scrambled desperately to catch up. Tonight . . . she wanted to go out with him tonight?

Perhaps he was dreaming? He placed his palm against his heart, feeling the steady, hard thump of the elevated rhythm—the same rate he experienced on a jog.

"Are you available?" she pressed.

"Yes."

"Oh."

Oh? She sounded disappointed? Why would she be disappointed he was available to go out with her tonight when she'd just asked him if he could? The pleasant fog of that something-like-a-runner's high dissipated.

"You don't want to," she said.

What?

"No. That is not at all what I—" Whatever this enchanting whirlwind was, he was doing a good job of messing it up. Grant drew a fresh breath and cleared his throat. "I would enjoy seeing you tonight, Sage. Can I take you to dinner?"

"No, I don't do restaurants much."

"Oh." Then what?

"I'll pack a picnic. You pick me up at seven. Okay?"

"A picnic?"

"Surely you can think of a good spot, right? Or we could just go to our place on the river. That would be easy, if you'd rather . . ."

"No, I know another spot." What was he saying? Where would he take this woman he barely knew for a picnic so close to sundown?

"Perfect. I'll see you at seven, then?"

"Yes."

"Lovely. Goodbye, Grant Hillman."

The click of the disconnection sounded before he could respond.

Grant stared at the phone on his desk. What had just happened?

He'd landed a date for the evening.

Was it a date?

He had no idea, really. Sage Greene was an exhilarating swirl of mystery and surprise. Not really his type at all.

But he was caught up in her gust just the same. And yes, it was thrilling.

· · · · ● · ● · · · ·

Sage waved a hand in front of her face, attempting to clear the dust from her field of view. Light filtered into the dreary space through the grime of the far attic window, stubbornly determined to subdue the gloom of this long-neglected area.

Her nose twitched, and then the tickle traveled upward until it produced a sneeze.

"Good grief." Sage itched her nose and tried again to move the floating debris from her face. "I'll add the attic to my project list." She twisted her mouth to one side. "Gramps will love that."

More likely he would forbid it, just as he had her digging a garden in the backyard.

Sage laughed. The morning after he'd given her a hard *no* to the garden pitch, she'd gone to town for a shovel, returned with the shiny new tool, and found Grandfather with one of his own—though significantly less shiny. Or new.

He'd already dug up a quarter of the square she'd marked out with an old, cracked hose.

"Don't stand there gaping at me, girl."

"You said no."

He'd nodded at the spade in her hand. "Clearly you didn't care."

"You're like ninety years old."

"I am not," he'd barked and then gestured to the freshly turned dirt. "And I can still dig, can't I?"

"But—"

"If you ain't gonna dig, then we can forget this whole thing."

"Yes, sir." Sage scurried over the space from the corner of the house to the garden patch and got to work.

They spent the remainder of that afternoon working together, Gramps leaning heavily on his spade as the tool worked double time for turning soil and operating as his cane. No words. Just digging. It was a rather beautiful day.

Sage smirked at that memory and then looked around the dimly lit space. A thick layer of dirt covered shapes of all sizes, most draped with cloth tarps. Furniture of some sort, likely. She wanted to uncover what each was—perhaps she would find evidence of whatever story Grandfather had lived. Maybe the reasons why he was the crochety old man that he was.

Or she'd simply find old furniture that, more likely than not, should have been sent to the dump long before now.

Either way, that wasn't why she'd pulled down the narrow attic stairway and scrambled her way up into this dusty gloom. She'd been looking for something specific—a basket. Because every picnic needed a basket, obviously.

Sage set herself to that task, starting with a neat stack of boxes at the corner farthest from the window. Some bore labels that piqued her curiosity—things like *china* and *music* and *quilts*. The handwriting was distinctly masculine, but the words proclaimed feminine possessions.

Who had they belonged to? Grandma Clara? Had they been together long enough to accumulate such things?

She moved from that pile to the next thing—a large box, sort of like a trunk, but longer and shallower, kept shut with three latches. Sage couldn't resist a peek. The opening of it produced a hollow smacking sound, and another puff of dust burst toward her face. Again waving at the stuff that would certainly provoke another sneeze in the near future, Sage leaned closer to see what treasure might lie within.

A cello?

Lifting the lid more, she reached in with her other hand and delicately stroked the strings. Yes, a cello.

Whose?

Did Grandfather play? He didn't seem like the type.

"Girl!"

Sage started at the harsh growl coming from the stairway at her back. She closed the box and pivoted on her feet, nearly jumping to a stand before remembering that the ceiling was low. "Be right down."

"What are you doing?" He sounded none too happy. Then again, he always sounded none too happy.

Placing a palm on her hammering heart, Sage demanded her pulse settle back to normal. After all, he was just a frail, sickly old man. Nothing to be afraid of—especially since she'd had glimpses of a fellow who *did* in fact care about her, even if she was his estranged great-granddaughter.

The distant offspring of a child he had apparently never wanted.

Her stomach twisted painfully. That seemed to be the legacy of her family line: Men who made babies they did not want. Men who could not love.

Not that she would know anything about *love*. Except perhaps that it only existed in fiction, where all impossible ideas resided. As much as Sage loved a good romance, her family legacy had taught her that such a thing was not real.

"Girl!" Gramps's bark was a sharp demand. One Sage could not ignore.

Sparked into motion, she bounded down the narrow steps, grabbing the opening of the ceiling as she descended so that she would not knock her head on it as she went. "Here I am." She smiled as sweet and as innocent as she could muster.

"What are you doing?" Gramps's watery eyes bored like needles into her face.

She shrugged, as if he did not intimidate her. "Looking for a basket. I'm going on a picnic."

That sharp glare softened. "A picnic?" His face tilted with a suspicious look. "Alone?"

"No. With Grant Hillman. He's taking me on a picnic this evening."

"Why?"

Sage laughed at the nearly accusatory question. "So that we can get to know each other better. I can have a friend in Big Prairie, can't I?"

"What sort of friend?"

"A nice one, I hope." Placing her hands on her hips, she dropped down the last two steps and then leaned toward Gramps. "He is a nice person, right?"

"Told you. I dunno."

"He doesn't have a criminal record or anything, right?" Sage looped her arm through her grandfather's thin one. The sagging skin hinted space for what might have been well-used muscle at one time.

Gramps stared at her, clearly insulted by her invasion of his space. But then . . . then a long sigh left his frail body, and he shuffled forward, his cane making a soft thunk in the run of green carpet smothering the hall floor.

Sage moseyed at his side. "Surely he can't have a record, or they wouldn't let him work in the schools. And he did try to rescue me from the river, even though I did *not* need rescuing."

She shot Gramps a pointed glare, the silent exchange harkening back to his command that she not jump from the ledge anymore.

"Men are rarely trustworthy." Gramps shrugged her off his arm so that he could reach for the railing before he started down the stairs for the ground floor.

How had he managed to come upstairs without her hearing him, anyway? Also, that was quite a statement.

"Is that a self-indictment?"

A low grunt was his only response.

The risers creaked and moaned as he lowered one leg down and then the other, a painful, methodical descent back into the domain he normally occupied. How long had it been since he'd come up to the second level?

He paused three-quarters of the way down. "There's a basket in the back part of the pantry. On the floor."

"Oh." That was . . . helpful.

"It's gonna be filled with dirt. Maybe holes. Don't know if it'll be any good."

"I can clean it."

Gramps resumed his slow *step, plant cane, step* procession. Eventually he reached the kitchen at the base of the stairs. He limped two paces forward and then turned to wait for Sage to reach the ground level.

"He comes to the front door before you leave."

Sage drew back. "I'm sorry?"

"You don't go if he can't manage that."

"Gramps, I'm twenty-five years old." And he was hardly the type of relation who could make demands on her personal life, considering he'd never even met her until she'd shown up on his doorstep a few weeks ago after a little adventure involving a train, a bus, and the local public transit (a '90s minivan with a pay-n-ride sticker on it).

"Age has nothing to do with anything. This Hillman fellow can come to the front door like a decent man, or he can run into the woods at the report of my gun."

Swallowing, Sage gawked at the old man. He was serious.

She was shocked. Appalled.

No.

She was . . . surprised and a little besotted. This grouchy old man was trying to protect her. Having never had a father figure in her life, she found that to be terribly sweet.

A little late, but sweet nonetheless.

"I'll tell him," she said.

"Shouldn't have to tell him. Man ought to know."

Sage tilted her head to one side. The world had changed quite a bit since Gramps had been a young man. "Think he does?"

"If he's worth the trouble of a picnic . . ." Gramps turned to limp his way back to his recliner. "Stay out of the attic."

Sage bit her bottom lip as a grin slipped onto her mouth. Seemed like as good a test as any. And as for the attic business . . .

She glanced over her shoulder and through the window that peeked at her freshly seeded garden in the back. Next week she'd go buy some tomatoes and peppers to tuck into the freshly churned soil.

And then she'd explore the attic.

CHAPTER SIX

STANDING IN THE MIDDLE of the produce section at the Big Prairie Market, Grant puzzled over the series of text messages. And not simply for the lack of punctuation—though that was off-putting.

first test

where will you pick me up

don't tell me though

I can't give you hints

it's against the rules

please don't fail

What on earth? He'd go to the front door and knock on it like any self-respecting, grown man would do. Where else would he go? She didn't actually think he'd meet her on the other side of the river again, did she? Like a sneaking teenager, or something even more ridiculous?

And test? Who said anything about taking a test?

Well, life in general was a bit of a test, was it not? She might have him there.

That aside, if this was a test, did that mean it was also a date? Like, a *date* date?

Grant hoped so, but he didn't believe so. Sage did not come across as a woman who went out on an old-school date. She seemed more like a whimsical little elf who had been born in his tired and lonely imagination.

One who would flirt and tease and eventually flit away—off to find new hearts to break.

That was not an issue. Grant had no intention of putting his heart on the line for an elf he might have dreamed into existence.

He hadn't conjured her up, had he? He lifted his cell phone and scrolled through the series of fragmented messages. No. He would not make up *any* of that.

He would never imagine any part of his interaction with this woman—he was not that clever. Or fun.

This Sage Greene was a strange one, and once again he found his mind whirling with an odd concoction of confusion, mild irritation (use punctuation, for the love of English!), and a sense of being . . .

Mesmerized.

After a quick check of his heart—ensuring it was safely fastened in the *she's a friend* zone—Grant allowed a small grin to poke at the corners of his mouth and took up a texting hold on his phone.

I will pick you up at seven. You will hear three knocks on the front door, and that way you will know it's me. Tell your grandfather I am looking forward to meeting him.

PS: Dipped strawberries or blueberries and cream?

There. See. Punctuation makes a difference. That small grin gave way to a full smile as Grant reread his response. As far as friendly flirting went, that was not half-bad, was it?

He couldn't be sure—he had never been good at flirting and had never dabbled in the friendly sort.

Why was he even wondering about such things anyway?

Right when a frown threatened to pull down that light grin, Sage's response lit his screen. A happy face with heart eyes, followed by *blueberries and cream*

No punctuation. Again.

But right then Grant Hillman did not care.

Enjoying the light sensation in his chest, as well as the smirk that moved his expression away from forever being serious, Grant tucked his phone into his back pocket and reached for a package of blueberries. That tucked into his basket, he strode toward the dairy section and grabbed a small carton of heavy whipping cream.

"Grant Hillman."

He shut the refrigerator door and glanced over his shoulder toward the woman who had spoken his name.

"Miss Jane." His heart felt less light and his expression less easy. Though it had been months, this kind old woman's subtle rejection still jabbed against him. "How are you today?"

"I'm quite well, thank you."

He had to appreciate her use of proper speech, even if Miss Jane had sunk a thorn into his heart. It shouldn't bother him so much, her disapproval. Throughout his life he had experienced more than one person's rejection. That came with the odd-duck territory.

But this was Miss Jane. Miss Jane loved everyone. She was kind to everyone. She *accepted* everyone just as they were.

Except, apparently, him.

"You have been on my heart, young man." Miss Jane reached her hand out, and those long, narrow fingers settled on his arm with a gentle touch.

Grant immediately drew back, though the action was not intentional. Swallowing, he forced his muscles to ease and then fixed a shallow smile. "I have? That is surprising."

"No, it isn't. Brenna's wedding is less than two weeks away." She lifted her hand from his arm and folded it with her other one, which was wrapped around the handle of her shopping basket. "Are you okay?"

"Of course." Why on earth did she want to talk about that? After all, Miss Jane had made it clear she did not approve of Brenna being with Grant.

What was this?

Compassion deepened in the woman's bright-blue eyes. "Truly, Grant? I know you cared about her."

"I am glad she is happy." Grant stepped to the side. "I am very sorry, Miss Jane, but I have someplace to be this evening."

"Do you?" She brightened at that. "Someplace fun, I hope? With, perhaps, someone lovely?"

What in the world was Miss Jane up to? Was this . . . guilt?

Grant could feel a scowl press his brows together. He schooled the reaction and plastered that shallow grin back in place. "A sunset picnic with a friend."

"Oh!" A wistful smile made the woman's expression warm. "That does sound lovely." She reached for his arm and squeezed. "I am glad to hear it."

He nodded and took another step away.

"Grant Hillman."

Tugging back a ready sigh, he turned to look at her again.

"I do earnestly pray for your happiness." Her smile faded as a heartfelt seriousness locked in her expression. "As I said, you have been on my heart. And in my prayers." A brief nod closed her little speech, and then she continued on her way in the opposite direction.

Grant was left entirely befuddled and with a building urge to chase after the older woman to ask her why she would say such a thing. Why had she pushed him away when he'd been dating Brenna only to be all compassion and care for him now?

Chalk it up to one more thing in his world that did not make sense.

Rather than pick at it, as Grant was prone to do with any sort of puzzle, he pushed away the Miss Jane encounter. That evening he was going on a sunset picnic with a whimsical elf who made his heart feel light and his smile surface easily.

Let it be a passing thing—he was going to enjoy the beautiful mystery of it. Even if that was the most un-Grant-ish thing he'd ever done.

Two hours later, Grant parked at the far end of the long, rutted dirt drive in front of Old Man Teller's. The house looked different from this angle. A little less haunted perhaps, though not any less the victim of neglect. From the front there was scant evidence of use. A wooden rocker on the sagging covered front porch, set to the side of the front door in a utilitarian place that cared nothing for aesthetics. Open blinds on the first floor—and one of the two on the second.

And a spring wreath of forsythias and forget-me-nots on the door.

Surely that was *not* Old Man Teller's doing.

The slip of a grin on his face was becoming more and more familiar. Seemed every time something provoked a thought that had anything to do with Sage, there it was. Uncoerced and with the unique ability to make his chest feel open, light, and distinctively . . . adventurous.

Perhaps he should be concerned about himself.

Rather than dwell on that all-too-practical and very-Grant-esque thought, he snagged the bundle of a dozen white tulips from the passenger seat and shut the vehicle door. Halfway up the drive, he untucked his free hand from his jacket pocket and stretched his fingers.

At the less-than-stable-looking front steps, he paused, rolled those fingers into a loose fist, and drew a deep breath.

It's not a real date. She is not really a dateable woman. Right. So nothing to be nervous about.

Except for the fact that Sage had a way of making his mind spin in the most bizarrely delightful way. And that she invaded his thoughts way too much.

How could he like a woman to this extent who was the extreme opposite of him? It was unexplainable. And likely dangerous.

But it's not a date.

Nor would the wedding be a date. Well, it was, but not a *date* date.

Grant shook his head and nearly growled out loud. For once he was going to enjoy something fun and unexpected and not calculate the outcome of it. Couldn't he do that?

Certainly.

He climbed the two stairs quickly, as he didn't trust the risers to hold him for longer than a second, and crossed the shallow porch to the front door. There, he knocked three times.

"Aha!" Sage's smiling voice floated from inside. "I told you, Gramps."

Grant straightened his shoulders, wondering if the old man would be the one to open the door. The solid wooden entry burst open, and there she was.

His heart rate surged and his breath caught, though both reactions were stupidly cliché.

"You pass." She reached for his hand and pulled him into the dim room.

"I pass?" There it was again. The woman's ability to befuddle him with no more than two words.

Biting her bottom lip, Sage dipped a nod while her brown eyes danced with mischief. She continued dragging him farther into the gloom of the old house until they were standing in a 1950s relic of a parlor room. There, in a vintage recliner that Grant thought must have been orange at one time, sat a man who looked more thin and frail than intimidating.

"Gramps, this is Grant Hillman." Sage looped her arm through Grant's and did a little hop, as if she'd won a prize. "He came to the front door."

The old man locked a hard study on Grant, his dark eyes as sharp as his scowl was firm. Then he grunted. "There's that."

Sage giggled. The sound seemed so out of place that Grant peeled his study from the great obscurity of Old Man Teller—a sighting not many in Big Prairie could claim—and looked down to the elf woman at his side.

She gazed back at him, all fun and eagerness. "Are these for me? Or maybe you brought them for Gramps?" She winked.

He wasn't sure which was the right answer. "Perhaps you would both enjoy them." And then he felt dumb. He shouldn't have grabbed them as he passed the florist's shop downtown. It had been a spontaneous purchase—another very-not-Grant thing to do.

"Yes! We'll enjoy them together, won't we, Gramps?"

He grunted.

Sage took the flowers and then swept toward the grouch in the chair. Without a hint of hesitation, she bent to kiss the old man's cheek and then turned to leave the room. "I'll just get these in water."

And then . . . then it was just Grant and Old Man Teller. Ahem. Perhaps *Mr. Teller* was a more appropriate title.

The room felt chilled and dark—more so the second Sage had vacated the space, taking her warm smile and exuberant energy and leaving them with just what they could spark for themselves.

Not much.

Grant cleared his throat. "I hope that you are okay with me taking Sage out this evening."

"Girl does what she wants." His voice sounded gravelly—as if it suffered from a long-term lack of use.

Nodding, Grant looked around the room. An old box TV sat in the corner, off. The oddly shaped coffee table in the middle of the room looked freshly polished—Sage's doing, no doubt. He let his inspection travel around more and found, tucked behind him against the wall that separated this room from the next, a twin bed. Made neat as a pin, the covers a masculine but faded blue and red plaid, with a single pillow at the top.

Mr. Teller's bed, no doubt. Something sad and weighty pressed in Grant's gut as he realized he was looking at the old man's whole world. Everything right there in that dreary little room with peeling floral wallpaper and sculpted golden carpet that had faded into something dingy and ugly.

It was terribly . . . depressing.

"Here we are." Sage nearly danced back into the room, and immediately Grant felt warmer by degrees. She placed the vase—a brown thing left over from decades before—now full of happy white tulips onto the weird eight-shaped coffee table thing and stepped back to admire them. "They're lovely. Just what this room needed."

Turning to her grandfather, she waited for his response. He looked from the flowers to Grant, and it seemed that the deep carving of disapproval eased from his forehead. Mr. Teller looked back at Sage. "Back before ten."

Grant nearly snorted at the command issued to a wild sprite of a woman of twenty-something who would clearly do exactly as she pleased and nothing else.

"As you wish, Gramps."

Gaping, Grant watched as she leaned back down to the old man to plant another kiss on his cheek.

And then she turned to him with a brilliant smile.

Grant wasn't usually a sentimental man, but he thought he felt his whole world take on a new trajectory.

CHAPTER SEVEN

SAGE SLIPPED INTO THE front seat of the truck, squeezing Grant's elbow as she passed him while he held the door. She mindlessly tugged on the seat belt while she took in this little bit of unexpectedness. The cab smelled of earth and working man and perhaps faintly of dog. None of which aligned with who she thought Grant Hillman might be.

After climbing in and starting the engine, Grant shifted the truck into gear, and they went bouncing down the poorly maintained dirt road, going north rather than south—the direction that would have taken them toward town. Another blip of a surprise.

"I didn't think of you as a pickup man." She winked at him, though he likely didn't catch it, as he was driving.

He did snort a muffled laugh though. "I'm not. This is my cousin's. I borrowed it for tonight."

"Just for me? Going all out, are we?"

As a faint blush feathered up his neck, Grant shook his head. "You told me to pick a good spot."

"I did. Where are we going?"

Grant glanced at her, and she thrilled to see the eager joy in his eyes. She might just like that better than the thorough confusion she'd plucked from him at their first, and part of their second, meeting.

Maybe. She'd have to try for them both a few more times to know for sure.

"A wheat field," he said. "Also my cousin's."

Sage surveyed the landscape as they came out of the treed area that lined the riverbed. Rolling hills stretched in all directions, farming fields a patchwork of color. Some were fallow and brown, and some were a carpet of bright spring green, while others were a mix of yellow and green grass that was much taller—likely pastures.

She had been a lot of places in her life. None were quite like this Nebraska prairie. So wide-open and vacant. One could imagine that they could escape everything here and never be bothered. Or that they could be taken out and dumped in this great wide middle of nowhere and never be found.

That could be unnerving.

Turning a suspicious look to Grant, Sage employed a dramatically wary tone. "You're not going to kill me and leave my body out here, are you?"

"Hmm . . ." Grant rubbed his chin, then turned a mischievous expression toward her. "Now is not a great time to consider that sort of danger. What would you do?"

"Fight, obviously. Kick and scream and scratch and claw . . ." She broke her serious tone as a chuckle bubbled from her chest. "But of course, I won't have to. We've already established that you're not a villain."

"I am glad you think not."

"I *know* not." She settled in a position that gave her more of a view of him than the scenery out the window. "So you're not a villain and not a pickup man. What are you, Grant Hillman?"

He shrugged. "I already told you that. I am exceedingly boring."

"This does not seem like a boring-man thing to me."

"No? Taking a beautiful woman to a wheat field for a picnic does not scream uninteresting to you?"

"Not one bit." She paused, biting her bottom lip as pleasure bloomed in her middle at his description of her. What girl didn't love to be called a beautiful woman? And as to this picnic on a green field, no one she knew could claim that experience, which made it exceptional. "Seems . . . creative. Out of the ordinary. In other words, exactly what I hoped for."

Grant chuckled again. "I am relieved to hear that you do not have high expectations."

"That is not at all what I said." Sage studied his profile while he maintained focus on the dirt road. "I have fantastic expectations. I begin every morning expecting something fresh, with laughter and, hopefully, a surprise or two tucked in. This"—she motioned toward the road—"meets that perfectly."

Grant's eyes crinkled as he allowed a small grin. That was his sole response—but somehow it was flawless. Honest, unadorned with flattery, and wonderful in candor. Things that usually didn't capture Sage's pleasure, but perhaps she'd never truly experienced them.

"Now," she prodded, "what does a creative, not-a-pick-up-man-nor-a-villain such as yourself do?"

His gaze remained steady on the road. "I'm a counselor at the school."

"Ah. Do you lean more toward academics or psychology?"

"I have a degree in child psychology. But I do enjoy academics. However, most of my clients are younger. I'm usually at the elementary school."

"I see." Sage paused to take him in. He had a good profile—one Sage quite enjoyed tracing as they traveled. Dark hair and a rather steep-sloping nose, with well-defined brows and a gentle yet determined mouth that seemed not as prone to smiling as Sage usually liked. But she had summoned more than one smile from him, hadn't she?

That seemed a victory, though she wasn't sure why or even if it should. Sage was not one to let mysteries hang around unbothered for long.

The truck slowed, and Grant guided it from the road to a turnoff that looked as though it disappeared into a broad field of waving green. He backed and then parked. Finally, after cutting the engine, he reached behind him to the tiny half seat in the back and retrieved a bulky gray blanket and a small cooler.

His brown eyes found hers. "What about you?"

"Me? I have zero degrees in anything. Entirely uneducated."

"Not in theater?"

"Ah, so you've caught my dramatic flair?"

He chuckled. "It's rather hard to miss."

She batted her eyes. "It's endearing, isn't it?"

"Something like that." His steady gaze lacked the flirtatious gleam she'd hoped for. Even so, she did like his warm eyes on hers. There was something anchoring about it, about him.

"How is it that you've landed in Big Prairie?"

Sage shrugged. "My great-grandfather."

"I think no one around here knew that he had a granddaughter, let alone a great one."

"Yes. I only met him when I showed up on his sad front porch."

"What prompted that?"

Twisting her mouth to one side, Sage considered how much of this strange story she was willing to share with Grant. He was, after all, basically a stranger. But as she lifted her eyes back to his, finding that calm, trustworthy patience sitting there watching her, waiting for her, she found a sudden desire to confide. To have at least one person know of her family's twisted past.

Perhaps he would help her unravel some of the messiness of it?

Sage twined her fingers together and shrugged. "I wanted to know him, mostly."

Grant nodded, his expression concealing whatever reaction he had to her vague statement. "Shall we?"

Sage found the concoction of interest and shy hesitancy in his voice endearing. She felt herself smile as she nodded, and then, after grabbing her picnic basket, she followed his exit—only she went out of her own side of the vehicle and walked beside the truck bed until she met him at the back. Grant plopped his armload of goods into the truck bed and lowered the tailgate. Using the tire as a step, he climbed up and arranged the blanket.

"A picnic in the bed of a truck? Sounds like part of a country song . . ." She raised a brow, provoking his blush.

"I, uh . . . This is . . ." Rubbing the back of his neck, he stood straight. "Not what you assume."

"I assume nothing of anything you're implying, sir. And . . . I love it." Setting her picnic basket onto the tailgate, Sage held a hand up toward him, and he reached down for her.

With his help, she scrambled up and settled herself on the blanket. Grant leaned on the opposite sidewall of the truck bed. For a moment, he held still, his gaze trained toward the western horizon. Distant and hidden.

Perhaps wondering what to say next—he didn't seem to be at ease with meaningless conversation. Or maybe he was simply enjoying the view.

It *was* lovely.

Sage let him slip away, taking in the scene as well. The rolling green grain swayed in the cool evening breeze, the tips of wheat gilded with golden light as the sun slipped toward the distant place where earth met sky.

There was breathtaking beauty in the simplicity. Sage found herself captivated by it, and she continued to watch the sun lower until it met the line of the horizon.

"It's stunning," she said.

"It is." Grant's low tone drew her attention, and she found his study had switched from the setting sun to her face.

Her pulse skipped as something pleasant oozed from her chest to her belly. Had any man looked at her like that? There had been many dates in the past. Men who would pay her such compliments as Grant had just done, and laugh, and fly about looking for fun and adventure alongside her.

But had any ever wrapped her heart in such warmth with one long gaze?

Grant shifted, busying himself with the cooler. Sage found herself in a strange place of quiet intrigue, and he remained silent.

What was it about him?

She didn't even really know him. And what she did see—what she suspected—indicated he was *not* like any of those other adventurous, fun-seeking men she had gravitated toward before. The type who ran with her for a while until they both got tired of the other and then moved on.

Flashing her a look that wasn't quite a smile, but still pleasant, he reached for the picnic basket. "Shall I?"

She nodded, pondering the rareness of that small phrase. As rare as this quiet, polite, mysterious man. Goodness, but she wanted to know him. And, of all things, for him to know her.

Was that safe?

"I'm a vocal artist." She volunteered that info into the lull between them. Quite intrusively. "I narrate romance novels, mostly."

He glanced up at her, considered for a moment, and then nodded. "That fits. And explains our first meeting."

His comment managed the very rare thing of summoning heat into her chest. Not that she would allow it to creep up her neck. She arched one brow, as if issuing a challenge. "Not too strange of a thing?"

"Not at all." A response that served to deepen her desire to know him more.

Grant possessed a steady seriousness that was taken aback by her playfulness. Hadn't she caused him to gape at her several times in their few interactions? And how much fun had that been? But her occupation didn't throw him off—as it did most people. Which was also nice.

He seemed deeply reserved, except in those moments he had flirted back. Moments that she guessed were rare treasures rather than normal occurrences resulting from years of practice.

But she couldn't be sure of that, could she? She was making assumptions. Building a character in her mind that might or might not be real. That was definitely *not* safe.

"Grant?"

He paused, halfway done unwrapping a chicken sandwich. "Yes?"

Sage started where they had last left off—the wedding she was to attend with him. There must be clues in that. "Tell me about this bride. What's her name?"

"Brenna."

"And you dated her?" She wondered if he'd be bothered that he hadn't been all that opaque about that part.

"I did." He finished unwrapping the food in his hands.

Not bothered, apparently. How hard was she going to scratch at this? "Was she your first love?"

He ducked and then reached to place the opened sandwich onto a plate. Perhaps that had been too much.

"She was my first—and only—girlfriend."

Only? Huh. How . . . unusual. "How long ago?"

"We broke up last fall."

"Whoa. Like six months ago?"

He shrugged and then pulled an orange out of the basket. "A little more than that, I think."

"And she's getting married next week?" That was a fast turnaround, even for Sage. And Sage wasn't one to hold on, look back, or *not* jump into the next thing as soon as the opportunity presented itself.

Also, surely having an ex-girlfriend get herself engaged to another man that quickly had to sting.

"To her high school sweetheart, yes." Finished peeling and distributing the orange, Grant sat back again, propping an elbow up on one knee. "It really is not that surprising."

Ah, the plot twist—at Grant's expense. "Sounds a little tragic."

"No. Nothing tragic." He shook his head. "Well, I take that back. There has been tragedy in Brenna's life. For both her and her fiancé, Craig. Her younger brother died in an accident, and Craig felt responsible. It was one of the reasons they broke up, and I believe a big reason Craig left Big Prairie and did not return for seven years."

"Wow. That does sound awful." Sage picked up the plate of orange segments and sandwich that Grant had set in front of her. "Somehow you ended up dating her while he was gone?"

"Yes." His eyes pinched, and he turned his attention back to the sunset. "I had a crush on her for years. Seemed almost too good to be true . . ." His voice trailed off.

Several beats went by in silence. In it she could nearly hear him finish that adage *I should have known it was . . .*

As a surge of irritation plowed through her at this Brenna woman, Sage poked a slice of orange into her mouth. She was disappointed at the lack of flavor and juice in the fruit. Sometimes things just didn't live up to expectations.

A lot of things, actually.

She managed to temper that billow of ire toward the other woman—and at life's letdowns—reminding herself that there were two sides to every story. Anyway, Grant's side didn't seem to hold Brenna with resentment. Just . . . maybe a hint of pain?

"Did you love her?"

Grant continued to stare out toward the distance. He inhaled. Then exhaled. Shook his head and finally dragged his attention back to Sage. "I do not know for sure." He brushed at the leg of his jeans. "I would have stayed with her, but I could see what she refused to see."

"What was that?"

"That she still loved him."

"So you let her go?"

His lips pressed into a line, and he nodded.

Not the normal response from men—at least not from the men Sage had experienced. Those who would insist that they were the better man, the better choice. The one who would love best. In books that seemed so romantic. But right then, as she watched Grant manage the ache she was certain he must feel, she thought perhaps this was the more noble character.

The one who let love go free when it was better for the other person. The one who chose pain over possessiveness.

Did that mean that Grant thought he couldn't love Brenna better than the other guy? Or maybe he thought he was unworthy of her devotion?

Or maybe his selflessness was what love was supposed to look like? That part . . . she wouldn't know. She didn't believe in love, really—the romance kind—in real life.

She dropped her attention to the sandwich on her plate. Maybe Sage should stick to narrating stories rather than making them up for other people. Fiction and reality didn't blend well.

Or maybe she should embrace the role she'd been cast in this part of Grant's life. Setting the plate aside, she scooched her way closer and covered his propped-up knee with her hand. "Tell what me to do."

His serious brow drew inward. "Do?"

"At the wedding. Tell me what you need from me. Am I to be the smitten new girlfriend? How would that look for you ideally? Do I hang on your arm and dote on you? Or am I prim and proper, only sneaking covert glances of adoration? I can do either."

Grant's brown eyes held her with that look again—the one of utter bafflement. He blinked and leaned away. "I do not need you to play a role."

"But—"

"I would rather you simply go with me as yourself. As . . . whatever this is right now." He motioned between them. "Or rather, before you asked that."

"What is this to you?" Such a forward question for a first date. Who really knew what *this* was? It was a picnic in the back of a truck. A shared sunset on a quiet wheat field. It was nothing consequential. Yet something . . . something entirely lovely.

Gentle brown eyes searched hers, and then he chuckled quietly. "This is . . . an unexpected pleasure. A break from my normal boring predictability—one I would never look for and did not know I wanted."

Delight stretched on her mouth. "I like that."

He covered her hand, squeezed, and then took up his plate of food.

"But the wedding," she said. "You asked me as your date, right?"

"I did." Grant held her with an honest look. "I do not want to be the object of collective pity at an event most of this small town will attend."

"Right. And so?"

"I told you—do not come to play a role. Be you, whoever you are."

"That seems risky. You don't know me."

That unexpected little grin moved his lips again. Sage was quickly finding that subtle look—all shy but pleased at the same time—a bit on the sexy side. The temptation to tell him so was nearly overwhelming—because certainly he'd blush. Which was also a touch thrilling.

"Tell me one thing I should know about you," he said.

Sage knew one thing he *must* know about her. She was relieved to have the chance to get it out there in the open—for both of their sakes. "I am a bird. I flit around through life, free and unattached. I never stay in one place for very long, and I don't ever want to have my wings clipped."

His brows lifted a small way, and he studied her while he processed that. Sage allowed the quiet moments and then turned his question back on him.

"Your turn. Tell me one thing I should know about you."

Tipping his head to one side, his look was measured, as if gauging how much he would trust her with. For some odd reason, she hoped it would be everything. "Remember, I never stay in one place for long, and I don't know anyone in Big Prairie. Whatever you tell me will stay with me."

Grant chuckled. "It is no big secret, really. I am more of an observer of life than a participant."

"Why?"

"So I can understand. At least, so I can try."

"Understand what?"

"People."

Sage looked skyward and laughed. "Is that possible?"

"For me? It is a constant struggle."

He was serious. Sage sobered quickly. "I'm sorry, Grant. I didn't mean to make fun."

That half smile—the rather shy one that Sage liked so well—poked on one side of his mouth. "I am not offended. I am admittedly an odd character. You can laugh."

"You aren't going to find a better sort of stranger to take to this wedding?"

"I like you so far." He met her eyes. "Even if you are entirely my opposite."

Perfectly said. Sage shifted her position so she sat beside him and then looped her hand through his arm. "I knew it."

"What is that?"

"We'll be the closest of friends."

He didn't respond with words. But when she lay her head on his shoulder, he reciprocated by leaning into her space. Another perfectly simple reply, which wrapped her heart in something gentle and lovely and a little bit foreign.

Into that charm came a thread of warning, a whisper she did not welcome. *Friendship* was one thing—all well and good. But that was all she could give this gentle, quiet man. She needed to proceed with caution. The very caution she'd just issued him—she was a flighty bird, always on the go.

Grant was the steady, rooted sort. More, his heart—what she had glimpsed of it so far—was too rare and beautiful to break.

CHAPTER EIGHT

HE WAS TOO ENAMORED of her.

Even in the early hours of the morning, time he had, years ago, set aside to soak in the Word of God and seek His presence—and Grant was disciplined about this practice, just as he was in every area of his life—he could not train his mind away from Sage.

No one had ever been that distracting.

Grant sat in his quiet house—too quiet—his Bible opened on the dining table in front of him but his mind preoccupied by a red-haired beauty who did not really fit into his world at all.

It did not make sense. He had spent all of two or three hours with the woman. She was, on every examination, not at *all* his type but rather the *fly into the wind just for a thrill, never hold on too tight* kind. He felt pretty sure on that. In other words, his opposite.

More, she used her genuine love of laughter as a mask. Of that he was more than pretty sure, though he did not know why.

Perhaps that was the real attraction—the need to understand. To study, to puzzle, and to solve.

Grant had learned how to read beneath the surface. It was something most people thought to be an intuitive gift. In truth, he worked hard at it. He had to, because his secret reality was that the social side of life did not make sense to him. At all. He watched and studied and silently dug for reasons and motives to understand what did not come naturally to him. It was the only way he could make sense of the world around him.

This, however, was *not* making sense. *He* was not making sense. Unless it was simply that driving need to gain insight.

He did not think that was the whole truth—and for Grant, truth was paramount. In this, the truth was that he was entranced with Sage Greene on a whole different level than was normal.

This . . . captivation could prove disastrous. In terms of psychology and relational happiness, Grant had the education to know that studies had shown the adage *opposites attract* was hardly a launching point for a satisfying long-term relationship.

Opposites might attract at the onset. But they rarely stayed happily attached. In fact, the pervasive belief in that claim led to any number of *un*happy relationships.

And why was he even thinking such things anyway? Grant had surmised with fair certainty that Sage was not the long-term-relationship type. After all, she had declared herself a flighty bird. As for himself, he was still licking his wounds, so to speak. Clinically, he'd tell himself to give his disappointing breakup with Brenna more time to heal before seeking out a new relationship.

Life, as it was turning out, was not clinical. As Brenna had pointed out to him during a few *discussions*, book knowledge and actual experience were not the same. Something he had conceded in their talks but was, at that moment, becoming more acquainted with in reality.

Because in reality, he could not pry Sage Greene from his mind, even if she was his opposite and that did not bode well.

One taste of her exuberance for life and he'd somehow become addicted. He longed to hear her charming laugh. Wanted to know her story and every bit of how she saw life. He craved a glimpse of her dancing brown eyes and that lovely flirty smile. If she woke every morning searching for joy and a surprise or two during the day, he wanted to experience both with her.

But he was boring, predictable Grant Hillman. The intense, introverted man who stood back from life, observing others at a distance. He liked stability. If Sage sought adventures, she would not find them with him. He was as tethered to routine as a flag was lashed to a pole.

They simply would not work. He'd known this from their first meeting, and the two after that had served only as confirmation.

Except, she had liked his quiet wheat field. Had thought the sunset lovely and had seemed genuinely happy to sit in the bed of Clayton's truck, her head tucked onto his shoulder, arm snaked with his.

When he'd dropped her off at precisely nine thirty—a full half hour before her grandfather's demanded curfew—she'd smiled at him with warm joy, the sort that exuded genuineness. Rising to her toes, she'd brushed a sweet kiss against his cheek and said, "That was delightful. Thank you, Grant Hillman." Then she'd squeezed his hand and slipped into the house.

Nothing of any of that had hinted that she'd been unimpressed with him. That she had thought him dull and awkward.

And there was the hang up. *She* seemed interested in him, despite his clumsy plainness.

One date. That could determine nothing. Besides, she'd said they'd be friends. The closest of that, but *friends* nonetheless.

Grant had no doubt that repeated comment had been intentional. A gentle warning to his heart not to get entangled.

He wouldn't let his heart, then. After all, he was the master at reining his emotions, directing them so that his actions aligned with what was right. Did not matter if he found Sage captivating in beauty or distractingly mysterious. They would move forward into this friendship with clear expectations: They would be the closest of friends. Nothing more. Nothing less. That was a perfectly acceptable arrangement.

Grant forced his mind toward the psalm that sat open before him. With more effort than it should have required, he set his fascination and worry aside and focused on the words of Psalm 139.

You know when I sit and when I rise; you perceive my thoughts from afar. You discern my going out and my lying down; you are familiar with all my ways. Before a word is on my tongue, you, Lord, know it completely. You hem me in before and behind, and you lay your hand upon me.

Inhaling, Grant put his heart to soak in those words. Considering the intimacy of God's knowledge of him, of his heart and his struggles, his far-off hopes for a life shared seemed as unlikely as a football career had been. Grant felt himself tremble.

No one knew him like that.

He shut his eyes as the wonder of it swelled. *But You do. And You will not forget me—You promised, right?*

Though he felt, on many occasions, alone and misunderstood, God—the one who'd made Him, who'd knit him together in his mother's womb, and who'd had entrusted him with this unique personality that usually set him apart from others—God *knew* him.

His memory summoned that very promise of remembrance from Isaiah 49, and he spoke the verse out loud. "'I will not forget you! See, I have engraved you in the palm of my hand.'"

The unrest he felt about Sage and about his unusual and immediate attachment to her, stopped thrashing. It did not disappear, but it stopped clawing at his peace. In that moment of surrender, Grant was able to pray with a clearer purpose.

Claiming his favorite slim-point Sharpie, he wrote out his simple but clear request in the spiral notebook he kept as a prayer journal. As he did so, he sensed a heavenly approval. As if God confirmed *This is why I brought her to Big Prairie. To you.*

Whatever this friendship with Sage would be, let it be for good.

•••••••••••

are you free

Grant glanced at the text and, surprisingly, rather than the normal irritation he'd experience at the lack of proper capitalization and punctuation, a touch of warmth filled his chest.

That would depend. What are we talking about here?

The dots at the bottom of the conversation scrolled.

tomatoes

What? The woman was as random as the wind, but not nearly as irritating. Not irritating at all, in fact, which, given their opposite tendencies, Grant found fascinating.

Sage was fascinating.

I need tomato plants for my garden

I found out that june is way too late to start them from seed

who knew?

She used a question mark on that last text, which was interesting. Why did she choose that one to punctuate? Was it because it was a question? Or was that entirely random as well?

Grant had no idea why these things that would normally put him off, make him shake his head and put some chilled space between himself and such a person, now seemed like a wonderful mystery he wanted to discover.

so are you free

No question mark on that query. What was her method?

Maybe Sage didn't have one. How did one survive life without a method?

Grant rubbed his jaw and became suddenly aware of the grin that stretched on his mouth. Rather than ponder the meaning of that—which he was more than likely to do later—he employed his thumbs on the screen.

I know of a place. We have a good greenhouse in town.

YAY!

meet me at that diner off the highway

what is it called

oh! Do you have time to do that?

More random punctuation. Grant chuckled.

Yes, I have time. Are you referring to The Grill?

that's the place!

Apparently exclamation points were always employed.

when

I'm so excited

let's do lunch k?

Grant sat back against his office chair and looked at his smart-watch—1:45. *You have not eaten lunch yet?*

Her response was delayed. Then a simple *no* flashed on her screen.

In that case, you had better make your way to The Grill immediately.

A heart-eyed emoji appeared. And that was all. But it was enough.

Smiling ridiculously, Grant tucked his phone into his shirt pocket, placed the report he had been working on into the file on his desk, put the package into his filing cabinet, and pushed his desk chair in. With a quick glance around to ensure his space was tidy, he then locked his office door and strode out of the school.

It was a good thing only minimal staff worked during the summer—and on that particular day, everyone else had already cleared out—because he had no doubt his expression would provoke a few questions.

· · · · ● · ● · · ·

Sage smiled brightly at the man walking toward the booth she'd claimed. Goodness, he was a good-looking specimen, even if he did wear way too

many button-downs and was meticulous about his hair. Those serious
brown eyes met her gaze and triggered an electrical jolt in her veins with
the way they lit up at their connection.

She shouldn't like this man quite so much. He wasn't her type—the type
searching for all fun and nothing much beyond that. More to the point, she
wasn't his type—the kind who was steady and reliable.

He shouldn't like her. But by the way his smile bloomed the moment
their gazes met, he did. Not to mention he had literally stopped whatever
he was doing to meet her on a whim.

Do not mess with this man. He's too nice . . .

Sage noted the warning, folded it neatly, and tucked it away for future
reference. When Grant stopped at the table she'd claimed, she patted the
top of it. "Saved this just for you."

"Thank you." Grant slid into the bench across from her.

"I ordered for us already too."

"You—" He blinked, folded his hands on top of the table, and leaned on
his elbows. "You ordered?"

"Waffle fries and a cheesecake shake."

By his furrowed brow and the slight wrinkling of his nose, Grant was
not impressed.

"Oh no."

"My thoughts exactly."

Crossing her arms, Sage slumped back against the bench. "You're the
healthy type, aren't you?"

One well-formed dark brow arched. "Let us just say that I am not the
type who calls waffle fries and ice cream lunch. Have you had anything good
for you today?"

Sage molded her best sassy face, which must have been a good one,
because Grant fought against the corners of his mouth nudging upward.

"I noticed the blueberries in my fridge this morning—left over from this charming wheat-field picnic I recently attended."

"You *noticed* them?"

"I did."

"Did you *eat* them?"

Sage shrugged. "Not yet."

"Why not? Blueberries are delicious."

"There wasn't any cream left."

"What happened to all that cream?"

With a bounce of her brows, Sage drew two fingers across her lips and pretended to toss away the proverbial key.

"Oh, Sage . . ." Grant sighed.

A large man with a large white apron interrupted their banter—the same man who had taken her unhealthy lunch order. His glance at Grant held a touch of curiosity. "Hello there, Mr. Hillman."

"Good afternoon, Wes."

"I made up some of that watercress and cherry salad you like today."

"Perfect."

"No waffle fries?" Sage shook her head and feigned sadness. "And here I thought we'd be such good friends."

"We can't be friends if I don't have waffle fries?"

Amusement crossed the server's face as he stood there, his look volleying from Sage to Grant and back again. "I wouldn't trust a man who didn't eat waffle fries either, young lady."

Sage scrunched up her best distrustful face. "I am questioning every-thing between us now, Grant Hillman."

The tinge of red creeping into Grant's cheeks made Sage's day.

The large server boomed with laughter. He looked down at her. "Now I must know your name."

"I'm sorry, Wes." Grant waved one hand toward Sage. "This is Sage Greene."

The burly man wiped his meaty hand on his apron and then nearly swallowed her outstretched hand in his massive grip. "Wes Morris."

"Wes owns The Grill," Grant said.

"My lovely wife, who is the brains behind this operation, would tell you that The Grill owns us." The large man, with an even larger smile, crossed his arms. "And I personally approve of your lunch choice, Sage Greene. However, for the record, this healthy fellow here is a good one, even if he eats rabbit food rather than waffle fries." He leaned down and dropped his voice to a conspirator's whisper. "I happen to know for a fact that he enjoys a peanut butter sundae on occasion."

Thoroughly delighted with the banter, Sage smirked at Grant. "That's passable. I think our friendship might survive."

"So am I to understand that I must eat a peanut butter sundae in order for this relationship to survive?"

"You understand correctly."

"That is a ridiculous demand."

"Be that as it may, you must comply."

"Or?"

She masked a deadly serious frown and drew a finger across her throat.

After a heartbeat and a blank stare, Grant snorted and then laughed. "If I must, then. Wes, I will need a sundae with my salad."

With a gleam in his eye, Wes nodded. "Coming up." He looked down at Sage again. "Impressive. Maybe you need to come work for me." He turned and left the pair.

"That was fun," she said.

"Buckets of fun."

"Why don't you eat waffle fries?"

"Grease does not agree with me."

"All grease?"

"Pretty much all grease."

"So no cheese curds?"

"Oh gosh." He grunted and covered his belly, as if he could feel the twisting of his gut for just speaking of such food. "No cheese curds ever."

"I am in deep grief for you."

"You would be much more so if you witnessed what cheese curds would do to me."

"Very well. I will eat them for you." Sage covered her heart as if swearing allegiance to a beloved king.

"Promise me forever."

The way Grant's eyes danced made Sage's heart delightfully light. She covered his arm and leaned in closer. "I promise."

Their gazes locked and held. In the space of a few heartbeats, the easy repartee that had passed between them sank into a much weightier silence. Not a bad weight—not at all. In fact, it felt soft and warm. Like . . . like . . .

Home.

Grant lowered his look toward the table. Sage sat back, pulling her fingers from his shirtsleeve. The pause between them shifted from comfortable to uneasy. After too many moments of that, Grant pulled his arms back into his sides. "Tell me something I should know about you."

Sage peeked at him, finding those serious eyes holding on to her. That red-flag warning waved in the back of her mind again. The one that frantically begged her not to damage this man, that he was too nice of a person for her to toy with his heart.

"I do not believe in love." She spoke the confession quietly. As if she regretted it. She didn't . . . except . . .

He sat back, stunned. "Don't you narrate romance novels?"

Nodding, she went stiff. "Yes. And they're fun. But all of that only lives on the page. I think it's best to know the difference between real life and fiction."

"What about all the people in the world who fall in love?"

"They fall right through it, I think. Because it isn't real. Think of all of the divorces. All the breakups. All the disappointed hearts in this world. All because they believed in something fictional."

"That is . . ."

She arched her brows. "That is what?"

"Sad," he said flatly.

Though she'd expected him to expand on his response—try to tell her where she was wrong—Grant didn't. He leaned back and held his peace.

Sage did not like the return of that uncomfortable silence between them. "Tell me something I should know about you."

For a long moment, Grant looked thoughtful. Then a half grin lifted one side of his mouth. "I don't eat waffle fries."

"That has already been covered."

"Then you have it all. Everything to know about Grant Hillman: I am predictable—most would say boring. I watch people in a vain attempt to understand the social rules that elude me. And I prefer salad to fries. I think that pretty much covers it."

"I don't believe that."

"No?"

"Not one bit."

"Hmmm . . ." He rubbed his chin. "I suppose there might be one more thing."

"Yeah?"

"I think I am prone to agree with you."

"About love?"

"No. About life. That it is best to know the truth."

"Oh." A sharp stab of disappointment sank into her chest, and Sage couldn't determine exactly why.

CHAPTER NINE

SAGE PULLED THE NOISE-CANCELING headphones from her ears and rolled her neck one way and then the other. Blowing out a breath, she set the headphones on top of the tablet she had been reading from and slouched back against the chair.

She was off today. Her characterizations fell flat. The story did not come to life. It was all vanity. A waste of time, and Sage could not make herself fall into it.

A session in her new garden it was then.

Sage highlighted the section of the book to mark her place, made sure her recording equipment was shut off, and fluffed the cushion she'd placed on the wooden chair that kept her posture erect. Once all was situated in her makeshift recording booth, she left the cramped little room and made her way down the narrow stairs and into the galley kitchen.

"How are you doing, Gramps?" she called while popping ice cubes from the tray she'd pulled from the freezer.

The muffled sound of some black-and-white TV show was briefly interrupted by the old man's grunt.

"Are you hungry? I can make us some sandwiches."

"It's eleven."

That meant no. Gramps did things by the clock. Breakfast at eight—two eggs over medium, a slice of wheat toast covered with butter and Miss Jane's jam, and a glass of cranberry juice. Lunch—though he called it *dinner*—at noon. Supper at five.

"Need some water?"

"Got my coffee."

And there was that—the bottomless mug of coffee. Black, stout, and steaming hot. He brewed at least three pots a day.

"Okay." Sage made her way around the corner, through the hall that separated one side of the farmhouse from the other, and into Gramps's room. "I'm going to go out and put those tomato plants in."

Those watery eyes lifted to search her face. "You ever grow anything in your life?"

"Not once." Sage shrugged. "How hard could it be?"

Gramps grunted as he sat forward, forcing the footstool of his recliner back into place. The old chair squealed a ghastly protest.

The churn of emotions toward this man continued to surprise her. At best she should feel indifferent. After all, he'd had nothing to do with them in all the lifetime she or her mother could remember. But he'd allowed her to push her way into his home. He'd grunted and grumbled and grouched . . . and then opened his door to her. Then there was the whole leaving the house and property to her mother. Why would this man do that?

And to add more confusion to the mix, he had those moments when there was a peek at a genuine care he held for her.

She glanced at the white tulips sitting in the middle of that coffee table. *Back by ten*, Gramps had commanded. Because he was a control freak? She didn't think so. He sure was a grump though.

Sage pushed away the brew of conflict in her heart. After all, she was after joy and adventure. If she could find that here, even with this grumpy old man, that would be a win.

"We should get you a new one of those." Sage pointed to his chair. "They make them much nicer now."

"Been planting my backside in that for more than fifty years, girl. Another year or so won't make much difference." Gramps gripped his cane. "Now, what do you think you're gonna grow in my dirt?"

Sage smiled. "Tomatoes. Peppers. I already planted the green beans."

He nodded, then shuffled toward the back of the house. Rooted to her place, wondering if he really intended to go out and *help* her, Sage watched him until he reached the back door. There, wearing a severe scowl, he motioned for her to follow.

"Get moving, girl."

"Yes, sir." She nearly skipped as she made her way toward him, then opened the door and stood back while he hobbled his way down the back two steps.

He turned and looked back up at her. "Go fish those eggshells out of the garbage."

"From this morning?"

"And yesterday."

"What for?"

He gave her his back without answering, limping his way toward the seedlings she had purchased at the local greenhouse Grant had taken her to yesterday.

Twisting her lips to one side, Sage debated whether to go through the trash to pull out used eggshells. That was gross. Was there a point? Maybe the old man she'd taken to calling *Gramps* even though he didn't deserve the title was giving her a hard time. Making a fool of her because she was an imposition on his solitary life.

Then again, he'd ratcheted his creaky old body out of his comfy chair to help her plant tomatoes in a garden he hadn't wanted but had helped dig. And he'd given her an ultimatum about a man taking her out, complete with a curfew—his cross way of protecting her.

He cared.

It didn't make sense, but Gramps cared about her. Sage was certain of it, and it made the hard spot in her heart—the place she tried with all her determined might to plaster with happy faces and laughter—all soft and squishy. It also made her wrestle more with confusion about who he was and why he had done what he'd done.

Why he had started this family curse that she was now stuck with.

What would make a man who seemed as stubbornly grounded as Gramps reject his wife and his son? How did that reconcile with this old version of the same man whose bark was much worse than his bite?

"Girl!"

Sage started at his sharp call, finding herself still standing in the doorway looking at him but not seeing him at all. She swallowed and summoned a bright smile. "Yes, sir?"

"Get going. I ain't gonna stand here all day and wait."

"Right." Spinning on the ball of one foot, she set off to dig in the trash. As she did so—and ew, there were wet, used coffee grounds, used napkins, and the foam meat tray from the chicken she'd made yesterday—Sage let the stories she'd been told about Gramps cycle through her mind.

He and Great-Grandma Clara had had a whirlwind romance. She had still been in high school when it started, and he'd been an ambitious young man with a touch of a wild streak. He'd wanted adventure and success, and Clara had a thirst for the same. Mostly, though, she was starry-eyed over him. Would do anything to please him.

They married in a rush, and James Teller was born within two years. Somewhere in that time, the boil of romance had chilled, and Harold had grown tired of Clara and the responsibility of being a dad. He'd sent her and his son away. As callous and coldhearted as any villain Sage had ever read in a novel.

The consolation of her family had been this: Harold Teller was a nothing. He lived the rest of his days alone in Big Prairie. Exactly where Sage had found him, on what was left of his family farm, most of that having been sold in the eighties—another flagship of failure for the man.

No less than he deserved.

Was this the story of the man examining tomato plants out back?

Grabbing an old Tupperware bowl, Sage puzzled at that. It could be, couldn't it? Didn't regret wear pride off of a man? Perhaps, like the announcement of Gramps's intention to leave the house to her mother—an offer that had made Mom roil—this chilled kindness was something of penitence. A man living in his sunset years might want to make peace with his past any way he could.

She placed the eight eggshells she'd recovered into the bowl and moved to the sink to wash her hands.

How did she feel about being the vessel of Harold Teller's atonement?

She felt curious about his life—his part of the story. Did he regret sending Clara and their baby away? If so, why had he never reached out to her? To Sage's knowledge, the only time Harold ever attempted contact with the family was at Clara's funeral. Too little, too late. But if he'd spent his life alone here in this dump as penance, why hadn't he tried to make amends sooner?

And she felt mystified by the way he was with her. From day one Harold had been an odd concoction of bristling old man with a soft, maybe even bruised underbelly.

She'd shown up unannounced and determined not to let him see her tremble when he'd answered the door with a harsh "Go away, girl. I ain't interested in hearing about your church ideas. God and me are in a personal battle."

"I haven't any church ideas, mister. I'm not really religious at all."

He studied her for a moment, a trace of hesitant curiosity in his watery eyes. "What are you doing here? Don't you know I'm dangerous?"

"I heard that you shoot at anyone who comes near your front door." She peeked around the partially open door, making a bit of a show of it. "I don't see a gun though."

The old man grunted, then began to shut the door in her face.

"I'm Sage Greene. Your great-granddaughter," Sage had blurted.

And that had worked. His head had come up slowly, that watery gaze still cautious. "Why would I believe that?" His tone, and the recognition in his eyes, betrayed that he already did.

Likely because Sage was the image of her great-grandma Clara. She'd seen a black-and-white of the woman, made when Great-Grandma had been young—likely in high school. When Harold had taken up with her. Same curly hair. Same oval face. Same thin lips. Same determined chin.

Same wild, free-spirited expression.

We are birds, Sage. Always ready to take flight. Don't let a man clip your wings. We were not made to stay in one place.

Words passed from Clara to Sage's mother and then from Mother to Sage. Advice more than likely tinged with bitterness because the women in her family line had discovered the faithlessness of men. It was their curse. Every one of them—including Harold's son, who went by Jimmy. Jimmy Teller grew up to be exactly like his absentee father. Reckless. Irresponsible. And he had died of liver failure, a pathetic, lonely man.

Sage had never known her grandfather. But she'd taken the lessons the women of her line had learned by generations.

Better to keep your heart free than to let it be broken.

Better to be a bird flitting from one place to the next than to be a rooted tree cut down by an axe. Even if it meant denying the quiet longing for a home, for a place to belong and to call your own.

Even if it meant denying the existence of enduring romantic love. Even if you wished with all of your guts it was real.

Sage wiped her dripping hands on a kitchen towel, pushing that bit of introspection back down to the bottom of her heart. Toward that cold, hard place she kept covered with smiles and fun.

Gramps was simply trying to make amends at the end of his life, and Sage would allow it. After all, people shouldn't die in bitter loneliness—despite what Mother claimed. There was just something in Sage that couldn't allow that. If her being there in that wreck of a house helped the old man build a bridge from his selfish, broken past, to a better end of his life, then that was good.

Though she might be a flighty bird without a home, she wanted her life to count for good.

Right now, planting tomatoes with her estranged Gramps seemed like a good means to that end. Sage hung up the hand towel where it belonged and, with a well-rehearsed smile, took herself outback, Tupperware of eggshells in hand.

"I've got them." She stepped down the back stairs.

Gramps didn't look up. He stood at the rickety old table she'd found out back and had claimed for her gardening bench, pulling leaves off her plants.

"Hey!" Sage jogged over to him. "What are you doing? I paid good money for those."

He swatted at her hands as she reached to rescue her seedlings. "I know what I'm doing." Pinning a glare on her, he then lifted one four-pack of plants and regripped his cane. "Bring the others."

Sage studied the two remaining four-packs. The tomatoes only had four leaves left at their spindly tops. A spark of irritation ignited from that hard spot at the bottom of her heart. She hadn't asked him to come out here. Snagging the plants and piling them on top of the silly eggshells, Sage marched herself over to the garden patch where Gramps had just arrived.

"You don't have to sabotage me."

"I ain't." He pinned another hard look on her. "Grew up farming, girl. I told you—I know what I'm doing." Pushing the four-pack he had into her middle, he shook his head. "Lay them out."

"What?"

"Lay them out the way you think you want them. But I can tell you already, if you want those three rows of beans to stay put, you're not going to be able to fit all these in this tiny little space."

"There's plenty of room." Sage bent to place the bowl of eggshells on the ground and then marched into the freshly turned soil to point where she wanted her plants. "Look. Here, here, here . . ." Every foot, she poked her finger into the ground. "Lots of space besides."

"You gonna grow a hedge?"

"A hedge?"

"The fruit will be tiny, you do that. And you'll likely end up with powdery mildew."

"What?"

"Look, you got to give things space to grow. Room to spread their branches out and thrive." He limped his way into the garden and took the four-pack he'd just shoved at her back into his hands. Pinching the bottom of the plastic, he loosened the seedling and pulled it free. At one of her poked holes, he laid the plant on the ground. Then he repeated the action, placing the second plant at her third poked hole.

"*That* much space?" Sage popped her hands on her hips, casting a none-too-sure look at him.

"*That* much. These are sauce tomatoes—they'll get big. Give 'em room."

"What about the peppers?"

"They can go closer. Eighteen inches, I'd say." Gramps straightened after placing the fourth tomato plant. "Unless you're planning to do some canning this fall, four tomato plants should be good for just you and me."

Irritation dissipated, Sage let a small grin soften her expression. Not only had she discovered a way to pry words from Gramps, but he'd just indicated he wouldn't be opposed to her staying there with him long term. For a girl who claimed to have only wings and no roots, she sure did warm to the thought of it.

"Do you like tomatoes, Gramps?"

"Only if they're fresh. Jane Hopewell brings 'em to me in the summer, from her garden."

"Ah . . . Miss Jane." The only person in Big Prairie who willingly came out to the Teller place. Except Grant Hillman, but that was a different story. Sage raised her brows. "How about you tell me about Miss Jane?"

His scowl came back in record time, and those brown eyes grew dark and sharp. "Ain't nothing to tell. The woman insists on bringing me stuff. I ain't never asked for it."

"That's *awful* nice of her." Sage couldn't help the suggestive tone in her voice.

"Whatever that means, girl, you keep your thoughts pure when it comes to Jane Hopewell. She's a good person. Best person this town ever saw. Don't go presuming anything else."

As a touch of guilt heated her gut, Sage looked toward the ground. She hadn't meant an innuendo. "I can see that, Gramps."

"Good. Now, get to work, why don't we? Don't want to be out here all day."

Sage did as he commanded. The first hole she dug was too shallow for Gramps, though the little plant fit exactly into it.

"Deeper. Give it good roots, and crumple an eggshell into the bottom of the hole."

By the time her little planting hole gained his approval, Sage figured she was basically burying the tomato. Only those four remaining leaves poked from the soil, making the plant look sadly stubby and not impressive at all. But she did as Gramps said—or barked.

By the time she had her seedlings tucked in, her hands were dry and dirt had packed under her nails. But when she glanced up to Gramps, who had stood watch the whole time, repeating instructions as she went, she caught a ghost of a smile. Just a hint. It was something light and lifelike.

It made her like him more. And more determined to discover his story.

CHAPTER TEN

HE DECIDED TO RISK the dirt road with his Altima. After all, borrowing Clayton's white pickup truck might have been a perfect option for the wheat-field picnic, but this time they were going to a wedding. Even if they would head out toward the vineyard after the ceremony for the reception, his car was the better choice.

Man, he overthought *everything*.

Truth was, he very much doubted his vehicle choice would make any difference to Sage. The woman jumped into the river fully clothed. She thought a wheat-field picnic had been brilliant. She wouldn't care about his mode of transportation.

Why did he? What was this desperate need to impress her all about? She bemused him, and from the moment of their first meeting, his thoughts had become a tangled mess. Had he been this way with Brenna?

He didn't think so.

As he sat in the driver's seat wondering about things that were irrelevant, the front door to the old farmhouse swung open, and then . . .

Then there she was. Dressed in a knee-length green dress that gently hugged her feminine curves, her wonderfully wild, curly hair pulled back loosely, and that happy-go-lucky smile making her face shine.

She was stunning. And that smile? It was for him.

Grant thought he might die, with the way his heart clenched and his breath stalled. Good heavens, what did this woman possess?

With a hard exhale, Grant exited his vehicle, stood straight, rolled his shoulders back, and fixed his tie. What he couldn't do was make his racing heart come back down to a slow, steady, *reasonable* rhythm.

Sage, as usual, threw him completely off kilter. Only this time she hadn't even said anything. She made him completely *unreasonable*, and the most bizarre thing about it was that he enjoyed it.

Don't be a fool. With that firm command, Grant moved forward, reaching her as she stepped down the last step. "Good evening."

"Hi." The sound of her soft laugh made him think of a gentle breeze ruffling his hair after a good run. He wanted to close his eyes, tilt his face toward the heavens, and savor the delight.

That would be so weird, even for him.

Instead, he focused on being a gentleman. That, he did know how to do. "I would have knocked on the door if you'd waited."

"I have no doubt."

"Your grandfather would have preferred that, I'm sure."

Sage shrugged. "I wore Gramps out today. We planted tomatoes—apparently, I am woefully ignorant on how to do such things, so it was a good thing I have him."

"He *helped* you?"

"Well, more like he stood outside and gave me commands. But still . . ." The smile she sent up to him spoke of victory and fondness.

That was also mysterious. How had Sage carved out a relationship with a man known best for being angry and shooting at people?

"So he's sleeping?"

"No, but he's resting. I'm afraid he'll not be his best self to you right now."

Grant couldn't stop the snort. "His best self?"

"Yes." She winked. "I think he's sore from bending and pointing, and that is making him grouchy." With a slip of her hand beneath his bicep, she nudged him toward his waiting car.

Grant fell into step beside her easily enough, though he couldn't peel his study from her face. There was an earnest layer there, even with the dancing laughter in her eyes. "I think I'd like to know the story between you and your grandfather."

She tipped her head to one side, her expression thoughtful. "It's a developing tale."

"You didn't know him at all growing up?"

"No. I only saw him once, briefly, when I was eleven. He came to my great-grandmother's funeral. He spoke to no one—which is understandable, since my mother and grandmother loathed his presence."

Near the nose of the car, Grant came to an abrupt halt while he pieced that bit of information out. "Your great-grandmother . . . his wife?"

Sage clearly read his puzzled thoughts. "His ex-wife."

"He went to her funeral?"

Her nose wrinkled, and then she nodded her head. "There is something unknown in his story. Something off . . ."

Grant refocused on her, finding her attention fixed back on him. "Is that why you came here?"

"No. I came fully expecting to fight a drunk old man."

"That seems . . . unwise."

"Stupid. That's what my mother said."

"Why did you do it?"

"When I read the letter from the lawyer . . . I don't know. It seemed wrong for us to simply take a man's property after he died when we'd never made an effort to know him at all. And it seemed terribly sad to think of him dying alone."

At the evidence of a tender heart, layered beneath her free spirit and firm claim to not believe in love, Grant knew a fresh longing to know her. To really *know* who Sage Greene was, beyond the laughter and determined fun that seemed both true and a mask.

Reaching past his deeply introverted and cautious normality, Grant held out a hand, and when she slipped her palm against his, he drew her nearer. For a long moment, her gaze fastened to his, and there was a silent space of something warm and beautiful and intimate.

She broke the connection, looking toward the car. "We were going to a wedding, right?"

"Yes." His voice felt rough and forced, and he wanted only for her to look back at him as she'd just done.

With a bright smile—too bright—Sage squeezed his fingers and then moved around the nose of his car. "Off we go to it, then. Unless you want to make a scene by being late?"

No. He didn't want that. The whole reason he'd asked Sage to go with him was to deflect attention from himself.

Perhaps that had not been the *whole* reason.

· · · · ●· ● · · · ·

The bride and groom made a stunning pair.

As Sage and Grant passed through the open double doors of the quaint but impressive lodge by the vineyard where the reception was to be held, Sage made a surreptitious but careful examination of the bride in particular. She was a beauty—a shorter woman with blond hair and crystal-blue eyes who seemed to be well loved by everyone in attendance, and *that* seemed likely to be the whole town.

Big Prairie's sweetheart, Sage mused, and then she imagined that adorable creature on Grant's arm rather than on the arm of the larger, good-looking man in the tux.

She didn't like that image much at all. In fact, she experienced an unfamiliar twist of something hot and distinctly unfriendly in her middle. What was that?

Envy.

That was . . . out of place. One was only envious of another if they possessed something one wanted for themselves. As Sage lived her life free and unattached, a legacy passed on to her by her mother, who had gained it from her mother, Sage couldn't possibly be jealous over another woman on Grant Hillman's arm. Sage had no long-term claim on the man who was her date that evening.

And anyway, she wasn't jealous. Couldn't possibly be. Brenna Blaum had just become Brenna Erickson. That made everything about Sage's physical and emotional reaction to the beautiful bride entirely ridiculous.

That settled, Sage turned her examination to her surroundings. The log structure was open and airy, with a vaulted ceiling and a series of windows on three of the four sides of the building. Every pane offered a view of the vineyard, which would likely be stunning had it not been for a once-in-a-lifetime flood that had coursed through Big Prairie two months before—Gramps still talked about it. The panorama of the now normal-sized river, however, *was* stunning.

There were etches of tragedy and triumph in both views.

The river had left deep scars upon the land. But the flood waters had receded, and the people who worked the damaged land were showing their resilience. They stayed. They worked. They hoped.

The vineyard owners, for example, were in the process of replanting the grapevines that had been lost to the flood. Small wisps of green stretched heavenward, reaching for the cross supports that had been installed for them. Their efforts whispered hope despite great loss. The determination to continue forward, no matter what had been destructive in the past, was admirable.

"I wish you had seen it before." Grant spoke quietly, clearly having caught her gaze beyond the building. "Lance worked for more than a decade to make this place something special. Losing it . . ."

"A near tragedy?" She glanced up to find sympathy carved deep in the lines around Grant's eyes. *A man who can feel others' pain . . .*

That seemed incredibly rare. And was wholly attractive.

Grant nodded. "Lance was as close to broken as I've ever seen him—and he and his brother have not had an easy life to begin with."

"Is he a good friend?"

Something dimmed in Grant's look as he glanced toward his feet. "I am not sure one could say that. We graduated together though."

"Would you claim anyone as a close friend?"

His lips seamed as a look of being caught—and not the delightful kind that she had thrilled at before—transformed Grant's face. Again, he looked toward the floor, and she felt him put subtle space between them.

She did not want that. Reaching for his elbow, she slipped her grip around his bicep and stepped nearer his side. His silent study on her seemed to whisper a timid *Can I trust you?*

The honest answer would likely be no. When It came to hearts, she'd inherited clumsy hands. He shouldn't trust her with any part of his. And she shouldn't want him to—she never had before.

But she fixed her gaze on his, felt her mouth move in a tender lift, and saw the intensity of his brown eyes deepen.

She couldn't help herself. "Perhaps you will claim me as one?"

"I hope to." His response came without hesitation, as if fully from the heart and not something he carefully considered at all.

That should have terrified her. For both of them.

"Grant." A woman with glossy black ringlets and a friendly smile reached to shake Grant's hand. "It's good to see you."

Sage felt her date stiffen.

"How are you, Sophie?" he said.

The woman's dark-brown eyes glittered as she latched on to the tall man wearing a cowboy hat at her side. "We're good."

The tension in Grant's muscles eased. "Married life is going well?"

The cowboy looked down, and there was no mistaking the joy in his face as he met the woman's upturned gaze. "Married life is good." He turned his attention back to Grant, encompassing Sage in his look.

"Do we get to meet your guest?" the woman asked.

"Yes, of course. I am sorry." Grant moved so that he could place his hand on the small of Sage's back.

She thrilled at that. As well as at his warm expression.

"This is Sage Greene, Mr. Teller's great-granddaughter." Grant motioned first to the woman. "This is Sophie and her newly acquired husband, Lance Carson. They own this lodge and everything you see beyond it."

Ah, the very man they'd just been talking about. They seemed on friendly enough terms, though Grant had just said he wasn't sure they'd qualify as *good* friends.

In response to first Sophie's offered hand, and then Lance's, Sage shook both as they exchanged the standard, "Nice to meet you."

"Mr. Teller's great-granddaughter, hmm?" Lance asked.

"Yes, though I'm guessing that's a surprise."

"A little bit." Lance nodded. "No one seems to know Old Man Teller's story—other than he doesn't want to be bothered."

"That seems to sum Gramps up. But he's not nearly as mean as he puts on."

"His bark is worse than his bite?"

"Exactly."

The conversation died there. Grant and Lance seemed perfectly fine with that.

Sophie broke the span of silence. "How did you two meet?"

Sage glanced up to Grant, wondering how much of their first meeting he would appreciate her sharing. For her part, she thought it the most unique and fun story she'd experienced in a long while, and she loved it.

Grant though . . .

"I was out for a jog, and Sage was swimming in the deep part of the river behind Teller's farmhouse. We happened to be at the same spot at the same time."

Well then. Now she knew exactly how much he wanted to share—which was not much. Usually one to delight in telling a good tale, Sage found herself surprisingly okay with that.

Perhaps because she knew he already felt conspicuous at this wedding, being the recent ex-boyfriend of the bride.

"Grant is one of the only people I've met in Big Prairie, so I latched on to him." She winked up at her date.

He rewarded her with a small secretive grin and a hint of a blush.

"Oh goodness, we can fix that." Sophie stepped back. "Nearly everyone from town is here."

She felt the man at her side stiffen.

"Actually, Grant and I were just talking about a dance." Sage couldn't tell if that was a save or if she'd just made Grant's discomfort worse.

Grant slipped his hand over hers and nodded at the new Mrs. Carson. "Thank you though, Sophie."

"Of course. It's nice to meet you, Sage." The couple stepped to the side, allowing Grant and Sage to pass them as he led her to the middle of the floor.

Over the speakers, a smooth tenor country voice sang to the music of a steel guitar, something about the keeper of the stars.

She had found herself in a cliché country wedding. Not really the unique, adventurous sort of storyline Sage preferred. But when Grant turned her into his arms, she discovered she didn't really mind.

He leaned in close before they moved. "I am not a great dancer."

With one hand on his shoulder, she leaned back just enough to make eye contact. "I'm not much for two-stepping. But here we are." She winked. "Shall we see how this scene plays out?"

He rewarded her exactly as she'd hoped, with that gentle, kind look that she was alarmingly becoming addicted to. At least, she probably should be alarmed.

"If we use our imaginations," she said, "we could pretend that rather than dancing to a country love song, we are engaged in a fantastic sword fight. Both require a little choreography."

At his lead, they were two-stepping—quick, quick, slow, slow. "Why would we do that?"

"Because then you wouldn't worry about who is here and what they think." She found his pace and moved easily enough with him.

He guided her backward, and she discovered that he had underreported his ability at this. He moved steadily, smoothly. "I am certain a sword fight would be far less conspicuous."

"Perhaps not, but your attention would necessarily be entirely on me."

At that shocking comment, the intensity of his look became narrow and nearly electric. "I find that is possible without a sword."

Her pulse zipped and her belly summersaulted—both sensations exhilarating.

Turned out this dancing-at-a-wedding cliché wasn't nearly as lame as she'd thought. Grant hadn't tucked away his ability to banter with her, even if the situation was outside his scope of comfort. And even better, *the man could flirt.* In the most sincere, thrilling way, Grant Hillman possessed the ability to flirt.

Sincere flirting—was that even possible? For this man, yes, it was.

Sage savored the discoveries. "Do you feel conspicuous?"

"Yes, a little." Grant glanced about the lodge and then focused his attention back on her. "It is a relief, however, that the looks are of a curious nature rather than pity, and not really focused on me at all."

"Your scheme played out, then."

"Perfectly."

The admiration in his study, held firmly on her, triggered a flood of warmth to wash through her chest. There was a distinct possibility she was blushing in his arms.

"It's only because I'm the girl they don't know. The mystery they want to uncover."

"You are a mystery." He leaned nearer and whispered, "But I would wager they stare because you are lovely, and that jade dress perfectly complements you." Then he dared to wink.

Grant Hillman, winking! At that point Sage was pretty sure she knew him well enough to know that action would absolutely cause a ripple of whispers. Grant was not the winking type. He wasn't the daring type. Dare she hope . . . He wasn't the flirting type. Not normally. Only, he was different with her.

That was why his doing so was so exhilarating.

Was she imagining all this? She enjoyed the moment—and this story—far too much to care whether she'd made it up or not.

"I wondered if you would notice my dress. Actually, I suspected you would."

"Why would you guess that?"

"You're a details guy."

"Who told?"

"Your texts. All capped and punctuated properly. And your promptness. Both dates on time exactly, right when you said you would be there. Then there's the state of your car."

"What is wrong with my car?"

"I didn't say there was a thing wrong with anything. Only that your car is cleaner than most hotel rooms, and my closet would be jealous of the organization of your glove box."

"You looked into my glove box?"

"Of course I looked into your glove box. I always check a date's glove box. You can tell a lot about a man by the situation in his glove box."

"Hmm." Grant let that be his only response. Then, "Do I pass inspection?"

"You surpass all expectations." She didn't mean to say that so . . . sincerely.

For a moment—a breathless, beautiful moment—their gazes held. His was open, warm, and intense. She shivered at the sensation of his thumb tenderly caressing the small of her back. He leaned in, down, hovering deliciously in her space. And then . . .

Then he pulled away. The hand on her back went flat and stiff, and his arms lengthened as he put space between them. Those kind brown eyes grew distant. For the remainder of the song, they simply danced.

Sage wondered what he was thinking. Had she offended him? She couldn't think why he would take offense. Had she given him some kind of signal that told him she wasn't receptive? That would be impossible. The buzzing of her body and the throbbing of her heart told her there was no way she could have communicated anything but *absolutely receptive!*

But she felt his slow, quiet withdrawal, and it made her sad.

Desperately sad.

The music ended, and they stilled on the dance floor. When Grant stepped back, releasing his hold altogether, Sage moved forward, gripping his arm and silently demanding his eyes find hers again.

And they did. In that look, caution mixed with that warmth that she liked so much. She wanted only the warmth, only the thrilling intensity she'd experienced moments before.

"I'm glad this isn't *your* wedding, Grant Hillman." Her heart raced as the words slipped from her mouth.

What was she doing? There were implications in that kind of statement. Things she really couldn't mean at all. Could she?

Grant stared at her, his long, silent watch measuring and powerful. And then the openness she'd glimpsed earlier shuttered. He stepped backward again, taking her hand in a gentle hold. With a small squeeze of her fingers, he looped her arm through his and guided her through the maze of couples remaining on the dance floor.

She'd said something terribly wrong. Waiting until they passed from the crowded lodge and onto the sparsely populated deck, Sage turned to him. "Grant?"

"Thank you for coming with me tonight."

"But—" Sage sighed. "But I just upset you. I didn't mean to—that was a thoughtless thing to say." Had that been it? She'd knifed his already wounded heart about this wedding of his ex-girlfriend's? It had been badly done, for sure.

"No. I am not upset."

"What are you?"

"I—" He looked toward the gray-orange sky, a sight that she should have found entrancing because she loved sunsets. She didn't at that moment.

Grant's expression grew more pensive. "I am awkward."

"I make you awkward?" There was truth to that—and she'd rather enjoyed it. The way she baffled him with her flamboyant ways was wholly amusing. And she rather thrilled when his shocked look morphed toward curiosity and then to pleasure—and *that* he tried very hard to smother.

But not this. She didn't enjoy this. Not the sort of awkwardness that made him feel bad.

"No. You make me—" Turning from the sunset display back to her, he shook his head.

What had he been going to say before he cut himself off? Sage wanted to know his every thought, and the reason this gentle, tender man held himself aloof from the world. Didn't he know his charm? Didn't he understand the wonder of the depth he possessed?

Didn't he know she was captivated by him?

That's not safe . . .

"I am simply awkward." With one hand, Grant motioned toward the scene back inside the lodge. "This kind of situation . . . I do not know how to fit in. I do not understand the rules."

Rules? What rules? "You were—"

"Grant." A woman's voice—elderly by the sound of it—snatched the illusion of privacy away, stealing Sage's turn to speak. Grant's shoulders repositioned as he resumed his perfectly straight posture and adopted the sort of expression that one would expect at a professional meeting.

Composed, cool, and a touch distant. Exactly as she'd seen at the wedding ceremony. To everyone around him, Grant Hillman was a closed book. Everyone except for a few treasured moments, to *her*.

That privilege could be intoxicating. And the mystery of it was commanding.

A familiar woman with bright blue eyes and silver hair pulled back in a loose updo walked from the open doors of the lodge toward their spot near the deck rail. "I'm so glad to see you here," she said.

The man at Sage's side grew noticeably stiffer. "Thank you, Miss Jane. It is good to see you as well." He motioned to Sage. "May I introduce you to Sage Greene?"

The older woman chuckled. "You may if you like. But I've already met Sage. A few times, in fact."

Wondering about his reaction—did he not like Miss Jane? —but not wanting to allow Grant to feel any more awkward, Sage smiled warmly. "Miss Jane delivers a box of goods to Gramps every week."

"Oh yes." Grant's tone took on a neutral quality Sage couldn't read and didn't like. Where had the warm, enthralling man she'd just danced with gone? What were these steel bars he was putting up all about? "I believe you told me that already. My apologies."

"None necessary." Miss Jane either didn't notice Grant's coolness or ignored it. Perhaps this was normal between them? In any case, she pushed past the fences Grant was silently placing between himself and everyone else and reached to latch on to his free arm. "I saw the pair of you dancing just now, and I was so happy to see you doing so."

"Thank you." Grant's cardboard voice only made the strange response weirder.

Miss Jane continued, undeterred. "I have wanted to see this lovely young lady out and about town for weeks now. A girl as lovely as she should not spend her life hidden away with that grumpy character all the time." She chuckled as she referenced Gramps.

A fingerling of defense touched Sage's heart. "Gramps is not so bad."

"No, Harold is certainly not bad at all. Once you get past his scowl." Miss Jane reached across Grant to touch Sage's hand, which was still wrapped on Grant's opposite arm. "I have known him since we were both much younger and better looking." She lifted a cheeky grin and then sobered. "And he has reasons for keeping others away. I am ever so glad that you've come. He's waited . . ." There, Miss Jane's voice drifted away. A sadness stole the joy from her expression. And her hand fell from Sage's arm.

"He's waited?" For Sage? Or perhaps for Sage's mother? Neither made sense. Great-Grandfather Harold hadn't bothered to contact any of them—his son, his granddaughter, or his great-granddaughter—until just a few months before.

If he'd wanted them to be a part of his life, he should have tried a long time ago.

Miss Jane held Sage with a tender look, one that she lifted to Grant as well. "Sometimes that's all one can do."

Was this a code? Did Grant have any idea what this woman was talking about?

The exuberance reentered Miss Jane's countenance. "Now. Let's talk about when I get to feed you."

"Feed . . . me?" Grant gawked at her.

"Yes. You, Grant Hillman. You haven't been to my shop since . . . well, for months. And I find that does not sit well with me. I think that since you've pulled the lovely Miss Sage away from her grandfather's seclusion once, you certainly could do it again." She winked at Sage. "Couldn't he?"

Grant made a throaty noise—perhaps he was choking? "We aren't . . . I mean . . . Sage and I aren't . . ." He pinned a panicked look on Sage.

Part of Sage was amused—Grant was adorable when thrown off-kilter. Part of her felt irritated—as if *she* were the only woman allowed to throw this buttoned-up man from his balance. Part of her wished he could ease up a bit.

All of her wanted to see him again, even if it meant sharing him with the quirky Miss Jane.

Sage met his pleading look with a sweet grin. "I would enjoy that."

She felt the rush of breath leave his body. "Oh." He cleared his throat again. "Then . . ."

"When should we come?" Sage looked around Grant at Miss Jane again.

The older woman squeezed Grant's arm as she made a triumphant little sound. "Let's not waste any time. Monday?"

"Monday is good for me. Grant?"

He glanced between the women, a touch of cute bewilderment still on his face. "I have a meeting at school Monday morning and a client scheduled in the afternoon."

"Lunch?" Miss Jane was not going to be put off.

"Uh . . . yes. Lunch would work."

"Excellent. Come to my shop." With a pat on his arm and then a squeeze of Sage's hand, Miss Jane pulled herself away. "Don't bring a thing," she said. "I will manage everything."

She floated back into the lodge, leaving Sage alone with Grant again. Sage glanced up to the man who wore befuddlement on his face, and she chuckled. "I like her."

Grant's stare held on to the spot where Miss Jane had just been before she disappeared into the crowd. "She doesn't like me," he muttered.

"What? That woman?" Sage shook her head. "I can't image such a person has the ability to *dis*like anyone."

"She didn't like *me*," he repeated. Then he looked toward his shoes. The expression of bewilderment slipped away entirely, leaving only one that spoke of rejection and defeat.

Sage resented whatever had happened that put that in his heart.

CHAPTER ELEVEN

WHAT WAS IT ABOUT her? What was it about her *with* him?

Grant sat in his desk chair, which he'd turned toward the six-paned window, and stared through the glass at the starry night. His house was, as always, still and quiet.

So quiet.

What was this pain in his chest? He had expected that going to Craig and Brenna's wedding would be a challenge—but not in this way. Not at all in this way.

Shutting his eyes, he allowed—likely foolishly—the memory of Sage in his arms to replay. Hours later the sensation of her body so close to his still warmed him. He inhaled, and the scent of something warm and sunny filled his senses—all only the memory of her. And then there was that moment . . .

That breathless moment when magically the people around them faded into gray nothingness. He'd gazed into her eyes and saw the longing he felt staring back at him.

He'd nearly kissed her.

Right there in the middle of a wedding-reception dance—one he'd been dreading since the day he'd broken up with the bride. All thoughts of what was expected or proper or assumed had disappeared. Every feeling of being the outsider faded until they were nothing.

There had been Sage in his arms, her upturned face so near that the warmth of her breath had scattered enticingly across his neck. And her lips, parted slightly. Inviting. Nearly irresistible.

As the ache of yearning hummed through him again, Grant opened his eyes and forced himself to see reality. The stars muted by the town lights. The partial moon cloaked in wisps of clouds.

His quiet, empty house.

What had happened to him? He was not that man. Not one to stare at a woman as if he'd become lost and hoped never to be found again. Not a man to make a scene—and certainly kissing Sage in the middle of a country two-step at a wedding would absolutely make an unforgettable scene.

Even so, part of him wished he had done it.

Heat climbed his neck. No, he did not wish it. The last thing he wanted was to be the talk of the town. Actually, that was the second to last thing he wanted. The last thing was to fall for a woman who would not fall for him. That certainly would include a woman who had told him up front that she did not believe in love.

She was a bird, flitting through life, never staying in one place for long. Never wanting her wings clipped. Those had been her words. That, and she didn't believe in love in real life. It was only for fiction.

She had been clear.

What *had* happened?

Grant had never in his life been swept away so entirely. The few times he'd come close had certainly not involved a public dance or a country song. To be honest, the only thing he could remember moving him so deeply had involved his cello. He was much more likely to be moved by Vivaldi or Mozart than by Tracy Byrd and a steel guitar.

So then it had not been a factor of Mr. Byrd's thanking the keeper of the stars that was to blame.

It was Sage. It was him with her.

Running his fingers through his hair, Grant allowed one last moment from the evening to take him away. After that near kiss, he had pulled himself back from the precipice, kept himself properly in check for the rest of the evening. They had been appropriately social. He'd introduced her to everyone who'd crossed their path—including Craig and Brenna—though the constant interaction wore him to his core.

And then he had taken her home. At the end of the long, rutted drive, he had stopped his Altima, came around to her side of the vehicle, and pretended he did not feel electricity when she slipped her arm through his. An energy that rejuvenated what had been exhausted by hours of interacting with a crowd.

Silently they'd walked to the front steps, accompanied by a cool northern breeze, a distant chorus of frogs from the river's shores, and the intermittent call of an owl. All of it peaceful and lovely. A comfort to what had been dizzying chatter. He had felt himself, with much relief, shedding the tension of the evening and sliding back toward comfortable ease.

Before he could climb the first riser, Sage tugged on his arm, and then they faced each other. Her ready smile was bright, but whatever she had thought to say did not make it past her lips. For the second time that evening, he found himself caught in a gaze he wished would never end.

Sage blinked first, then looked down as she unwound her arm from his. When she again found his face, that too-bright smile was back in place. "That wasn't so bad, was it?"

"No, it was not." He already missed the warmth of her so near to his side and wanted the comfort of her arm twined with his. He wanted to brush away this mask she'd put into place and to have instead the steady sincerity of the way she'd looked at him while they'd danced. The way she had just moments before.

As if she understood his silent wishes, that playful expression changed again. Sage leaned close and lifted a hand until her palm cradled his jaw, thumb caressing his cheek. "Thank you, Grant. I had a good time." Then she lifted to her toes and brushed a light kiss against the spot her thumb had just been.

Before he could move, she'd slipped up the two steps and into the front door. Grant had stood there, alone and in turmoil for several moments before he had turned to take himself back to his car and then home.

That turmoil still churned within. Because he knew Sage was a kind but playful creature. Because he knew he had no real place in her world.

He knew this was a *closest of friends* thing—Sage had said that loud and clear.

But he also knew that he had never felt this way before. Not with Brenna. Not with anyone. In truth, had never expected to.

But now that he did, he yearned for more.

The longing, the strong current of emotion demanded some kind of release. Grant sought it from his cello.

Long into the night, with the winking stars as his silent, celestial audience, Grant pulled his bow across the strings, allowing the beautiful, haunting tones of his favorite classical music to speak the desires of his heart toward heaven.

· · • • · • • • · ·

I cannot make it. I am sorry.

Sage read the text that had surfaced on her phone only moments before she had parked Gramps's truck. Was he dodging her? Or maybe more likely, Miss Jane?

She shook her head, remembering his proclamation that he would never stand a woman up. If he was anything, Grant Hillman was a gentleman and a man of his word.

Hooking her arm over the cold, hard steering wheel of the 1970s Chevy truck, her phone still in hand, Sage stared at the small shop just beyond the cracked windshield. Should she still go in? What excuse could she make for Grant?

She didn't want to make excuses. And though she enjoyed Miss Jane and would like to get to know the woman better, she wasn't sure she was up for this on her own. No, perhaps that wasn't the problem.

Truth was, she wanted to see Grant. It had been a whole day—little more than twenty-four hours since she'd kissed his cheek and bid him good night after the wedding. Sunday had dragged on for an eternity as she had listlessly wandered Gramps's house and property, trying to put away the memory of that silly dance and the sensation that Grant had wanted to kiss her.

Why hadn't he, dang it? Any other guy she'd dated would have. Kissed her long and good, and she would have grinned coyly, and maybe they would have snuck off somewhere to make out.

And that would have been the end of it.

Why did Grant leave her feeling fitful and confused?

Now this. She looked forward to seeing him, to teasing a blush from his neck up into his face. What was it she wanted from this man? He was too kind to toy with but too endearing to walk away from. Where she was flighty and silly, he was rooted and too serious.

This path had all the makings of a disaster. Sage should cut it short and walk away. But there she was, disappointed that the very man she should want to leave alone couldn't make it to a lunch thing.

Sage blew out a breath, then sat back and reached to restart the truck. But before she had the key turned, Miss Jane appeared at the big picture window and waved.

No disappearing then. Not from Miss Jane—and not from Grant.

Brushing up her perky smile, she slipped from the truck and sauntered her way into Miss Jane's shop. The tinkling bell chimed cheerfully as she passed through the front door.

"Ah, Sage Greene. You made it to town." Miss Jane waved her in and toward a table set for two.

"Barely," Sage said. "Gramps's truck is a rickety thing at best."

"I can hardly believe that hunk of rust still runs." Miss Jane peered around Sage at the truck in question. "Harold almost never uses it anymore."

Harold again. Interesting that the two of them were on a first-name basis. Once again Sage wondered at the tie between the pair.

"Grant called about twenty minutes ago." Miss Jane pulled out a chair and motioned for Sage to sit. "He had a last-minute appointment and can't make it. So, it's just us girls."

So she didn't need to make his excuses. Sage should have known he would call for himself. "He texted me."

After retrieving a tray of food from her butcher-block counter and placing it on the table, Miss Jane walked to the front door, flipped the lock, and then hung a sign that read *Closed for Lunch*.

That was curious. "Isn't lunch a busy time for a café?"

"It is." Miss Jane strode back to the table and plopped onto the chair across from Sage. "But I prefer the currency of friendship to a dollar." Without preamble she distributed bowls of something purple and creamy, garnished with a blueberry and a pair of mint leaves, plus plates of buttery croissants and two glasses of something tea colored with sliced peaches floating among the ice.

She removed the tray and folded her hands. "Well then, we're set. Shall we thank the Lord?"

Sage sat back. "Umm . . . sure?"

One slivery brow arched upward at Sage's hesitant response but was quickly overcome with a firm nod and then a bow of her head. "Lord, you have been good. We praise You for it. And now, as we get to taste and enjoy the delicious provision of Your hand, we pray that You would guide our words and fill our hearts. May we delight in You, Father, as beloved children should. Amen."

While Sage appreciated the poetry of Miss Jane's words, she wondered at her prayer. She'd not been among praying people much. Really, the only time she'd remembered witnessing a spoken prayer was at her great-grandmother's funeral. Her memory was vague on that, as she'd been young, but it seemed that prayer had been an odd, cold thing full of words she didn't understand and language that was formal and out-of-date.

"Let's eat!" Miss Jane rubbed her palms together and dug in.

Sage followed her lead and discovered the purple stuff was cold blueberry soup—and it was amazing. She moaned in appreciation.

Miss Jane smiled. "That is my Daisy's favorite dish, so I hoped you'd like it."

"Daisy is your daughter?"

"No. My great-niece. She is staying with me for a while and working out at the Carson place."

"Oh. Oh! She was the blond woman in your truck that first day we met."

"The very one." Miss Jane nodded.

They ate in quasi-comfortable silence. Then Sage asked, "Do you have children?"

"No, my girl. I never married, never had children." In Miss Jane's pause, something distant and wistful passed over her expression.

Sage would have guessed there was a tinge of regret or pain in that.

But then Miss Jane's bright smile returned. "I have had the privilege of seeing most of the town's young people grow up though. And call them my special dears. Many came through my Sunday school class, and there is a wonderful bond when you learn about Jesus together."

Discomfort ribboned through Sage's chest. Was this whole encounter going to encompass God and Jesus? She had no experience with dealing with that.

After taking in two more spoonfuls, Miss Jane wiped her mouth with a napkin and set it on the table. "You have come to meet your great-grand-father."

Sage nodded, relieved to have moved to a different topic.

"How is that going?"

"He is . . . not entirely what I expected."

"What was that?"

"Well, he was supposed to be a mean drunk, was what I'd been told."

Miss Jane scowled at that. "Harold doesn't drink."

"Since I've found no trace of alcohol in the house, I believe you. He is, as you've said, an old grump though."

Amusement shone in Miss Jane's eyes. "He tries very hard to be. I would wager, since you've been here several weeks, that you have worked your way around that."

Sage chuckled. "He is all bluster and no storm."

"Hmm." One firm nod confirmed Miss Jane's agreement. "We must remember that we are all wounded souls. And how do you find our Grant Hillman?"

Having just put a spoon of blueberry yumminess in her mouth, Sage nearly choked on her soup. She coughed and sputtered, holding her napkin over her mouth.

Miss Jane merely laughed. "You will find, my dear girl, that I am direct."

"Apparently," she choked.

"Grant was one of my Sunday school boys, and I have a soft spot in my heart for him."

Folding her napkin, Sage quickly thought back to Grant's reaction to Miss Jane. If Miss Jane was going to be direct, then Sage could be so as well. "I find that a little surprising. He thinks you don't like him."

Understanding, rather than shock, was Miss Jane's response. "I know that." Sighing, she laid her spoon onto her table and sighed. "I handled some things last fall in a way that has hurt him, I fear. It was not well done."

"Things?"

"With Brenna—the bride from Saturday's wedding."

"Yes, Grant dated her."

"He did."

"And you didn't think he should have?"

"No, that was not what I thought. I thought she should not be dating him. It was not honest."

"That's not the same thing?"

"No, it isn't. But as I said, I handled the situation in a way that hurt Grant, and it has sadly taken me all these months to realize it."

"What made you come to that conclusion all of the sudden?"

"God."

Sage blinked. "God?"

"Yes. God. He placed Grant on my heart only a few weeks past, so firmly and consistently that while I have prayed for him, I have also taken a look back and have seen what I clumsily did to Grant."

Sage had never heard of anything quite so bizarre. "Perhaps you should not have interfered at all?" She wasn't sure she meant that, even if this was a weird conversation. For all she knew, if Miss Jane had not interfered with Grant's dating Brenna, it would have been Grant's wedding on Saturday.

That was a disruptive thought.

Rather than responding with offense, Miss Jane took that in with careful thought. "I have not sensed that conviction, Sage. Only that I have wounded Grant by communicating dislike when that was not what I intended."

She reached across the table and touched the back of Sage's hand. "He is a good man. A tender soul. And God has shown me that I need to mend some things between us."

There was God again. Sage slipped her hand from Miss Jane's touch.

"You don't believe in God, do you?"

Stars and sun, this woman *was* direct. Sage wiggled in her chair. "I think there is a power out there—a god. I can't imagine all the things I see on earth having come from nothing—that is too farfetched even for me. But this god you speak about . . ." She shrugged. "I don't know of a god who would care about my life and what I do the way you seem to think your god does. If there is a god watching us, he doesn't seem too involved in my life. I wouldn't call him good."

Silence followed Sage's stumbling speech. The truth was, she hadn't given much thought to God. She spent more time fighting against a heritage that she'd been planted in, her determination focused on not becoming the statistical fatherless child that permeated her family line. The rest of her energy was spent on the flip side of that determination—the drive to live successful, happy, and free.

It consumed her.

"You were surprised to find Harold not as you were told?" Miss Jane's interruption of the quiet felt out of the blue.

Why had she gone back to that?

"I was." Sage pinned a curious look on the woman.

Miss Jane's warm expression was knowing. "It is always better to discover for oneself what is true about another."

That felt like . . . like perhaps it had a double meaning.

"Most people seem to think that Grant is stiff and a little too self-disciplined to be around. Perhaps even a touch of a snob. Would you say that is true?"

"I don't know anyone around here, so I don't know what they think. But if that is what they assume, I would say they don't really know Grant."

"Well said, my dear girl." Miss Jane's smile held full approval. "That is well said indeed."

And then the uncomfortable conversation closed. Miss Jane moved on to talking about the beautiful spring it had been and asked about the garden she'd spied behind the farmhouse. When their lunch ended, Sage was once again comfortable and drawn to this likable quirky woman.

All the way until the end of the visit, when Miss Jane walked Sage to the side of Gramps's truck. There the woman touched Sage's arm. "I want to tell you something, dear girl. The God I know is the author of joy and peace. He gives life and blesses it—because He is good."

Sage smiled, thanked the woman for lunch, and pointed that old bucket of rust back toward Gramps's house, all the while determined to silence the last of Miss Jane's words.

But the encounter had an impact. One Sage found she could not ignore. The seed had been planted, the implied question sown deep.

How could she say that she couldn't call God good if she did not know Him at all?

Chapter Twelve

Sage tugged her earphones from her head and sighed. Such a melancholy had taken her that morning. While she wanted to pin it wholly on the story she was narrating—the pair who had discovered the thing that pulsed between them was the opposite of contempt had now found that their lives were not at all compatible.

No matter how they felt, they could never be.

Wasn't that how all romance stories went? Boy meets girl, they fight the attraction but fall in love, only to find that it is too hard. There are too many barriers. It won't work. And for that black moment, all is lost.

They go their separate ways, hearts irrevocably broken.

That morning, as she read the parting of the captainess and her pirate, Sage's heart ached—as it had never done before—with the emotion of it. She felt fitful and empty and battled the bizarre temptation to sob.

Sob!

Good grief, she was a sap. More so than ever. Certainly it had everything to do with this silly romance novel she was working on—which was so dumb. After all, she knew how these stories went—it wasn't like they weren't predictable every single time.

And yet there she was, feeling the loss of it. A sap for sure.

Her emotions couldn't possibly have anything to do with a shy, brown-eyed introvert whose look on her the night of the wedding had . . . Her belly fluttered with the mere fringes of that memory. A full week had gone by. Surely in that time the powerful effect of that near kiss had dissipated.

Nor could her wonky mood be tied to the talk she'd had with Miss Jane the Monday past. She didn't believe in romance, and she didn't need Miss Jane's god—whether he was good or not.

Both were still true.

And yet there she was. Her heart feeling like a tangled mess, her thoughts running hither-skither, and her reaction to the black moment in a pirate-romance way too strong even for her.

Never mind. She needed a swim. A crisp morning plunge would be just the thing to shake her from this silly funk.

Shutting off her recording equipment, Sage stood and gathered her hair at the top of her head. She wrapped the mess of curls with a satin-covered elastic while she clomped down the stairs, then through the kitchen. At the sink, she paused, her attention snagging on the coffeepot.

It was still nearly full. Only the cup that she'd poured herself over an hour before, after she'd made the brew in the early dawn of the day, was missing from the transparent carafe.

The pit of her stomach clenched. Something wasn't right—Gramps usually had at least half the pot gone by now. With a cautious draw of breath, Sage crept right, toward the parlor room where Gramps basically lived.

The room was dark, the shabby olive curtains still drawn, no TV flashing light. No Gramps in his ratty old recliner.

Full panic zipped through Sage's heart as she stepped into the gloom and turned to look at the twin bed Gramps had somehow managed to put in that room long before she'd arrived in Big Prairie. He lay unmoving.

Deathly still.

An icy chill fell over her shoulders as her breath stuck in her lungs. *Dear sun and stars above!*

Hands shaking, she crept toward the form on the bed. Was he dead? A sob caught in her chest as surprising emotion claimed her heart. She didn't want him to be dead!

I was just starting to like you, you grouchy old thing!

He couldn't die yet—she had questions.

Reaching the side of his bed, Sage sucked in a deep gulp of air—for courage—and reached for the bony, arthritic hand resting atop the faded plaid bedcover. Though his fingers were cool, the hand wasn't icy, nor was it entirely stiff.

A soft, wheezy groan filled the room. Sage knelt, sagging with relief.

"Gramps," she whispered, squeezing that hand. "Can you wake up?"

Another rattling groan, this one louder.

"That's it." She covered his shoulder. "Come back to me now. You don't get off that easy."

Watery eyes blinked open, clearly struggling to focus. "Clara . . . " he wheezed in soft wonder.

Sage lifted his hand to her chest. "Sage. I'm your great-granddaughter, remember?"

He blinked and then looked away with a grunt. The sound was more put off than anything else.

"There's my surly old fellow."

Though clearly weak, Gramps pushed her touch away. "Let me up." His breath rasped as he scraped out the words.

Fresh concern pulsed through Sage's veins. Gramps was sick. "Maybe you should stay in bed."

"Ain't—" Whatever else he was going to add got lost in a cough. Even so, Gramps propped up on an elbow and struggled to a sitting position. He caught his breath, then shot her a scowl. "Move."

"I don't think—"

He swatted a hand toward her, not hitting her, but his message was clear. He was getting up, and she wasn't going to stop him. Sage stood. With a toss of the covers, Gramps swung his legs toward the floor. Paused to cough again.

"Gramps."

He glared, then with both hands pushed himself to stand. Once on his feet, he staggered, and Sage reached for him.

Again he swatted her away. "I don't—" Another coughing fit claimed him, knocking him off balance.

Sage lunged forward, but before she could direct his fall toward the bed, Gramps collapsed against her and then crumpled to the floor, taking her down as well. His breath wheezed, his cough crackled, and he groaned pathetically.

"I'm calling an ambulance." Sage scrambled back to her feet.

"No."

"You need—"

"No." This time his bark sounded more desperate than demanding.

The strong surge of emotion that had taken her moments before, when she thought he was dead, reactivated. Blinking against the heat in her eyes, Sage knelt beside him again. "Gramps, we need help."

His eyes shut, and he focused on breathing.

Cautiously, Sage took his hand again. This time he responded with a weak grip. Then he looked up at her, and the pleading she saw in that look sank clean through her heart.

"No hospital," he said.

"But—"

He shook his head, that imploring demand remaining steady on her.

"I don't think I can get you up by myself." Her voice quavered.

"We'll manage."

They tried. She helped him sit up. But when she attempted to get him on his feet, they discovered his legs were too weak to accomplish it.

"Gramps."

"No hospital." A fresh fit of coughing claimed him.

"You can't stay on the floor."

"I'll just . . ." more coughing ". . . just wait . . ." still more ". . . get my strength . . ." yet again ". . . back."

A heavy cloak of helplessness draped over her while she watched him struggle. What could she do? She should override his stubborn demand and call an ambulance. But that look . . . so sad and begging and somehow trusting. She needed help though. Gramps was too weak to get from the floor to his bed, and she wasn't strong enough to lift him.

Grant.

Surely between the two of them, they could get Gramps back into bed.

He would help her, wouldn't he? With the gentleman he'd proven himself to be, that wasn't a question.

He might, however, insist on taking him in to see a doctor. That would not go well. *One problem at a time . . .*

Scrambling, Sage snatched the pillow from Gramps's bed and wrangled him up enough to ease it behind his head. Then she grabbed the blanket and tucked it around him.

"I'm calling for help." She bent to kiss his forehead, noting that it burned with fever.

"No hospital."

"I'm calling Grant."

His eyes pinched as he processed that. A bout of coughing shook him before he sputtered, "Only if he comes alone."

Sage didn't bother with an answer. Instead she raced through the kitchen and back up the stairs to retrieve her phone from the studio. With three quick taps her phone was ringing Grant's and she was begging him to pick up.

First try was a failure. It clicked to messages on the fourth ring—which meant he'd seen her call and hadn't accepted it.

If this was a social call, she'd feel disappointed and give up. This was not a social call. She redialed. "Pick up, Grant."

"Hello?" His voice was hushed.

"I need help."

"What is wrong?" Though still a whisper, his tone was clearly worried.

"Gramps fell, and I can't get him back in bed."

The sound of a squeaky door opening came moments before his answer, this time stronger. "I am coming. Be there in ten minutes."

And then the call dropped. Sage sagged against the folded quilt she'd hung up against the closet wall for noise-dampening purposes. "Thank you," she breathed. She wasn't sure to whom, but it didn't matter.

Grant was coming to help her, and she was thankful. There didn't seem to be a need to think much beyond that.

· · · ● ● · ● ● · · ·

With a flick of his wrist, Grant checked his watch as soon as he hung up. He had promised ten minutes, and the church was over fifteen minutes from the old Teller place.

Grant Hillman *never* exceeded the speed limit, but he was about to. He also had never walked out of the sanctuary of that little church while the pastor was still preaching. But he just did.

There were a lot of firsts happening these days. Grant wasn't sure how to process that. For the time at hand, he pushed away the need to seek a resolution for the anomalies and instead let the flow of warm adrenaline racing through his veins take him where it would. Hopefully, fast, because Sage sounded alarmingly upset.

Grant had always cared for others—*the gift of empathy*, a teacher had once called it. Which seemed to him, even to that very day, such a strange contradiction. He did not understand the social aspects of life, but he felt deeply the distress of others.

How was that possible?

The answer to that had never surfaced, though he had often questioned the juxtaposition of it. However, that gift of empathy, and his determination to study others where he lacked intuition most, had by nature made him particularly good at his job.

All that being mildly interesting, none of it had bearing on that Sunday morning. Grant buckled up, started his car, and raced out of the gravel parking lot—another first for him. The more pertinent element of his current state of mind was that while he'd always cared for others, his worry over Sage's distress was something new entirely.

He felt her panic and wanted—no, needed—to fix it. Not simply that he wished her troubled morning would ease for her, but *he* wanted to be the one to smooth out the way.

He wanted to be the hero in her story.

As he pressed the accelerator, his speed already twenty miles per hour more than the legal limit, Grant intentionally ignored the professional warning flag that flapped against this sudden drive to become that main character. He was aware of boundaries and human limitations, thank you very much. And anyway, nothing about his interactions with Sage had been *professional*.

What should have reasonably taken him sixteen to eighteen minutes had been cut down to nine when Grant turned his Altima onto the horribly potholed dirt drive. This time he drove the car all the way on the pocked path, stopping a mere few feet in front of the sagging front porch. Not bad at that—the drive was not nearly as hazardous as he had previously thought. A few large dips, a handful of ruts. Nothing all that terrible.

With a quick flick he shut the car off and climbed out, then jogged the short distance to the front steps, which he leapt over and opened the screen door. The thing screeched a warning like a cantankerous old woman. Conveniently, that alerted Sage of his arrival—either that, or perhaps the rumble bouncing of his car as he'd come down the drive. In any case, there she was, opening the solid wooden door.

"You're here." She brushed a stray lock of curls from her face, tucking it behind her ear. "That was quick."

The fact that Sage looked adorable in her loose gray T-shirt and black-and-white polka-dot jammie pants and her hair a gloriously curly mess at the top of her head did not escape Grant. It had been more than a full week since he'd clamped his eyes on her, and he wanted to take in his fill of such loveliness like a man starved would inhale food. However, the more gripping part of her appearance was the deep pull of her auburn brows and the lack of laughing mischief in her brown eyes.

This was not a time to act the part of the smitten fool.

"You said there was trouble." He cupped her elbow and gave it a gentle squeeze.

Gnawing on her bottom lip, Sage nodded and turned to lead the way through the dim house. "Gramps wasn't up when I came down for a break." Sage glanced back, her expression making it clear that was very unusual for her grandfather. "I went to check on him and thought he was dead."

"Oh, Sage." The catch in her voice caused a sharp pinch in his chest. "I am sorry."

"He's not dead." Blowing out a hard breath, she stopped at the far side of the kitchen and turned to him. "And he insisted I *not* call an ambulance when he went down and couldn't get back up." She crammed her fingers into the mass of hair at the top of her head. "I should have anyway."

"Let's get him into his chair, and then we will make an assessment."

Her bottom lip went beneath her teeth again, and the worry in her gaze made Grant's heart squeeze again. "I barely know him, Grant. But I need answers . . . I need him to . . ." She pinned her lips closed and looked toward the gray room on her left.

Grant stepped closer, taking her arm in a gentle grasp again. "We will do what is needed, Sage. Do not assume the worst yet."

When she dipped her head and leaned into his shoulder, Grant could not resist wrapping her in a gentle embrace. She shuddered against him, stirring a curiosity about her relationship with this hermit of an old man. What answers did she seek, and why would Old Man Teller have them?

What did Sage need from this grandfather she'd barely known?

Filing the questions to a safe place where he could examine them later, Grant gently set Sage back and moved past her and into the dark room where he'd officially met her grandfather weeks ago. "Mr. Teller." At the crumpled body on the musty carpet, Grant stopped and knelt. "Can I help you up?"

"You a doctor?" the man rasped. His lungs rattled with his breath.

Grant glanced at Sage, who shook her head. Technically, yes, Grant was a doctor—he had earned a PysD—Doctor of Psychology—alongside his education specialist's degree. But that was not what Mr. Teller had in mind. "I am not a medical doctor."

The man grunted, then motioned for Grant to lean down. Nearer.

Grant complied.

Mr. Teller gripped Grant's blue button-down shirt near the collar and tugged him even closer. Brows furrowed, Grant looked at the man, assessing if he actually thought to threaten Grant while he lay helpless on the floor.

He did not. Instead, Mr. Teller picked his head off the pillow and strained toward Grant's ear.

Grant leaned in so Mr. Teller did not have to try so hard.

"Need the lavatory."

Empathy engulfed Grant's whole being. He nodded and whispered back, "Yes, sir."

When he looked back into Mr. Teller's eyes, he found humiliation in that pleading stare. He guessed why. Pulling back, Grant looked at Sage. "He would like to get dressed. Can you give us a few minutes?"

"Sure." Sage nodded, her tone relieved. "I'll make some eggs, Gramps. How would that be?"

Mr. Teller grunted, and then Sage spun away from the parlor and moved out of sight. Grant put his attention back on the helpless man on the ground. "How about I get you to the bathroom and then I come back for your clothes?"

After a hard swallow, Mr. Teller looked toward the curtained window and nodded.

Grant tossed aside the blanket Sage must have covered her grandfather with, then shuffled his position to help Mr. Teller sit up. The pungent smell of urine touched his nostrils, stirring deep compassion in Grant's heart all over again. He repositioned again, coming behind Mr. Teller and securing a hold beneath his arms and around his chest.

"Just lean back on me, and I will get you up."

Mr. Teller did so, though he tried to press on the floor with his arms to launch the motion. Grant locked his forearms firmly at the man's chest, hoping that the man's ribs were not brittle and that Grant would not cause any harm. This would have been safer with a gait belt.

After a series of grunting and foot scrambling, Grant had Mr. Teller upright. At one point, it seemed likely the elderly man was about the same build as Grant, but now he was at least an inch shorter, likely two, and a good twenty pounds lighter. Grant would not complain about either given their situation. Coming to the man's side, Grant locked a hold on Mr. Teller's arm. "Point me the way to the restroom."

Not making eye contact, Mr. Teller motioned toward a back cove, likely a small room tucked under the stairway that ran into the kitchen. Grant nodded, and the pair shuffled their way in that direction.

The bathroom was tiny. Room enough for a small toilet, a slender shower, and a camper-sized sink.

"Did you add this room to the house?" Grant made casual conversation while he helped Mr. Teller with his flannel pajamas. With all his heart he did not want the man to feel the humiliation of the moment, especially when the wet bottoms confirmed what Grant had already known.

"Dozen years back." Mr. Teller nearly choked out the words.

Grant was careful not to make eye contact. Not in that undignified moment. He simply worked as if the business of changing a full-grown man was nothing at all.

Inside, he wanted to cry for him.

"What inspired that project?"

"Arthritis."

"Ah."

"Other one is upstairs."

"With the bedrooms, I would guess."

A grunt confirmed it to be so. Grant had him securely seated on the toilet and gathered the soiled clothing. "If you tell me where to find them, I'll get your change of clothes."

Still without looking at Grant, Mr. Teller managed a small wave of his hand. "Drawers at the end of the bed."

"Yes, sir."

"I need a shower."

Halfway out the bathroom door, Grant paused. He leaned back to look inside the small space of the shower, then shook his head. "I do not think that is wise just yet. There is not a grab bar in there."

"Need it anyways."

Turning, Grant planted a sympathetic look on the man. That head, covered with thin silver hair, slowly came up, and a defeated look met Grant's. It was a pathetic, heartbreaking scene: this once strong, mean fellow reduced to sitting half stripped on a toilet begging to be allowed to clean the smell of humiliation off himself.

Grant rubbed his forehead with his fingertips. "Do you have a chair we can put inside the stall?"

"Kitchen."

"I will fetch it. Will you sit tight until I get it secured?"

Those sad eyes lowered, and then the bent head moved in a resigned nod.

"I will hurry up about it. Perhaps you can work on the buttons of that shirt?"

"I can manage my own clothes," Mr. Teller grumbled.

Grant had to swallow back the hard lump in his throat. He made a swift exit, heading to the kitchen. Working at the stove, Sage turned at the sound of his footsteps.

"Is he in his chair?"

"No. He needed the restroom."

"You left him there?" Her eyes went wide.

"He is safe for the moment." Grant held up the wad of clothes in his hand. "Is there a washer nearby?"

For a breath, Sage's expression was of confusion, and then her shoulders sagged as understanding dawned. "Oh dear. Poor Gramps."

"Do not say a thing to him. He is already humiliated."

"I wouldn't ever."

Grant nodded and then gestured with the clothes again. Sage turned off the burner on the stove, wiped her hands on a towel, and silently led him around the opposite side of the stairway and onto the enclosed back porch. There, he found a harvest-gold washing machine and dryer set—which matched the refrigerator and the oven in the house.

"Must have been a package deal." Grant tried for a light tone.

"It's a miracle they all still work."

"Do they?"

Sage nodded, but the smile she tried for barely moved her lips. "Grant . . ."

He deposited the clothes, ran his hands under a stream of warm water at the utility sink beside the washer, and turned to face Sage. "These things happen."

"I don't know how to take care of an old man." She blinked and looked toward the floor. "In truth, I don't really know how to take care of anyone besides myself."

Taking care of the elderly wasn't really on his expertise list either. "We can get him to town after he gets cleaned up."

Her head came up immediately, and with a surprisingly determined look, she shook off the suggestion. "He won't."

"He might not have the choice."

"But . . . but how could I do that to him?" A lock of curls fell over her brow and into her eyes. She blew it out of her view and then perched her hands on her hips. "I can't do that. He said no, and I just can't."

Grant studied her for several heartbeats, and when that lock of hair drifted over her face and landed alongside her nose, he reached to tuck it behind her ears. "What is it you think you owe him, Sage?"

Her face twisted with some sort of pain, but she shook her head.

"You barely know him."

"I know. But—" Emotion caught her voice. "He is a person, after all. And . . ."

Grant rubbed her shoulder. "Tell me."

"My great-grandmother died alone. Her son died alone. And two years ago, my grandmother died. Also alone."

A strange explanation—especially from a self-proclaimed bird of a woman who flitted through life unattached and apparently free. Grant puzzled at her strong, sentimental reaction to this situation. "Were you close to any of them?"

"No. I only met my grandmother a handful of times."

A family pattern emerged. *She doesn't want to be that wandering bird . .*

.

"Sage, I am not saying that you have to leave your grandfather alone at the hospital, but perhaps the best thing is to—"

"No." Sage lifted a stubborn chin at Grant and crossed her arms. "No. I won't. There has to be a different way. I'll figure it out." Spine straight and shoulders stiff, Sage turned and marched back into the kitchen.

Grant followed, wondering what exactly Sage thought she would do out there on her own with no medical training—and not even the ability to get the old man off the floor when he went down. More, he still turned over the intense reaction she'd had to her grandparents' lonely deaths. If he were willing to make a wager, Grant would bet they had led lonely lives as well.

A barrage of racking coughs came from the room beyond the kitchen. Reminded of the more important need of the moment, Grant strode toward the metal kitchen table and pulled a vinyl-covered chair from one side of it.

"He wants a shower. It will be a few minutes before he will be ready to eat."

Sage looked at the chair and then back up at Grant. "Oh dear. Do you want me to—"

Grant shook his head. "He most certainly will not want that."

"Oh." Her face reddened as her attention drifted toward the doorway separating the kitchen and parlor.

Reality was sinking in quickly. Once more Grant felt the weight of empathy pull in his chest. He picked up the chair and started toward the parlor but stopped when he reached Sage's side. "We will figure this out."

Wide brown eyes, so full of emotion and perhaps a touch of wonder, lifted to meet his gaze. "We?"

Grant nudged her shoulder with his. "*You* are not alone."

Chapter Thirteen

The grinding sound of the old washer at work played at her back while Sage dried the last of the dishes. In the other room, the low tone of Grant's gentle voice came intermittently with the harsher sound of Gramps's responses.

Thank the stars and sun for that man. He'd come immediately—hadn't even asked for details. Had apparently left church—a fact she'd discovered when she had observed over their eggs that he was all dressed up, for a weekend morning. That reply had stirred something uncomfortable in Sage's gut.

A church man.

Sage wasn't much for church or church people. They had too many rules. Too many stuffy people. Too many hypocrites.

Or so she'd heard. *How do you know what God is like?* Miss Jane's implied question echoed in her mind. It was easily enough transposed to *How do you know what church people are like?*

A prick of consciousness jabbed through her accusations. Fact was, she didn't know many of those church people she resented. Could be, in fact, that Grant and Miss Jane were the first real church people she'd spent any amount of time with at all. Miss Jane was a nice person, and Sage liked her—even with the awkward conversation they'd had.

And Grant was . . . wonderful, actually.

Her opinion on the religiously inclined had been formed basically from hearsay. Her mother's, mostly, and as she had shared a breakfast of eggs and orange juice with Gramps and Grant, Sage had pondered where her mother had gained such a view.

And then, in that moment at the sink that Sage had to herself as she finished cleaning up breakfast, she pondered the contradiction of who Grant was revealing himself to be against what she assumed of church people all over again. Yeah, he was a straight arrow. Buttoned up. Self-disciplined. But also . . .

Kind, respectful, gentle, selfless.

Mentally she ticked off the list, and as she did so, the hard corner of her heart—the place she kept reserved for things like resentment and dislike—softened.

But there was every possibility that those things—the whole list—was a factor of Grant being one of the most unique men Sage had encountered and had nothing at all to do with his being one of the church people.

Goodness, these were perplexing thoughts, especially for a Sunday morning. Sage swatted them away. She had enough to ponder with Gramps's situation without adding the complexity of a man she liked way more than was good for either of them, and his religious bent—whatever that may be.

She wiped her hands on the dish towel and hung it up on a hook above the sink, then wandered into the parlor.

"Your family homesteaded here?" Grant asked.

Gramps nodded.

"Was this the original house?"

"No. This was built in the 1920s. The original homestead was a soddy. Then a little clapboard thing that could barely stand up to the wind." Gramps finished with a fit of coughing.

Seated on the brown sofa, Grant leaned forward and pressed his elbows against his knees. "That sure sounds painful, Mr. Teller. I think a doctor could—"

"No doctor."

"Why not, Gramps?" Sage walked to the recliner and lowered herself to a squat. "They're not evil."

"They're expensive."

"Oh." Her shoulders drooped. Gramps had a point. "There's Medicare though."

"Ain't taking a government handout."

"It is not a handout, sir." Grant glanced at Sage and then focused on Gramps again. "Medicare is something you have paid into your whole life with social security tax."

"No." He coughed again, the rasping sound coming from deep within his chest.

Grant ran a hand through his hair. "What about a nurse? My cousin's wife is a nurse. If I call her to come check on you, will you allow that?"

"What cousin is that?"

"Clayton Hillman. His wife is Anne."

Gramps dipped a subtle nod, his expression turning mildly thoughtful. "His grandfather bought the north one forty from me . . ."

Sage wasn't sure what the *north one forty* was exactly. Land, likely. Nor could she tell if Gramps appreciated that sale or had resented it.

Grant's expression remained impassive. "Yes. That was my grandfather too."

"You farm?" Breath wheezing, Gramps stared at the ceiling, as if the information didn't matter much to him.

"No, sir. My dad got out of it when I was little. Clayton's dad, Robert, took over the family farm."

Brows lifting, Gramps pinned his attention onto Grant. "You were a different one."

Even from the distance between them, Sage could see Grant work his jaw. "Yes, sir."

"How about Clayton? He like his father?"

"I do not think one would say that either Clay or I are very much like our dads."

There was something in that response—an undertone of . . . resentment? Of chilled separation? From Grant Hillman? Sage couldn't reconcile that.

Gramps sputtered through another round of painful coughs, his breath rattling at the end of it.

"Gramps—" Sage stood. She looked from the old man to the younger one.

His jaw set equally stubborn, Grant held his attention steady on Gramps. "Anne is a good nurse, and she is not one to do things unless they are necessary. And she is your neighbor. That will matter to her."

Breath still shaky, Gramps aimed a furrowed brow on Sage. After a few beats, during which she was tempted to tell him he was going to the hospital and that was the end of it, his obstinate expression softened, and he nodded. "Just Anne."

"Just Nurse Anne," Sage agreed. *For now* . . . As to later, that depended on what the nurse said.

Grant rose from the ugly harvest-brown couch. "I'll go call Clay." He moved toward the kitchen, and as he passed Sage, he laid a hand on her shoulder and squeezed.

For a reason Sage couldn't identify, Grant's simple touch felt like the kindest thing anyone had ever given her.

Perhaps it was because for the first time in her memory, she wasn't in the middle of a struggle alone.

·········

Clayton and Anne Hillman arrived within an hour of Grant's call. Like the man who had helped Sage since the morning, his cousins were dressed in Sunday clothes. Sage and Grant met them both on the front porch, and Grant made quick introductions.

Anne was an average-built woman with straight honey-brown hair and an easy smile. She wore a pair of white pixie-cut skinny pants and a flowing teal top—the color setting off her blue eyes like a deep mountain lake on a cloudless day in Colorado. Anne carried a small bag in one hand.

As the group stood precariously on Gramps's sagging porch, she asked Sage about the morning's events. Sage filled her in, though she omitted the messy parts that Grant had taken care of, sparing Gramps's dignity.

Looking every bit a professional, Anne nodded and asked some questions. How long had he been feeling poorly? Sage had no idea—Gramps wasn't the type to complain about that sort of thing, she didn't think. How long had he been coughing? The worst of it had appeared just that morning. Sage remembered a few slight coughs here and there over the past couple of days, but nothing that gave her concern.

"The flu can come on hard and fast. I'll listen to his lungs. My guess is that his O2 sats were low, and that's why he fell. Without a monitor, I can't say for sure, but I'll take a look at what I can and tell you what I think."

"Thank you," Sage said.

Across from the women, standing next to the railing and to Grant, Clayton wore dark-wash jeans and a crisp white button-down, the sleeves rolled up on muscled forearms. His hair was darker than Grant's—closer to black than brown—and by the sprinkling of salt at his temples, Sage guessed him to be at least five years older than Grant, perhaps in his late thirties. A suspicion that seemed confirmed by the way Clayton subtly acted more like an older brother than a cousin.

Dark eyes that held kindness assessed Sage with a gentle wariness before Clayton turned to Grant. "Can I beg a favor from you while Anne is in with Mr. Teller?"

"Of course." Grant stood on the porch opposite Clayton.

"I got a call this morning from Lance Carson." Clayton crossed his arms. "I know cows aren't your thing, but I put out a small herd along the river stretch. I guess there was fence damage from the flood that I'd missed, and they got out. My boys are off with some friends this afternoon, so I could use another hand."

"How many?"

"Just eight. Lance said he figured they'd hang out down by the river most the day but wanted me to know because it's that section by the road."

Grant glanced at Sage and then nodded at Clayton. "Eight should not take long."

"Right. Should be back just in time to pick up Anne."

Again, Grant looked at Sage. "You'll be okay?"

"Of course." Sage summoned her brightest smile. She wasn't new at being with strangers—she'd spent her life flitting from one place to the next. Strangers were her normal, and Anne seemed perfectly nice.

The group split, the guys going to Clayton's white truck—the one that Grant had taken Sage on a picnic in—and Sage and Anne into the house.

Anne stopped at the kitchen sink and washed her hands. "Will he bite?" She leaned in and whispered, partly in fun, but some serious.

With a muted chuckle, Sage shook her head. "I don't think so. He knows you're coming—Grant talked him into it."

Though it likely wasn't intentional, Anne quirked one brow, and then her easygoing, kind expression smoothed out again. "For a man who struggles with people, Grant has a way with them, doesn't he?"

An interesting remark. Sage tucked it away to consider later. "Gramps is right in here." She pointed toward the parlor and then led the way.

Gramps was his normal burly self, with a hefty dose of hard coughing mixed in, while Anne introduced herself and got straight to business.

"You married a Hillman boy?" Gramps asked.

"I did." Anne winked. "Lucky girl, huh?"

Gramps grunted. Whether in agreement or not was only known to himself. "You like farming?"

"After twelve years, I'm almost adapted to it, I think. It's a lifestyle, isn't it?" She paused but didn't seem to expect Gramps to answer. "I like that Clayton likes it." From her small bag, Anne pulled out a stethoscope. "I'm just going to listen to your lungs for a minute."

With neither approval nor rejection, Anne pressed her equipment against Gramps's chest. Mild annoyance crossed his already scowling face, but he kept quiet. Anne took him through the expected routine of deep breathing and then helped him sit forward so that she could repeat the process against his back. She checked the other vitals one more time and wrote everything down on a small notepad that she'd pulled from her bag.

When she was done, she stood and stepped back. "Well, Mr. Teller, I'd say you likely have the flu—but remember, I'm not a doctor."

"Don't want to see a doctor."

"So I hear." She crossed her arms. "At this point, if you're not willing to come into town, all I can tell you is to rest and drink lots of fluids. If you were willing to come in and see Dr.—"

"I ain't."

"—then he would likely prescribe you Tamiflu, and that would maybe shorten the duration. But." She stopped there, emphasizing his stubbornness in the pause. "I can't do that. As I said, I'm not a doctor."

"What if he gets worse?" Sage asked.

Anne looked at Sage, waiting against the doorframe. "We'll hope for the best for now. He's better off staying in that recliner. Being a little upright, even when he sleeps, might help us avoid pneumonia or bronchitis." She looked back at Gramps. "But that's not a guarantee."

"I've had the flu before," Gramps muttered.

Anne chuckled quietly, then leaned down and patted Gramps's arm. "I'll check back with you in a couple days." She repacked her small bag and walked toward the kitchen.

Sage turned and led the way to the table. "Can I get you some water? Or coffee?"

"No, thank you. I had two cups at church."

Then Sage's suspicion was correct—they had been at church. "Do you go to the same one as Grant?"

"We do. You'd be welcome to come."

Sage shook her head. "I'm not the church type."

"Hmm."

"I didn't know Grant was there. I felt terrible when he showed up in a button-down and khakis."

"I would be shocked to see him in anything different." Anne winked. "We wondered what was going on when he snuck out of service. Don't think he's ever done that before. But I'm sure he didn't mind coming to help you." There, Anne paused and settled a meaningful, assessing gaze on Sage. "My husband told me to scope you out."

A spiral of discomfort feathered through Sage's middle. "Wary of outsiders?"

Anne laughed. "No, not that at all. Heaven knows this small town could always use a fresh face. Plus, if that was the case, Clayton would have never married me."

"You're not from Big Prairie?"

"Not even from Nebraska. Clay and I met at a baseball game in Colorado. He sat in my seat and decided that little mistake was a stroke of good luck."

"Wow, that's quite a story." The kind that Sage might narrate, although she preferred her romances to have adventure in them. Who knew—maybe Anne's did?

Anne waved it off. "One for another time maybe."

Guess she wasn't going to find out right then.

"Ah yes." Sage grinned knowingly. "Because right now we're investigating me."

"Exactly." Anne's teasing expression faded into something more serious. "We saw you at the wedding and of course were curious . . ." A thread of gentle warning hung in Anne's voice. "Clay is protective of Grant. They have some history together. And now, especially after Brenna . . ."

When Anne didn't complete that last statement, Sage felt something hard form in her chest. The same sort of firm ball that she experienced sometimes when she thought of Gramps's rejection of Grandma Clara and the silent distance he'd kept with the family until recently. If she were to do an honest evaluation of that reaction, she would likely come up with resentment. But Sage didn't dig into that sort of thing. She preferred to keep things on the happy side of life.

"She really did a number on him, hmm?" Sage gestured to a chair at the table.

"Oh no. Not the way that sounds. And we had wondered if you knew that Grant had dated the bride." Anne sat down.

"I knew."

"Brenna is a sweet girl, and I really think she cared a whole lot about Grant. In fact, I think if Grant had proposed before Craig came back, Brenna would have said yes and they'd have gotten married."

The thought of that didn't sit well with Sage. Yet another yucky thing stirred in her middle that Sage preferred not to have. "Maybe it's a good thing Craig came back when he did. Maybe it saved them from a mistake."

Anne looked toward the kitchen window, her expression thoughtful. "Perhaps. But I don't think Grant or Brenna would have been *un*happy together. They didn't have a whirlwind romance, but they were good together. I think they would have been okay."

That was *not* the stuff of novels.

"You don't believe in a soul mate?" Sage wasn't sure why she was pursuing this. Particularly since she herself didn't believe in such a thing.

Anne shrugged. "I don't know. I think love is as much a choice as it is a feeling."

"That doesn't sound very . . . romantic."

Anne raised her eyebrows. "Hmm. You don't think?"

Every book Sage had narrated had proclaimed that love was a rushing current. Unmanageable. All high emotion and untamable passion. This version Anne was talking about sounded . . . flat?

No, not that. She didn't know what.

Then again, Sage didn't think that love—the romantic stuff of the novels she made her living off of—was a real thing, so what did she really know about it? Maybe, if love existed in real life, it was more like Anne's version.

Might be interesting to ponder . . .

Something about that felt unsettling, so Sage brushed it from her mind. Hopefully, that would undo the strange twisting in her middle.

"So Grant would have made it work?" Sage got back to the question at hand.

"My guess would be that he and Brenna would have both made it work." Anne adjusted her sitting position and leaned her elbow on the table between them. "But that doesn't matter now. What I do know is that Grant is distinctly loyal, and he does what is right even when it costs him.

I know that he would choose to love, to keep his promises, and to work at happiness."

"Which brings us back to the beginning." Sage also leaned in. "Back to your husband telling you to get a read on me, right?"

A tender grin made Anne's face lovely. If ever Sage had wanted a real, close friend—something she'd not had in any of her wandering years—it might be with this woman. A tug at her heart accompanied that random thought—another unexpected reaction Sage had to tuck away.

"Grant is . . . special," Anne said softly.

"I can see that."

"Not just with his unique personality—though he is unique. Some see it as cold and entirely too formal, but, as I am guessing you've already discovered, that's not really true."

"No, Grant is not at all cold." Sage knew cold. Cold personalities didn't lean in and ask questions like *Tell me what I should know about you*. They didn't sit and listen, *really* listen, while you shared whatever came to mind.

"Not everyone is willing to see past Grant's layer of formal speech and rather rigid practices. They don't know why he is scheduled and organized and likes things done properly. They see him as boring and stiff and maybe even a little bit of a snob."

"He says he's exceptionally boring."

"What do you say?"

"I say that he is wonderfully unique." Sage straightened and pulled in a breath before she plunged ahead. "I can appreciate that you and your husband look out for him. I kind of got the impression that he was a little bit like Gramps—stuck here in this small town all alone. I'm glad to discover that's not true, because no matter who my gramps may be or what he's done, I don't think he should be an outcast. That goes double for Grant, because from what I've seen, he's a really good man. But here's the thing, Anne—I'm not looking for a man. I'm not looking for a relationship. And Grant knows that."

Anne's expression fell. "Does he?"

"I don't believe in romance, and I've told him so."

"You—" Anne stopped and processed, as if Sage had just declared the sky was yellow. "You don't believe in romance?"

"No. I think it's the stuff of fairy tales. And though I make a living narrating those sorts of stories, I think believing in them is a good way to live a disappointing life."

Lips pressed together, Anne sat mute for several seconds. Then, "And Grant knows this?"

"Yes. One of the first things we talked about. What is between us is, hopefully . . . the closest of friendships."

"I see." Anne spoke the pair of words with slow hesitation.

"You say that like you don't see at all."

Another beat went by, and then the furrow on Anne's brow cleared. She sighed, and then a soft grin returned to her lips. "I do see. And I'm glad you've been honest with him."

Sage held a steady look on Anne as she tried to gauge whether Anne thought Sage was trustworthy with this man she and her husband apparently valued and looked out for. The conclusion on that was muddled. Sage leaned forward until her middle pressed into the edge of the table.

"Grant *is* exceptional. Just not the boring sort. I would never want such a man to get hurt."

The rumbling sound of a vehicle bouncing up Gramps's drive filtered into the kitchen. Anne tucked a lock of her hair behind her ear, grabbed the bag she'd placed on the table, and stood. Sage followed, also coming to her feet.

For some reason, it was important to Sage to gain this woman's respect and trust. "Anne, I do mean that."

A gentle smile softened Anne's face. "I believe you, Sage." She stepped forward and stopped to touch Sage's arm. "I'll be back in couple of days to check on your gramps. In the meantime, if you need anything—or if you'd like to grab a cup of coffee sometime—call me." She squeezed Sage's elbow. "Grant has my number."

An offer of friendship? That was a rare thing in Sage's experience.

Anne left, and within minutes she and Clayton were backing down the drive in that white truck, leaving Grant and Sage standing together near his car. Sage took in his appearance—top button undone, sleeves rolled up to his elbows, and dark khakis wrinkled and bearing a smudge of dirt on his right leg.

She thought he looked kind of good. Then again, Grant was a handsome man—the state of his clothing didn't alter that all that much either way. However, she had a hunch about how he felt about his appearance.

"I didn't know you cowboyed."

Grant unrolled his sleeves to put them to rights. "I don't. Not usually."

"You're a little untidy, Grant Hillman."

"I know it." He met her teasing smirk and then looked down at himself, and when his face met hers again, his expression read *uncomfortable*.

"That bothers you, doesn't it?"

"Very much."

Sage laughed softly. Her hunch had been correct. She had no idea why Grant's preference for all things neat tickled her so, but it sure did. Even so, she didn't delight in making him *truly* uncomfortable. "Then you had better go."

He simply held her eye contact, and in that shared moment was an understanding. A silent look had never felt so . . . so beautiful. Nor so intimate.

"Call me if you need help."

"I will." Drawn to him, she stepped forward and lifted onto her toes to brush a kiss on his cheek.

Long after his taillights left her view, Sage thought about that silent moment of connection. And then her fairly innocuous kiss on his cheek—not the first time she'd done that. Her heart rate sped up at both memories.

CHAPTER FOURTEEN

GRANT SLOWED HIS PACE as he came to the bend in the trail. The one that would lead him to the river's edge and to Sage's swimming hole. Though the morning was significantly warm, he guessed she wouldn't be in the water.

His strides brought him within view of the Teller farmhouse. All seemed quiet. No splashing, no glimpse of a halo of dark-auburn curls moving about the backyard. Most likely she was in the house tending to her grand-father.

He'd never been one to act on compulsion. Not until Sage Greene had literally dropped into his world. But now that she had, Grant found himself doing things out of his routine—compulsive acts being on that list. Oddly, he didn't find that terribly alarming. Rather, he discovered that it uncovered a softness in his crisp personality.

That felt a little bit like unearthing a hidden prize.

So as he slowed to a walk and strayed off the cut path he normally kept to, he only briefly questioned why he was veering from his norm. Particularly on that morning, to find a few downed logs that would serve his intended purpose.

If he was to check on Sage in the middle of his morning runs, he'd prefer to do so without getting his feet wet. Just past Sage's swimming hole the river narrowed. It would be the perfect spot to scrape together a crossing—he just needed a few thick and sturdy limbs.

Within a few minutes he had identified at least four limbs with the needed girth and length for his project. Within a half an hour he had those four, plus two more for added width and stability, placed over the narrowest part of the water. The rough ends of the gray branches sank into the damp earth on either bank—if another flood should rip through the area, even one significantly milder than the last one, his small efforts would be washed away.

But no matter. For now, this would do.

Brushing the front of his wicking shirt, Grant tested the stability of the center three limbs with first one foot, and then dared to add his full weight with the other. His makeshift bridge wobbled slightly but not enough to be alarming.

He crossed the water in five strides, making it to Sage's side of the river with his feet dry. Mission accomplished.

Well, the first part of it, anyway.

Resuming his jog, Grant set his direction for the animal trail that angled up the side of the steep bank—the one that Sage had ascended in her wet skirt after their first meeting. The memory of her stopping near the top flooded his mind. Her smiling at him while the sun backlit her form, making that auburn mess a halo of glowing dark-red curls . . .

His breath caught—which was not a great experience while one was jogging up a hill. Grant slowed to a walk for the last few feet of the climb and continued through the taller wild grasses and then the mowed section of the backyard.

Had Sage mowed this?

Likely, yes. Though before Mr. Teller had come down with the flu, it seemed possible he might have done the job. Either way, Grant would take it over.

To be helpful.

His breath came back down to near normal as he approached the back door—the one that opened into the covered back porch where the washer and dryer had been. Was he a back-porch sort of visitor at this point? Perhaps he should walk around to the front door. That would be more proper.

With anyone else, he would have done exactly that. Instead, he stood there two feet from that crooked screen door and stared at the house.

It was in such rough shape. The foundation drooped into the earth on one side. The windows looked cockeyed. The roof sagged beneath the weight of at least seven layers of shingles—and the top layer looked worn thin and useless.

How had this place survived the spring flood?

Grant surveyed the land around him, turning a slow circle. Down the way about two hundred yards, to the east, was evidence of damage—trees uprooted and tossed to the ground. But closer to the house?

No sign of damage.

How had that happened?

Sage's swimming hole sprang to mind. Grant had run the path that went by the old Teller place for a couple of years—he had never noticed a deep hole there before. Maybe he would not have, not from the bank. However, he also enjoyed kayaking, and he'd gone past this place while floating the waters on several occasions. Surely on the water, with the river being mostly a uniform, rather shallow body, he would have noticed. After all, as Sage had observed, he was a details guy.

Now facing the river, though the height and position of Mr. Teller's house did not really give him a view of the water, Grant puzzled. He strode back across the yard the way he came until he stopped at the bank's edge—the overlook from which Sage had jumped.

Looking down on the water from that point, he could see the hole, and yes, it looked significantly deeper than the rest of the bed.

A sinkhole perhaps? One that had dropped under the weight and force of the floodwaters?

That would explain it.

"Are you going to try jumping?"

Grant whipped around at the sound of Sage's teasing. His heart rate spiked, and it was possible that condition was not entirely due to her startling him.

The screen door smacked shut behind her as she sauntered from the house toward him. The sun touched her head, making that hair shine with that soft radiance that had minutes before stolen his breath just from memory of it.

Grant stood mesmerized.

"It's an exhilarating thrill." Sage stopped beside him. "I recommend it."

"I was not going to jump." Grant commanded his brain to participate in the conversation rather than sit there in a muddle of attraction. Sage was a beautiful woman. He confessed it. Now, to behave like a dignified man. "I stopped to check on you and your grandfather."

"You stopped?" Sage turned at the waist, looking as if she could see the front of the house. "I didn't hear you drive up."

"That is because I was not driving. I was running."

She turned back and pointed across the river. "Running? The trail is on the *other* side of the river."

"That is a fact."

"Have you learned to walk on water?" Delightful teasing filled her look. "If so, please demonstrate."

"Let us not get blasphemous."

"If I understood what that meant, I might be able to banter back."

Grant chuckled. "It means that I am not Jesus." With a pair of fingers, he nudged her chin and redirected her gaze. "If you'll look at the narrowing of the water, you will see that I have built a bridge." He let his touch fall away.

It took a moment for her to identify the place, but when she did, her smile grew. "A bridge!" She looped an arm through his. "Brilliant."

She looked up at him with that expression that called him a hero to her. He had come to crave that look over the past few weeks and wondered for the briefest moment if there was anything he would not do to gain it.

Instead of pondering that—because doing so would also require an examination of emotion that could lead to murky waters—Grant covered her hand that remained on his bicep. "How is your grandfather today?"

A sigh sagged through her, pulling down that happy grin until it became a slight frown. "Still coughing. I am trying to keep him hydrated, but he is stubborn about it. I think he doesn't want his bladder to fill up . . ."

Grant nodded.

"He managed to get to the bathroom on his own yesterday evening, but goodness, was he wobbly. Every time I offered to help him though, he about bit my head off. Told me he didn't need some little bit of a girl to help him." She leaned her head against his shoulder. "Oh, Grant, what if I can't take care of him? What if he falls again? What if . . . what if I wake up tomorrow and he's dead?"

"Why didn't you call me last night?"

"You'd already been out here—and you left church to help me. I didn't want to bother you anymore."

"You don't bother me." She disrupted his sleep, provoked him to do things he normally wouldn't, and made his pulse race at the simple memory of her smile. But she didn't *bother* him. He turned and looked into her face. "I want you to call me. Please."

"Okay," she whispered. She stepped back, prying space between them. "Hey, Grant?"

"Yes?"

"Why are you helping me?"

Another muddy question. Grant went for the easiest, most readily available answer. "Because we are the closest of friends. Is that not what you said?"

"I did." When he expected the sunshine of her smile to reappear—the one that she often employed as a mask—Sage bit her bottom lip instead. "Can I tell you something?"

Anything. Everything. He wanted her to trust him with all that moved in her heart. "Tell me what I should know, Sage."

"I don't actually have any experience with having a *closest of friends* kind of friend." There was a rawness to her voice, a vulnerability in that confession.

Grant stepped into the small void between them and with a brush of his fingertips, he tilted her chin up so she would meet his gaze. "Me neither." As the hushed words left his lips, they hit him with a startling clarity. They were the truth—even with his belief that he had loved Brenna, which seemed like a sad contradiction.

How could he have loved a woman who had not been his closest friend?

The thought seemed both incredibly obvious while at the same time deeply profound. It provoked another query straight on the heels of its impact: Was it possible to *not* fall in love with a woman with whom he intended to be the closest of friends?

Sage didn't believe in love, so he had better not.

Grabbing on to that, Grant posted the fact of it in the center of his mind, where it would not be missed.

So then, back to the real reason he was there. "Let's go see how Gramps is, shall we?"

Sage nodded, and on they went. Grant felt secure in his standing.

· · • • • • • • · · ·

Gramps was nearly resettled in his chair. Sage wondered how terribly un-comfortable the old man had been all this time—but thanks to Grant's un-expected arrival, her grandfather could rest easier, having used the restroom and also showered.

Gratitude surged in her heart, and on the tail of that, wonder. What she had shared—so daringly, she might add—with Grant as they'd stood on the overlook had been the truth. Sage had little experience with true friends in general and none whatsoever with the very close variety. She went through life meeting all sorts of interesting people and enjoying limited interactions with them, but she never stayed around long enough to claim real friendship status.

For the first time, that struck her as sad. Why it hadn't before, Sage wasn't sure, but now, experiencing this faithful kindness offered by Grant Hillman, she felt the lack of it in the rest of her life.

She feared the lack of it when it was time to move on.

Who she was—who she had always been before—thrashed at that nig-gling worry, as if it was a threat to her independence.

The low murmur of men's voices distracted her from really thinking on that. Now that Gramps was showered and more comfortable, perhaps he'd be willing to put some soup into his belly. Sage reheated the canned chicken noodle she had tried to give Gramps an hour before Grant had arrived. After a few minutes, when steam curled up from the translucent yellow liquid, she placed a half-full bowl of it on a tray, alongside a plate of crackers and a half a mandarin orange she had peeled.

Entering the parlor-slash-Gramps bedroom, she found him sitting com-fortably, a soft blanket tucked around his legs, and his expression signifi-cantly less strained.

"The eighties were hard on most farmers. After I got through that, mostly in one piece, seemed a good time to get out of it."

Grant nodded from his seat across from Gramps. "My dad had been a teenager then and swore he'd never farm. Made Grandpa upset, from what I hear."

"Didn't take much to make Claude Hillman mad," Gramps murmured. Then he glanced toward Grant, a mild look of regret in his expression. "He was your grandfather though . . ."

Sage lowered the tray onto Gramps's lap. He glanced at her with not much more than an acknowledgment of her presence and then looked back at Grant.

"I didn't know him well," Grant said. "We lived in Lincoln most of my growing up years—Dad preferred the city. We only moved back when I was in junior high. Grandpa died before I graduated high school, and we were never close."

"Why did you come back?"

Grant shrugged, though he looked uncomfortable. "Dad thought it might do me good. Smaller school."

"You didn't like Lincoln?" A few coughs shook Gramps's shoulders, but nothing as bad as had gripped him the day before.

Grant shrugged again. "I did not feel like it made a whole lot of difference. I was the same person here that I was in Lincoln. Quiet. Not athletic. Liked playing my cello and reading. Did not like football or hanging out with other people."

Gramps nodded, as if none of this was news to him. "That bothered your dad?"

"Yes." Grant's answer was definitive and yet detached. That seemed a strange combination, especially since he'd just looked uneasy with this topic.

Gramps turned his attention to the food on his lap, as if suddenly that was more important than the rather significant conversation Sage had walked in on. A mild scowl folded his brow. "This looks like sick-old-man food."

Grant leaned forward and inspected the tray. "It looks like a decent meal to me." He then looked at Sage with calm approval.

Grateful for his presence, and a little shocked at the ease Grant had with Gramps, Sage walked around the coffee table and lowered onto a cushion beside him.

Brow still furrowed—but that wasn't unusual—Gramps studied the pair. "You two a serious couple?"

Sage laughed. "Oh, Gramps. You know we only recently met. Remember?"

"What does that have to do with anything?"

Grant cleared his throat, but his expression remained calm. Impassive, even. "We're not dating."

The way he said that, so matter of fact and firm . . . Sage's gut clenched. It shouldn't have, not in that painful way that it did. She summoned her brightest grin and aimed it first at Grant and then at Gramps. "Right. No dating happening here. Grant is entirely too serious for me."

One bushy gray eyebrow lifted on Gramps's face. "Typical woman," he muttered, stirring his soup.

"What's that?" Sage said.

He lifted a spoonful to his mouth and ate it, then pinned disapproval firmly on her. "I said, 'Typical woman.' Doesn't know a good thing when she's got 'im."

"Wait just a minute here, Gramps." Of all the . . . how dare Gramps? After all, Grant was the one who had just firmly, unequivocally declared they were not dating. She was simply affirming his position. Why was this her fault?

A gentle hand covered hers and squeezed. Sage glanced at Grant, catching the quirk of a half grin.

"Sage is right," Grant said. "We are opposites. As a psychologist, I can firmly say that *opposites attract* is a cliché of fantastic failure. Opposites almost never work out romantically. And anyway, neither of us is looking for romance, so we are friends."

Gramps stared at Grant. The room suddenly seemed small and stuffy and in need of more light and a good cleaning. Actually, come to think of it, everything in this house needed a deep scrub.

Smacking her legs with both palms, Sage popped up to her feet. "Now that that's settled, I have work to do."

"What work?" Gramps muttered.

As if she didn't do work. She spent her mornings narrating and then in the garden, her afternoons narrating, and her evenings making sure the old man of the house didn't starve. Sage rolled her eyes. Well then, if he wanted more, he was gonna get it.

"I've decided this place needs a deep clean."

"No."

"Not optional. I live here too now."

"I don't remember inviting you."

"Too bad."

"What?"

"I'm your granddaughter." She popped her hands onto her hips. "And you're sick. Now you're stuck with me. And since you refuse to go to the hospital, I'm stuck here with you. So this house is getting cleaned. Or perhaps exorcised. I'm not sure."

Gramps held her with a glare that was mostly perturbed but at least a little bit fearful.

Maybe she misread that?

He shoveled a few more spoonsful of soup into his mouth and then coughed again. "Do what you want, but don't go digging into my stuff."

Feeling victorious, Sage moved her attention to Grant. Rather than meeting her smirk, he held his attention on Gramps. There was concern in his study.

Sage wasn't sure why.

CHAPTER FIFTEEN

"You looked like you didn't approve down there."

Grant finished tugging the large highboy away from the wall. He and Sage were in one of the four upstairs bedrooms. She had covered her curls with a folded kerchief, while he had gone to work pulling furniture away from the walls, at her request.

Grant did not look back at her to answer. "I have no problem helping you clean. At least, not until two. Then I have to get going. I have an appointment at four, and it will take me twenty minutes to jog back to my car."

"That's not what I was talking about."

His shoulders pressed down, and he sighed quietly. The conversation belowstairs had been anything but comfortable from the beginning. In general, Grant did not like talking about himself. That was just his personality—he did not like attention, especially in a group situation. A group, by him, being defined as more than one person. But it had been more than that.

Mr. Teller had poked around into Grant's history. His family. His relationship with his dad. Grant preferred all of those things to remain omitted from conversation.

He wasn't close to his family—with the exception of Clayton. In a town like Big Prairie, and a culture such as farming, that sort of thing got noticed. And talked about. Grant did not have a good explanation for the situation.

He was simply different, that was all. More, when his not fitting in with the Hillman clan came up, it made him feel his oddness in a way that cut deep.

So Mr. Teller bringing up the Hillman group at all had been an awkward start. Then he went to the relationship status between Grant and Sage.

What Grant had said was the truth—they were not dating. But he liked her. He liked her so very much . . .

And then in a snarky response to her grandfather's rather sexist and demeaning comment, Sage had picked at something Grant felt certain was a wound. He wasn't sure what or why, but he saw the flicker of pain in the old man's eyes when she had declared that the house needed cleaned—or *exorcised*.

As if there were ghosts lurking there. For Mr. Teller, there likely were.

With a dramatic sigh, Sage flopped onto the double bed Grant had dragged to the center of the room. "Okay, I confess. I let him get under my skin, and I maybe responded with a little too much offense. But you have to admit, he had no business accusing me of not knowing a good thing. After all, I *claimed* you as my closest of friends first."

He could not explain why her dramatic ways amused him. Still, he could not school the urge to chuckle as he straightened and faced her. "I think if you decided to use this charisma you own to charm your grandfather, you would have him wrapped around your finger in no time."

Her eyes brightened and she smirked. "You think I have charisma?"

"You know you do, Sage."

She came off the mattress and stood in front of him, poking a playful finger into his chest. "Enough to wrap you around my finger?"

"Don't do that." He wrapped the hand she'd pressed against his chest in a gentle hold and lowered it back to her side. "I know what your mask looks like. What I do not know is why, in this moment, you have chosen to wear it. But I don't want you to. Not with me."

That bright, flirty smile faded. She held him with wide alarmed eyes and swallowed. She stepped back, and he let her hand fall away.

"I don't know what to think—or how to feel about my grandfather. Flirting with you seemed easier than thinking about him."

Her honest answer surprised him. "Why did you come here to stay with him?"

She sighed, lowering back to the edge of the bed. "My mom called me out of the blue one day—we don't talk much—and she was ranting about this letter she got from a lawyer. Basically it said that Gramps had changed his will, naming her and me the inheritors of his property. I guess before it was to be left for my grandmother—but she died last year."

Sensing this was only the beginning of a story she wanted to talk about, Grant simply waited for her to continue.

Sage played with the end of a thread at the hem of her loose-fitting tank top. "I didn't even know that heiresses or whatever got notified. Is that a normal thing?" She paused, but only long enough to shrug. "Anyway, Mom was certain there had to be something nefarious in it. Like he was leaving her stuck with a bunch of back taxes or something. So I used my charm to dig out some information from the lawyer's office, and I found out that Gramps owned this little riverside property in a charming small town and that everything was on the up and up."

Giving up on the thread that she'd been wrapping around her pinkie, she leaned back onto her hands. "That made me curious. Why would he leave his property to a granddaughter he'd only met once and had no interest in beyond that? It just seemed so . . . so odd."

Grant nodded his agreement, and she continued. "So I decided to come here. To see who this great-grandfather was who was leaving my mother and me his stuff. Mom didn't want me to—she said it was just an old man's ploy to appease his guilty conscious, and she didn't want anything to do with that."

After a long sigh, she shrugged. "I don't know—maybe it is. But he's not really what I expected."

Grant lowered onto the thick wood pine planks of the floor and leaned against the highboy he'd just moved. "What did you expect?"

She shrugged. "Like I told you before, a drunk. That's what Mom had called him. What Grandma had said. But guess what? I've not seen one bottle of alcohol in this place."

Rubbing his jaw, Grant nodded. That was an interesting discovery. "Most of the town has labeled him a drunk too. A mean one."

"Most?"

"Except a few. Wes, at The Grill. And Miss Jane."

Her expression softened. "Yes. Miss Jane is . . . different." There she sat forward. "Except you said she didn't like you?"

That familiar discomfort snaked in his gut—the one that told him he was different. Not the good kind. The too-subtly-different-to-figure-out kind. The kind people set aside and ignored because that was easier than feeling uncomfortable with him. He knew this about himself already. He disliked the indirect ways people reminded him of it. Their quiet distance and the lack of enough interest to get to know him beyond his social ineptitude were like small barbs into his soul. Nothing deadly, just the proverbial thousand cuts . . .

Enough self-pity.

Anyway, there was Sage. Not keeping her distance. Inviting him to share who he was, even if that was awkward.

Grant leaned forward, looping his arms around his bent knees. "I do not know, I guess. It seemed like Miss Jane did not like me." That did not fit quite right. Miss Jane had been his Sunday school teacher in junior high, and she had seemed perfectly fine with him. This disapproval had been only a recent thing. Rubbing his jaw, Grant considered that. "Perhaps it was more that she did not like me with Brenna."

"Why in the world not?"

With forced intention, Grant thought back to last fall, when it had seemed that Miss Jane was artfully sabotaging his relationship with his then girlfriend. Maybe she wasn't sabotaging. Perhaps she was shedding light on a truth he and Brenna both needed to see . . . the very same truth that Grant had realized. The reason he had broken things off with Brenna.

Brenna and Erikson were not finished. No matter how much they ignored each other. How much they wanted to pretend everything was *fine*. Indeed, the fact that Brenna could not stand to be in the same space Craig occupied had been revealing.

Had Miss Jane known the same thing?

Hmm. Perhaps he had more in common with Miss Jane than he had realized.

"Grant?"

There he'd gone again, getting lost in his thoughts. Puzzling things out while rudely ignoring someone. "Sorry." He lifted his attention from his hands to find that Sage waited without frustration. "I have not thought about it much, I guess. I just felt the poke of Miss Jane's actions. But now I can see . . . she must have known too."

"Known what?"

"That Brenna and Craig needed to work things out. That I was in the way of that—I was Brenna's hiding place."

"That doesn't seem like a bad thing, if she needed you to be."

He shook his head. "No. She was not getting past some things. Not healing, because she was angry with Craig. And because she still loved him—which was why she could not get past the anger. She *needed* to deal with things with him."

"Did you ever tell her that?"

"I tried."

"But?"

"She did not like me playing counselor to her. She said boyfriend Grant and counselor Grant needed to remain separate, or she would go crazy."

"Ouch."

He had understood, mostly. He understood that people assumed he was always analyzing them. Their actions and thoughts and feelings. And truthfully, he was. Just not for the reasons they assumed.

Not to fix them. Heaven knew, he could not even fix himself.

He just wanted to understand. How was it that he could feel another's emotions with such strength, but he could not for the life of him figure out how to connect with them in a personal way?

Skip it—that was the unanswered question of his life, and Grant felt nearly certain he would never find an answer. "It does not matter now."

"No? Your heart isn't broken?"

"No." It was a simple, honest answer. Not one he could have given six months before. Oddly, he wanted to tell Miss Jane—to tell her that she was right and all the sudden he understood why she had done what she'd done.

And that maybe they shared some things. Except, Miss Jane could not only read people, she could connect with them.

Sage's gentle smile was purely glad for him that his heart wasn't in shambles. "I have to tell you something, Grant."

His heart skittered, but he schooled his expression as he looked at her. "What is that?"

"Miss Jane knows she hurt you last fall, and though she didn't mean to, she is sorry. She said you are special to her."

Grant didn't know what to say to that as emotion bulged in his chest. It seemed such a small thing to be called special by Miss Jane. But it mattered.

As if to brush away the dust of their conversation, Sage brushed her hands together one way and then another and stood up. She turned a slow circle in place, inspecting the small room. "I think that after a thorough scrubbing, these walls need a fresh coat of paint." Tapping her lips with her index finger, she tilted her head. "A soft, warm yellow."

It would do some good, no question. "What will your gramps say?"

"I'll charm him."

One side of his mouth tipped up as Grant scrambled to his feet as well. "I am sure of that."

Placing her hands on her hips, she shook her head. "Actually, I think you have done that better than me. He likes you. And by the way, he isn't mean. Not really. Just . . . grumpy."

Grant nodded, knowing that she was referencing part of the earlier conversation. "It is amazing what you discover when you give people a minute."

Appreciation filled her soft brown eyes. "You're a pretty smart guy, Grant Hillman." Sage squeezed his arm as she passed by.

Grant relished that her voice held sincerity. And that she wasn't wearing her light-bright smiling mask.

For some reason, he could connect with Sage. Perhaps he wasn't entirely emotionally broken after all.

CHAPTER SIXTEEN

GRANT HAD HELPED HER move furniture and clean for the remainder of that morning, until the last possible minute he had to spare before he needed to resume that jog and get back home and then work.

And then he showed up the next day. And the day after that. Both times claiming that he was jogging by and wanted to stop in to check on her and Gramps. As she cracked six eggs at the kitchen counter, Sage wondered if this *jogging by* thing was the truth or an excuse. Likely, the truth. Grant Hillman was not the sort of man given to lies. Likely he despised falsehood, much as he disliked chaos, and as he'd shared the day before while they'd scrubbed the rough plastered walls in preparation for fresh paint, he was not a fan of surprises.

"Tell me something I should know about you." Sage turned what was evidently Grant's favorite conversation starter on him.

Squatting in front of a paint can, Grant paused his stirring of the "friendly yellow" paint and tipped his face toward the ceiling. After a thoughtful moment, he fixed his attention on her. "I dislike surprises."

"All surprises?"

"Yes. All surprises. I . . . I have a hard time adjusting to the interruption of my plans. And I do not enjoy feeling caught off guard."

"So you are inflexible."

"One might say that."

At the brief memory of that conversation, Sage grinned while she whisked eggs for two. (Or three. She'd cracked enough for three, in case Grant stopped in again. She hoped he would.) She could not pinpoint why she thought Grant being inflexible was adorable, but she did. More, she admired that he knew it and that he would just say it plainly. Didn't that speak of a man who knew himself—the good and the bad—and was simply willing to lay it out there in honesty?

She'd known few to no people who were able to be honest about their foibles. Most were more set on pointing out the shortcomings of others rather than owning their own. If they did own them, they used them as some sort of humble brag, which Sage found annoying.

Not the case with Grant. He simply knew who he was and was honest about it.

Eggs sufficiently scrambled, Sage poured the bright-yellow mixture into the hot pan. As she watched them cook, she wondered if the eggs Miss Jane had delivered the week before were farm fresh. She would guess so. Yolks that bright didn't come from a chain store. In a matter of minutes, the cheerful breakfast was cooked, and she plated a serving for Gramps.

"That young man of yours coming today?" Gramps rasped as she lowered the tray of eggs, toast, and orange juice onto his lap.

"He's not *my* young man. But I hope he stops by."

Gramps held a long stare on her, and when she looked to meet his eyes, he lifted both brows. "Bet it wouldn't take much."

Heat trickled into her face. Why, she couldn't say. Not like she hadn't liked a guy before. Not like she was a rookie at dating, either. But Grant wasn't . . . dateable. Not for her, anyway. He was the commitment kind, and she, as she'd told him, was a free bird. The noncommitment kind. She came from a long line of the noncommitment sort.

Starting with the man whose bushy brows had challenged her position on the situation a moment before. There, a surge of something that felt a whole lot like resentment pressed into her chest.

Know who you are and be honest about it, just like Grant. Well then . . .

Sage crossed her arms and narrowed her look. "*I* am not okay with breaking hearts, Grandfather."

When she thought he'd look down, maybe with a flash of guilt crossing his expression, Gramps nodded. "That would make you better than most."

Better than him?

The need to know overwhelmed her, as did this sudden, rolling tide of bitterness. "Why did you do it, Gramps?" She spat the question out more like an accusation.

A hard, guarded expression crawled over his face. Ignoring her, he busied himself with the breakfast she'd brought him.

"Don't ignore me! I was raised as a fatherless kid—as was my mother and hers before her. Do you know what the statistics are on that situation?" Sage pulled up from memory the research she'd done in her high school speech class—the statistics that solidified the beliefs about men that had already been passed down to her.

"Here are a few fun facts for you, Gramps. Ninety percent of all homeless and runaway children, over sixty percent of teen suicides, and eighty-five percent of children and teens with behavioral disorders come from *fatherless homes.* And that's just scratching the surface. We haven't even touched the percentage of fatherless kids who end up living in poverty, addicted to drugs, dropping out of school, or the best yet, winding up in prison." It was amazing how clearly all of that information had remained in her mind. Permanently inscribed there because she desperately did not want to be one among those devastating statistics. She most certainly did not want to pay them forward. "That is your legacy, Harold Teller. That's what you chose to pass on. I deserve to know why."

"Don't talk about the past."

"Why? Too many regrets?" Sage uncrossed her arms and rolled fists at her sides. It'd been a long time since she'd allowed anger to grip her like this. So long, in fact, that she had thought she'd mastered it. Had buried it deep and planted happy white daisies over the top of all that rage. Rest in peace. Do not resurrect.

Only live happy, and don't become a statistic.

The ugly grave split wide open, and out it poured. Anger. Resentment. More, it seemed, than she had buried as a teenager.

She stepped closer. "Too much guilt to deal with? Is that why you're leaving this house to me and my mother? As atonement?"

He met her molten gaze with a matching one of his own. But his lips remained pinned shut. Slowly, his glare softened and drifted. He stared out the window, which faced the road, and something clearly painful seized his emotions, as his face twisted.

Swallowing, he shook his head. "Ain't nothing good back there, girl. It's best left alone."

"You can't even admit it now, can you? Just say it, Gramps. You rejected your wife and your own son. The least you could do is admit it."

Gramps blinked, and his whole body went rigid. But he remained stubbornly silent.

Sage trembled all over, and she discovered with great irritation that warm liquid threatened to drip from her eyes.

No.

No. No. No. She would not cry over the heartlessness of this man. Nor of any of the men in her linage.

She would not cry over men in general. She had built a guard around her heart—they could not touch it. Not ever.

With her jaw clamped down hard, Sage spun and walked away from the room. From the old man who had miraculously managed to slip past those long-established defenses and from the crushing weight of disappointment she felt in him right then.

All men disappoint. All. Live free of them, like a bird. Don't ever let them clip your wings.

Mom's scathing words, likely hissed after one of the several live-in boyfriends she'd had over the years had left her, sizzled in the back of Sage's mind as she stormed through the kitchen, into the covered back porch, and out the back door. She paused for a moment, scanning the backyard—specifically the drop-off that plunged to the river.

Now would be a good time to stop by, Grant . . .

How stupid was that? Hadn't she just been reminded that men were always a disappointment, and she should never hang her hopes on one?

Oh the pathetic depths of her hypocrisy! One minute thinking of her mother's weakness in that she inevitably repeated the same stupid story again and again. Find a man. Fall in love. Let him move in. Let him break her heart. Seethe about men. Wash your face and return to step one.

Again and again.

Sage had looked down on her mom for it.

But the very next moment, there she was, searching the horizon for a man to show up and fix all her problems. Searching for him as if he was a hero rather than a villain—just like the beginning of their story.

Grant is different . . .

Ha! She'd heard that before—ad nauseum. It had never been true. Not a single time.

Propelled by that steaming anger that had broken from its chamber, Sage marched toward her garden—giving her back to the riverbanks. She snagged a hoe from the side of the house as she passed by, and with great gusto, she uprooted the tiny weeds littering the pathways between her tomatoes and peppers.

"Be gone, you little joy-wreckers. Die, you little life-sappers." Her arms burned as she energetically turned the soil, destroying the little sprouts of life that dared to threaten all the good things she had planted. She finished the tomatoes and peppers and started on the rows of beans. A medley of birds chirping sounded from her back pocket.

Sage ignored the incoming text. Whoever was messaging her didn't want to hear back from her right then. Especially if the one making her phone chirp again was who she guessed. And even more so, if he was letting her know he wouldn't be showing up that day.

Likely that. Of course he wouldn't. Not on the day when she actually needed him to drop in. Why would he want to prove her—and her mom—wrong about his species in general? That would be . . .

Winded by her aggressive weeding and the spiral her thoughts and emotions had taken, Sage stopped ripping ribbons into the ground and leaned against the handle of her tool. Her breath came and went with great puffs, and her arms trembled.

And dang it, those threatening tears still hung in the balance.

Wow. She needed to get a grip on herself. Starting with this fierce burst of irritation directed at Grant. He didn't owe her anything. If he didn't stop by, that didn't make him a lousy person. It made him a man with a life and a job, neither of which revolved around her, for heaven's sake.

Sage pressed a palm to her forehead as she calmed her riled spirit. Goodness, where had the black powder come from?

Gramps.

Poor excuse. He was sick. And anyway, the things she'd railed at him had happened more than sixty years ago. But wouldn't a person want to clear the air before they died? If Gramps felt bad for what he had done, couldn't he just say it?

Why did she need him to do that?

The phone in her back pocket chirped again. This time Sage reached for it. And found that she had been right—Grant.

I had a last-minute appointment come up. I am sorry, but I can't make it out this morning. Would it be okay if I drove out this evening?

The hardness in her chest eased, and her heart might have liquified a bit at his last question. Grant was . . .

Different.

He seemed to dislike that about himself. Sage was finding his uniqueness to be her favorite thing about him.

The phone in her hand chirped again.

I am worried about you and Gramps. He seemed better yesterday, but I asked Anne to stop by this morning anyway. Please do not be upset.

That seemed a little outside of Grant's normal procedure. He was helpful, always considerate, but he also had been careful not to overstep.

Was this an overstep?

The sound of a vehicle creeping up the rutted drive out front sidetracked her thoughts before she could decide. Heart rate settled back to near normal after her fury-driven weeding, Sage walked the garden hoe back to the side of the house, leaned it against the lapped siding, and wiped her hands down the front of her pixie-cut jeggings. Boosting up a smile—the bright sort that Grant had called a mask—Sage trekked around the house to the front in time to meet Anne as she popped out of an SUV.

"Good morning, Sage." Anne closed the car door and sauntered toward her. "I hope you don't mind the intrusion."

"No intrusion. Grant texted and said you might stop by."

"Of course he did." Anne's smile held genuine esteem for her husband's cousin. "How is Gramps?"

It did not escape Sage's attention that both Grant and now Anne had taken to calling her grandfather *Gramps*. She wondered how the old grouch would feel about that. Rather than pondering it too much, she walked toward the house. Anne joined her at her side.

"He seems better. He's able to move around on his own more."

"That's good news." Anne followed Sage through the front door, then touched Sage's arm. "And how are you holding up?"

"I'm . . ." Sage stumbled over that answer. "Tired."

Truth was, she was tired and an emotional wreck. She hadn't slept well in three days, getting up three or four times a night to check on Gramps and worrying about him in between. She wasn't sure why, exactly. Sure, she was concerned that he'd get worse or even die—a deeply unpleasant thought—while she lay in bed. But this level of concern felt deeper, more intimate than the general and natural fear of death.

Sage felt like she might be losing something important. Maybe it was the answers to those nagging questions about *why*? Or perhaps it was the slim opportunity that she and Gramps could reconcile the past somehow. Even that . . . Sage couldn't understand why that was so important.

Worse, given the conversation of the morning, reconciliation didn't seem likely. And had she really hoped for it?

Maybe what she hoped for most was something that would anchor her life.

What a contradiction to her free-bird claim.

Anne's gentle touch turned to a soft squeeze on Sage's arm. "That's understandable. Caring for the sick and the elderly is a hard and exhausting task. And Grant says you've added to it by taking on painting projects upstairs."

Grant was worried about that? The news cradled her heart with a gentle warmth. One that, though Sage was tempted to embrace with the mushy side of herself who loved a romantic adventure story, she instinctively pushed away.

Sage shrugged. "I can narrate for only so many hours a day—my voice gets raw, and the quality goes down if I overdo it. I need other things to do, or I'll go crazy."

"Understandable." Anne continued her way into the house. "But perhaps you could use a break? I could bring a cup of coffee by after my shift tomorrow. I get done at two."

Coffee with a friend . . . something Sage had seen on TV shows and in movies but didn't do much in real life. Mostly because that would require staying in one place and getting to know people deeper than surface level. Even so, it sounded lovely. "I'd like that. Thank you."

"My pleasure."

Sage led the rest of the way from the kitchen to the parlor, and Anne ran a quick check over Gramps. When she was finished, she looked at the old man. "Seems you're on the mend, Mr. Teller."

He grunted.

"Don't go running down the driveway or anything just yet though." Anne winked. "I still hear a bit of rattling in your chest. We don't want that to get worse."

"Girl takes good care of me."

Was that a . . . a compliment? Sage stared at Gramps, and his watery eyes settled on her. In that silent exchange, a truce nestled into the strain between them. The lingering burn of anger in her chest cooled, and Sage resolved to let the argument go. She couldn't force a confession, let alone an apology, from Gramps. And even if she could, what would it change, really?

Mom would hate him forever, no matter what. Just like Grandma had done and Great-Grandma Clara before her. And Sage? Sage had long since decided that hate was toxic, and she didn't want to drink the poison any more than she had wanted to be a fatherless-child statistic.

She desperately, more than anything, wanted to live a happy life.

The God I know is the author of joy and peace. He gives life and blesses it—because He is good. Miss Jane's claim sank deeper still into Sage's heart. Perhaps later she would really examine it.

Perhaps she would even ask Grant what he thought of it. But for now, Gramps was holding out an olive branch.

Sage took the four steps required to bring her beside Gramps, and she laid her hand on his shoulder. "I'm glad to do it."

The arm beneath her palm was thin and bony. The build of an old man not much longer for this life. All the reminder that she needed of why she was there—to make peace with the family drama, no matter what it took, so that maybe she could be free of its curse. Free to live happy.

Not a fatherless statistic but truly a girl free to fly.

CHAPTER SEVENTEEN

GRANT HAD NOT ONE but two last-minute sessions, one of which was with Trent. Seemed he'd had quite an outburst when Craig and Brenna had come home from their quick honeymoon to the mountains. For Trent, an outburst usually meant destruction. This time it was two tires on Craig's jeep.

"Tell me what I need to know, Trent."

Trent had sat stoic for several beats, but Grant waited him out. Most people couldn't keep their stories inside for long, and Grant had learned, even before his formal training, that staying quiet and listening usually was the surest way to gain trust. And, more often than not, the truth.

And the truth did come out. With the heartbreaking tears of a kid who had way too much fear pressed into his world.

"I slashed his tires."

"I see."

"He left us! He promised he wouldn't, and then he did!"

"You knew he and Brenna were going and that they would come back. They told you the plan."

"But . . ."

Yes, that *but*. *But* this kid had been left a lot in his life. Abandoned and neglected. In fact, Craig and his mom, Janet, and had been the first people in his chaotic little world who had been any source of constancy at all. Could anyone really blame Trent for his reaction?

For sure, Craig did not. The phone call Grant had with him this morning had made it more than clear that Craig had felt responsible for Trent's outburst, and he was miserable for it. *"I've taken us ten steps backward. What do I do now, Hillman?"*

Grant thought of the bird analogy he'd read in *The Connected Child* about trauma kids. How a bird would build its nest carefully and logically. But if a storm came in and wrecked that carefully-put-together nest, a bird would often come back and reconstruct it in haste and madness. No reason, no design. Just chaos . . . whatever it took to have a home again. To feel safe.

Trent had reacted in haste and madness. No, it wasn't sensible. Not to someone who didn't know the backstory. It had been emotional and reactional. And heartbreaking.

Craig had called Grant that morning, immediately after he found the damage, his voice rough and near broken. *"I thought he knew we were coming back. I really thought he got it and was okay."*

Though his heart squeezed for Craig and for Brenna also, Grant focused on Trent. "But you felt abandoned."

The boy's face fell, and a giant tear seeped onto the side of his nose.

"Sometimes we know things in our head, but they do not always connect with our hearts."

"I made Craig mad." Those big brown eyes lifted, wide with fear. "What if this time . . ."

Grant shook his head. "I know your life has shown you otherwise, but Craig won't send you away. He wants to be your dad. He won't leave you or Ashton. He has claimed you, and you are his. There is nothing you can do to make him change his mind."

"How do you know? What if he's just like everyone?"

"Do you know how long he has loved Brenna?"

Trent shrugged. "Not that long. Same as Ash and me, I think."

Taking a breath, Grant absorbed the truth of what he was about to share with Trent. It was quite something actually—the constancy of Craig's heart for Brenna. Something that, to be honest, Grant hadn't allowed himself to really soak in.

Enduring love was really quite something.

"Craig has loved her since he was seventeen. That is more than ten years, Trent."

The boy's face wrinkled. "Why he take so long?"

"To marry her?"

"Yeah."

Grant leaned forward and rested his elbows on his knees. "Well, like you and Ashton, Brenna and Craig had some hard things in their past. Things that, just like you today, they did not know how to handle, and so they handled them badly."

"Because of Brenna's brother?"

"Yes."

Trent swallowed and then nodded. Connection. Grant's heart lifted. They were going to be okay, this little instant Erikson family. And that was something to rejoice in.

"Craig loves big. And he loves you. He loves Ash."

"And Brenna."

"And Brenna, who also loves you."

"She not gonna make Craig get rid of us? We a lot of trouble."

"Never."

Trent chuckled quietly, the teary kind that was usually meant to hide hurts. "She just gonna make me talk right."

"That is likely. And for your good."

With a slow nod, Trent blew out a long breath. "I hafta help pay for the tires."

"Do you think that is fair?"

Trent eyed him. "Do you?"

"Yes, I do. It will show that you understand actions and consequences—and that you are taking responsibility. And more importantly, that you are sorry. And you are sorry, is that not true?"

His bottom lip trembled. "Yes."

"Have you told Craig so?"

He shook his head.

"Then you know what I will prescribe."

"A 'pology."

"Exactly. Mend the fracture in your relationship, Trent."

"Fracture?"

"A small break."

"But you say Craig love me."

"I do say that, and it is true. But do things feel right between you and Craig right now?"

Looking at his hands, Trent shook his head. "Craig mad."

"Trent, I think you should realize that although you are right—Craig does feel anger right now—you broke something on purpose. And the tires are expensive, and he can't drive his car without them—that more importantly than the car, what you did hurt him. That is the fracture. Your actions were both wrong and hurtful."

"Grown up men hurt?"

At that, Grant couldn't stop a small chuckle. "We never outgrow the ability to hurt, Trent. Not ever. Some will try to smother it with anger, or with drugs, or something else that is meant to replace it, but in the end, pain is part of life."

Trent's small shoulders sagged as disappointment seeped from his fallen expression. Grant reached across the space between them and set a gentle hand on his shoulder. "Life is not always hard though, Trent. It does not have to be."

Trent sniffed and then ran his hand over his nose—something that made Grant cringe inwardly, but he said nothing about.

"Make good choices, right?"

"Exactly so, Trent."

Grant could feel the tension ease beneath his hand, and he rubbed the boy's back, then leaned back and refolded his hands. "What else should you do?"

"Be honest." Trent sounded less confident in that than in the apology part, or even the good choices.

That, Grant understood intimately. Sharing your deepest insecurities was a hard ask—one he himself had yet to master.

They were out of time though, and so that was where Grant left it.

Later that evening Grant thought on that interaction while he drove toward the Teller house. He could not explain why, but his conversation with Trenton Fulton-almost-Erikson seemed relevant to his connection with Sage. As he navigated the washboard dirt road, across the bridge that had quickly been repaired after last spring's flood, and within sight of that old white farmhouse, Grant parsed out the fragments of his appointment with Trent and pieced them against his interactions with Sage.

Nothing fit quite right. Even so, there was *something* relevant. He sensed it, the way he could sense underlying distress in another person.

He pulled into the drive, navigated around the worst of the potholes, and parked near the front porch. The puzzle remained undone—which as usual, bothered Grant. But he intentionally sent it to the back of his mind. It had been a long day, with two extra appointments and worrying about Sage and Gramps.

And missing her smile.

Climbing the rickety steps (perhaps he should address those?), Grant felt the warmth of something pleasant move in his chest. To his thrilling delight, that same feeling flooded his bloodstream when the front door swung open before he knocked and there she was, her joyful grin lifting.

At him. For him.

He should not hope for such things—not the way he did. But contrary to everything in Grant's careful life thus far, he could not help himself.

"Exactly five thirty. Just as promised." Sage stepped forward and pecked his cheek.

Though he knew she meant nothing more than a friendly greeting, Grant's heart kicked into a jog. Hand on her arm, he leaned down and inhaled her. She was all warm sunshine, smelling like sweet lemonade.

He had the most distracting impulse to discover if she tasted so as well.

Instead, he straightened. "How is Gramps by now?"

"Better." Sage turned and led the way through the house. "Still wheezing a little, and he dozed most of the afternoon. But Anne says that he's on the mend." Now at the doorway between the kitchen and parlor, she stopped and gripped Grant's hand. "Thank you for that."

His mind was erased of everything but the awareness of her slim fingers in his. She was soft and warm, and he wanted only to know the sensation of her in his arms again, as he had on the dance floor.

Yikes, but his emotions must be raw today! That conversation with Trent had hit something deep within.

Or. *Be honest . . .*

He could not. It was too risky—she had already made her heart clear.

Self-discipline was a feat as he let her hand slip away. "Thank you for what?"

"Sending Anne."

"Oh." Relief feathered through him—though he could not be sure if it was at safely entering the conversation without making himself a fool or at her welcome of his mild interference in sending Anne. Either way, he relaxed his mouth. "You are welcome."

"We're having coffee tomorrow."

"We are?"

"No, not you and me." Her laugh was playful. "Anne and me."

As much as he would rather it be her and him in everything . . . no. Not that. He knew better than that . . . He was glad that she was glad.

"I am glad to hear it." And how about all that glad?

"Me too. Anne offered to bring me a cup of something fancy from Miss Jane's."

The brief memory of Miss Jane's reprimand last fall about his not knowing what Brenna liked flashed through his mind. "You'll have to tell me what you have, if you like it."

"What would you have?"

Grant shrugged. "Water, most likely."

Rolling her eyes, Sage wiggled his arm. "Oh, Grant. If you were having a treat, surely you wouldn't choose water."

She could not keep touching him—he would go mad. Grant stiffened and slid a step backward.

Sage blinked, dropping her hand. "Oh. I'm sorry. I didn't mean to offend you."

He was not offended. Not about the comment. Not about her. He was . . . captivated. Not at all his measured, controlled self.

What would she call it, if she was in her dramatic, novel-reading mode?

Besotted. Infatuated to the point of a drunken-like state?

At the moment, it seemed exactly so.

"I am not offended." His voice felt rough, and his heart hammered, like he'd just run a 5k.

He needed to clear his mind of this thick, pleasant fog before he did something impulsive. Even so, his gaze traced her face, following the lovely curves of her arched brows down to her cheekbones, over to her jawline, which led to her chin. Just a small lift of his eyes and he found her lips.

"It would depend on the season." He forced out an intelligent response through the fog of this attraction.

"Summer." Sage smiled—a sweet, pure, lovely grin that was the furthest thing from a mask or guile he'd seen on her yet.

Yes, intoxicated. He was in trouble.

"Raspberry lemonade," he whispered. Did his voice sound husky?

"Raspberry lemonade?"

Without permission, his gaze found her mouth again. Oh, he longed for a taste . . .

Stop this!

He licked his tingling lips and cleared his throat. "That is what I would get. For a treat. In summer."

"Sounds like a good choice and not terribly unhealthy. Why not have it every day?"

Why not indeed?

A rough cough broke into Grant's trance, and he may have been startled at the sound.

Gramps.

Gramps was sitting just over there in his chair. Observing this whole conversation? Watching Grant slip into a haze of delicious stupor?

Horrifying.

How had Grant not thought of the man? This was not normal.

How had he been hypnotized? Sage certainly hadn't done any-thing—not intentionally. Turning toward the old man, intending to make his way to the couch for a visit, Grant demanded his mind right itself. And his heart to stop thrashing about like a wild, untamed thing.

Sage fell into step beside him after he passed through the doorframe, her gait easy, her countenance light. As if nothing had just passed between them.

Was this really all one-sided?

"Raspberry lemonade," she spoke with lightness. "I'll remember, Grant Hillman. One of these days I'll surprise you with a treat."

"I don't like surprises, remember?" Grant questioned the truth of that claim as he quickened his steps just enough to get around the coffee table before her.

"Even gifts?"

He hesitated.

"Every man loves a thoughtful gift, girl." Gramps inserted his opinion with garbled authority.

Grant couldn't deny that, even if it had not proven so in the past. But in the past, gifts were usually something he did not want. He wasn't sure if that made him ridiculously picky (probably) and unusually hard to please (he cringed to think so), or if it meant that truly he had never allowed another person to know him well enough to find something he would enjoy.

Brenna, for example, had tried to bring him impromptu treats. He had tried to act grateful, because he *did* appreciate the gesture, but he never had owned the sort of politeness that lied. So when she'd shown up with some sort of frozen mocha thing shortly after they had started dating, he had said thank you anyway, but she could have it.

Coffee upset his gut, was the problem. But he had never told her that.

Same with greasy foods, like Hot Pies pizza. He simply did not relish the prospect of spending his evenings in the bathroom after that sort of dinner.

Those were personal details he had never shared with her though. Not in nearly two years of dating.

Why hadn't he? Counselor Grant would have advised honesty. But he had been boyfriend Grant at that point and was not well experienced at such a role, nor, frankly, anything close to it.

"Is that true, Grant?" Sage lowered onto the cushion opposite the side of the couch Grant had sat on. "If it was a well-thought gift, would you enjoy it? Or do you truly not like *any* surprises at all?"

Remarkably, there was no doubt or censure in her question. Just the desire to know—very much asked the way he would often say *tell me what I should know . . .*

Grant looked at Gramps, wanting to see his reaction to this conversation. That watery gaze met his, and in it was something of understanding. Of knowing, and not just at a head level. Truly *knowing*. The look sparked a fresh desire in Grant to understand who Harold Teller was—not just as Sage's grandfather or the town's mysterious recluse, but as a man made in the image of God, complete and complex.

What made him hide here in this old house all alone? Why did he allow the rumors to run wild about his drinking and temper, which were clearly untrue?

What had happened between him and his wife that had led him to this sad, lonely life?

"Grant?" Sage slid over onto the cushion in the middle of the couch.

"I think Mr. Teller is likely right."

"A thoughtful gift is an acceptable surprise, then." Victory danced in her voice. "That is good to know." She turned her attention toward Gramps. "And what about you?"

"What about me?"

"What would you consider a thoughtful gift?"

A flash of tenderness passed over the man's face. "You are here." The rest, though unsaid, was clear.

Sage being there, though the man had griped and groaned, was enough. No, it was everything.

And Grant could believe that.

Having one person, even if it was only one, determined enough to get past the rough edges, to care enough to stay and to learn the truth, was enough.

To be truly known would be near everything.

CHAPTER EIGHTEEN

Sage had found a friend. Not just in Grant—which was an exquisite friendship she wasn't entirely sure how to define. But also in Anne Hillman.

Seemed this little town of Big Prairie held all sorts of surprises for her.

Anne had come out after work, just as promised, bringing with her two heavily whipped topping-topped chilled vanilla coffees from Miss Jane's shop. Enjoying the treat, Sage sat across from Anne out back on a set of solid wooden chairs Sage had uncovered in the attic only that afternoon and had muscled down to the backyard.

"How on earth did you manage to get them down from the attic?" Anne wondered while she ran a hand over the smooth, wide armrest.

"They were heavy!" Sage laughed. "But don't let this wispy build fool you—I'm not as wimpy as I look. The bigger trick was talking Gramps into letting me do it."

"He didn't want them outside?"

"He didn't want me in the attic." Sage widened her eyes and made a *yikes* face. "His face turned beet red, and he gave me a good chewing out. Gave himself a wild coughing fit doing it." She shrugged. "I probably deserved the ear boxing. He had already told me to stay out of it."

"Uh-oh."

"Yeah. I'm a little bit of trouble like that."

"As in, you don't do as you're told?"

Sage smirked. "Something like that." She sipped on the delicious drink. "Maybe it was disrespectful of me. But I made up for it by practicing my narration of an epic battle on the high seas for him. He seemed to enjoy that."

"Epic battle?"

"The book I'm working on now—I'm almost finished with it—is a pirate-y high-adventure romance. It's pretty great."

Anne clapped her hands with giddy joy. "I must hear this when it's done."

"Sure." Sage flipped her hair over her shoulder and winked. "I'll get you a copy."

Nodding her thanks, Anne took a sip of her drink. "Now, back to the chairs and the attic. Was there a reason you did it?"

Sage shrugged. "There's a lot of stuff up there. Furniture covered in dust cloths. Boxes. Even a cello, I think. Seems like a cavern full of stories, and I like stories. I want to know them."

Anne laughed. "Is that what gets you into the most trouble?"

"Pretty much all. Curiosity kills the cat, right?"

"What stories have you found up there?"

Sage leaned into the backrest of the chair, soaking in the warm afternoon sun as her mind wandered over the things she'd explored earlier that day. "Mostly a bunch of lumpy, dusty mysteries. Like I said, there's a cello. I was stuck on that for quite a while. It seems like a find loaded with possibilities, don't you think?"

"Such as?"

"Who did it belong to? Was it Gramps? Or did it belong to my great-grandma Clara? Perhaps neither—this is the house Gramps grew up in. Did his mother play?"

"Which possibility did your imagination settle on?"

"Gramps—because he seems the least likely. Can you imagine my crusty old grandfather losing himself in the movements of Vivaldi's *Four Seasons*?"

Anne chuckled. "Actually, I could." She lounged back in her chair and crossed her legs. "Did you know Grant plays?"

"The cello? Oh yes!" Sage paused to wonder why she hadn't connected that more firmly before. "Gramps did mention something like that . . ."

"He's pretty good at it. Occasionally we can beg him to play at church. He doesn't like to—doesn't like the attention—but he'll do it if I ask him just right." Anne molded a look of innocent pleading.

Sage tapped the tips of her fingers together, as if she had a sly plan. "This I *must* investigate."

"Don't tell him I pushed you into it. In the years since I've been part of the Hillman clan, I've carved a good relationship with Grant. With an introvert of his level—and one who is extra guarded at that—that takes some intentional work, so don't ruin it. I rather like him, and I rather like that he likes me."

Sage could appreciate that. Grant's allowing one into his inner circle seemed like a special privilege. How she'd obtained it for herself was one of those beautiful mysteries she'd found in Big Prairie. She certainly didn't want to lose the honor either.

"Why is he extra guarded?" Sage asked.

Anne's grin faded, her expression slipping into something more serious and sad. "He just wasn't well accepted by . . . well, by much of anyone, I guess. Clay says Grant's dad was especially hard on him. He wanted an outgoing football star—someone like Craig Erikson. Introverted, studious, musically bent Grant wasn't on his hoped-for list. Clay sort of took on a protective position when Grant moved back to Big Prairie. Like I told you before, Grant is important to my husband, and Clay still looks out for him, even if Grant really doesn't need it much anymore."

Sage focused on the part about Grant's dad rejecting him. Grant had hinted that himself the other day when he'd been visiting with Gramps. Where all men prone to rejecting their offspring? In her experience, yes, but even so, it still seemed off. "Surely a father wouldn't reject his son because he wasn't bubbly and athletic."

With a sigh, Anne shook her head. "Men can be strange creatures."

"I guess." Sage closed her lips and let her attention drift from Anne toward the dip of land where the river ran. Initially her thoughts flashed to Grant—to their first meeting. To the way he looked at her as if she'd had four arms and a pair of wings. She'd thought he was adorable—once she'd determined he was harmless.

Grant was deeply reserved—she'd seen it the few times they'd been together in town. But she hadn't ever thought he was terribly awkward. What she had thought, in pretty much all of their time spent together, was that Grant was exceedingly kind.

How could his dad not want that?

For some reason, her pondering thoughts about Grant's father sent her musings sideways toward her own mother.

Men were not the only strange creatures.

Sage had never been able to understand her mother. The woman clawed to maintain her "unclipped wings," yet she had had no fewer than four live-in boyfriends while Sage had been between the ages of five and eighteen. Men who'd promised a life of adventure and fun but repeatedly had only sapped her mother of the few savings she'd scraped together and stripped her further of any real self-dignity.

The cycle then sent mom into a fresh fight for her freedom and independence, having her swear off serious relationships forever and pronounce all men disappointing liars.

The contradiction struck Sage afresh as she mulled it over. Mother hated men. But she couldn't seem to live without one.

She wasn't fighting for her freedom. Mother was a fugitive, running from her own bad choices. Straight into fresh ones.

"Are you still with me?" Anne's soft intrusion pulled Sage from the internal squall this line of thinking had provoked.

Brushing up a bright smile—one that certainly would cause Grant to frown and shake his head, as he would say it was her mask—Sage returned her gaze to Anne. "I think I have to show Grant the cello in the attic. Perhaps just seeing it will make the music in his fingers itch . . ."

"What then?"

"Maybe he'll play it for Gramps?"

"And?"

"And . . . then we shall see."

"What if he's mad?"

"Who, Gramps?"

Anne nodded.

"Oh, he will be." Sage swatted her hand in the air, as if smacking at a fly. "It'll be fine though. Gramps is a gentle soul beneath all his bluster. I'm beginning to think that everything I was ever told of him was a lie."

That was true. And for some reason, unsettling. But Sage didn't want to go into that with Anne. Not now, on this lovely sunny day.

Sage had lived to find joy. Digging into this mystery, though undeniably intriguing, felt like a threat against that quest. She'd leave the deepest parts be.

For now.

Chapter Nineteen

Grant arrived on the front porch with a cast-iron Dutch oven in his mitted hands.

Was it presumptuous to simply arrive, unannounced, with dinner? Normally, Grant wouldn't do such a thing. He would call or text, make a formal offer, and abide by the answer given.

Everything with Sage Greene had been askew though. How odd that he liked it that way.

The solid front door hung open, leaving only the screen door as a barrier to entry. Grant leaned on the jam and called through the screen. "Knock, knock. Are you in there, Sage? Mr. Teller?"

A loud grunt, followed by a cough, came as an answer. Grant took that as a *come in*, and using his pinky and fourth finger, he pulled the screen door open while keeping a hold on the Dutch oven. Stepping onto the light-colored plank wood flooring, Grant called into the house again. "It's Grant Hillman, Mr. Teller. May I come in?"

This time a clear *come in* came from the garbled voice in the parlor. How far they'd come in just a few weeks' time. Or maybe the rumors about Mr. Teller shooting at anyone who came near the front door were gross exaggerations.

Both were likely.

Grant made his way through the house, pausing to set the Dutch oven on the stove top before he wandered into the parlor-turned-bedroom. Mr.

Teller sat in his recliner, the TV across from him flashing images, though on mute.

"Good evening, Mr. Teller."

"Grant." The man nodded, and though he didn't smile, he did not point a scowl either.

"How are you feeling today?"

"Old."

Grant stuffed his hands into his jeans pockets. "You seem better than a few days back."

"Yes." One arthritic, gnarled hand ran over the thin mat of white hair on top of Mr. Teller's head. "I didn't tell you thanks . . ." His face drifted toward his lap.

"None required, Mr. Teller."

His gaze flickered back up and held. In that pause there passed between them an understanding—one of appreciation and of respect. Grant had known firsthand what it was to feel humiliated about things he had no control over. He could not help that crowds pressed panic into him—specifically when he was younger and had not yet learned how to cope with it. He could not help that he preferred the intricacies and emotion of music over the physical prowess and strategies of football.

He could not help that he was not who his father had ordered for a son.

None of those things Grant could change, just as Harold Teller could not help getting old, becoming sick, or losing his dignity for a moment. Grant was the last man who would intentionally humiliate him for it.

Letting the silence be his oath, Grant wandered around the eight-sided coffee table and lowered onto the couch.

"Your cousin stopped by today," Mr. Teller said.

"Anne texted me that she had. She said you seem to be on the mend."

He nodded. "I appreciate it. The girl does too."

Sage had been right. Harold had a soft underbelly. "Are you hungry?"

"Something smells good, that's for sure."

Grant smacked his hands together and rubbed his palms. "It's wild rice, roasted peppers, and chicken. High in protein—good for guys on the mend."

"You brought it for me?"

"Of course."

"Thought you'd be cooking for that girl." A mild and sly grin lifted his thin lips. "Not how we used to do things, but seems effective."

Heat crept up the back of Grant's neck. "There's enough for all of us." He shifted his attention toward the kitchen. "Where is Sage?"

"Upstairs. Recording, I think."

"Ah." Grant shifted in his seat. Should he go look for her? Man, he sure wanted to. The hope for her smile had propelled him to fix extra of his planned meal and drive over uninvited. Come to think of it, it was the hope for her smile that had him doing all sorts of not-normal things.

"Go on." Mr. Teller spoke into the length of silence.

Grant whipped his attention back to the man.

"You didn't come here to see me."

"That is not true." Not entirely.

"Go on and find her." That knotted hand waved in the air, shooing him off. Then he molded a frown that was not at all convincing. "Let me finish *Jeopardy* in peace."

Grant buttoned down his grin only until he reached the kitchen. There, he eyed the steep stairs, and that smile set itself free. He'd woken up that morning thinking of her. Wondering if she was already up and recording—she'd told him that sometimes she would rise hours before dawn, if she felt the twitch of story tickling through her veins. He liked the way her eyes sparkled when she told him about it.

As he climbed the risers toward the second floor, he allowed himself to imagine that same dancing look would greet him in a few moments. It was nearly all he had been able to think about through the afternoon—especially after Anne had texted to say that she'd stopped by and spent some time with her.

She's sweet, Grant. I like her.

Grant had pondered over how to respond. Not responding was rude, so that was not an option. But his honest response would be telling. Grant wasn't one to share his heart with many. But Clay and Anne had always been in his corner.

I do too.

He'd sent that text feeling exposed.

I like her for you, Grant.

That was . . . encouraging, and the part of Grant that still hung back, scared about the opposites-attract disaster issue, took a gulp of courage.

There was, however, still the issue of Sage's proclamation. The one about not believing in love. Also, there were other beliefs Grant needed to know about. But admitting that he liked her felt a little freeing. Like he was being honest with himself.

He reached the top of the stairs and strode toward the only room he had visited in this part of the house—the one he had helped Sage clean out and paint. "Sage?"

Something thumped above his head. Grant halted, glancing up at the ceiling. "Sage?"

"Grant?" Her voice was a muffled call from above him.

"Yes. Where are you?"

"In the attic. The access is at the end of the hall, left side, opposite the bathroom." Footfalls thudded softly while she spoke.

Grant followed the sound of that trail rather than her instructions—both of which led the same way. When he reached the end of the hall, he stopped.

"Hey!"

She startled him, though that was foolish. He should have expected her to meet him. He lifted his eyes to find her at the top of the narrow pull-down steps. And his heart lurched with joy.

Because, yes, she smiled. At him.

"I wasn't expecting you," Sage said.

"I know . . . is that okay?"

Her lovely grin spread wide. "I love surprises. Particularly good ones."

Though he didn't like surprises, he thrilled that she counted him as a good one. "Then let me add to it. I have brought you supper."

Her head fell back dramatically, and she clasped her hands together in front of her chest. "You are absolutely a hero, Grant Hillman. Despite what I thought when we first met."

Grant climbed the steps, ducking so that he wouldn't bonk his head, and stepped into the attic next to her. "When I saved your life?"

"When I thought you were going to violate me."

"You were quite something that day, Sage."

Her eyes danced as she reached to cup his jaw. "At my best." And then she winked.

Heaven help him. Every instinct and longing were to reach for her. To slide his hand around her waist and pull her close. To graze those playful lips with his and see what happened next.

Thankfully, Grant was a highly self-disciplined man. Which meant that though his mind had gone delightfully numb with that desire, his actions did not chase after folly.

Would it have been folly?

Sage watched him, her grin fading slightly. That laughing gaze turned serious, and she bit her bottom lip.

His heart ached and stuttered, then stalled. Did he lean toward her?

Swallowing, he ironed his posture.

Sage turned away. Disappointment clung heavily in the stuffy air. Or perhaps that was only in his mind.

Perhaps he had missed an opportunity. His chest clenched at the thought, and suddenly he wished he was a more impulsive man. More, he wished the moment back.

Too late though. She cut a trail through the piles of this and that hidden beneath drop cloths.

"Come here." Sage sounded normal. Bubbly. Too much so. "I want to show you something."

Grant realigned his thoughts so that he might have a conversation with her without sounding like a man lost. "Okay. What?"

"This." She stopped at the far end of the attic, having passed several pieces of furniture draped with coverings, and pointed to a long, rather flat box.

"What is it?" He followed her path and stopped beside her.

"Open it."

"Is this a prank?"

"No. I just want you to see what it is."

"Can't you simply tell me?"

"Just open it, Grant."

He had told her that he did not like surprises, right? Did she not take him seriously?

Taking his hand in hers, she knelt and tugged him down beside her.

Maybe he could learn to like surprises, if it meant she put her hand in his. Grant could not resist the longing to tighten his fingers around hers. For a breath, she froze. Then she lifted his hand, turned it so that his palm faced her, and examined his fingertips. Her index finger traced over the tips of his, and even beneath the long-won callouses that covered them, he thrilled at her soft touch. When she glanced up at his face, her brows raised with some sort of eager question.

He did not know what that meant.

Dropping his hand, she leaned forward and lifted the top of the box, whose lid had already been unlatched on both ends.

If his breath hadn't already been caught, it certainly was now. Grant impulsively reached toward the neck but stopped himself before he wrapped a grip around it. Instead, he grazed the strings—they were loose and in need of replacing—down to the upper bout and then traced the dust-covered spruce top down the waist and around to the lower bout. His touch was ginger, almost reverent. "It's beautiful."

"Is it?" She met his sideways glance. "I don't know cellos, but it seems lovely."

"It is." He nodded toward the box. "May I?"

"I think so, but it isn't mine."

"Gramps?"

"I haven't asked him yet. He doesn't know I'm up here."

Grant froze, his careful grip now closed on the neck. He eyed her. "You have not asked to go through his things?"

"I have."

Arching a brow, Grant released the instrument and shook his head. "Sage."

"I'll go through them at some point."

"That's cheerful." He leaned back.

"Don't look at me like that, Grant."

"Like what?"

"All disapproving. I don't want your disapproval." Sage reached and lay her palm on his bicep. "And before you settle on it, know that I'm not simply disregarding Gramps's wishes. I came here to know him. There are stories up here." She stopped and let her gaze roam the dusty space. "His stories. I want to know them."

"Then ask him."

She smacked her thighs with both hands and growled. "I have." With a huff, she stood. "Grant, I have asked and prodded. He says he doesn't want to talk about the past. But he isn't what I've been told, and I want to know who he really is—was. Not just the bitter ramblings of a half-crazy old woman and the sharp disdain of my mother. Mom never knew him, and something tells me that what Grandma Clara told isn't the whole truth."

Somewhere at the beginning of that speech, Grant had risen from his crouch and now stood looking down on her. Seeing her sincerity, combined with the increasing desire to do anything to earn her smile, Grant teetered on relenting.

He looked back down at the cello resting in the box. It was old and likely German-made. His look caressed the instrument—the lovely yellow-brown of the spruce tone wood varnished to a gleam—though dust and time had dimmed the finish. The dark contrast of the fingerboard and the darker wood of the scroll—maple.

Cleaned up, strings replaced, the instrument would be stunning.

Johanne Brahms's Cello Sonata in e minor played in the back of his mind, and his fingers twitched.

"You wanna play it, don't you?"

Startled from his private admiration, Grant shifted his attention to Sage. She grinned her best temptress grin and sidled up next to him.

He narrowed his focus on her. "How did you know I play?"

Reaching for his hand, she held it up and studied his fingers again. "These callouses came from something."

"You noticed my callouses?"

Dropping his hand, she gazed up at him with wide adoration.

Grant groaned and shook his head. "Don't do that with me, Sage. No masks. No stage. No games. What are you up to?"

Her facade fell, and she sighed. "Anne told me you played when I told her I found a cello up here. And Gramps had mentioned it too. Come to think of it, I think you said something about it to him the other day."

"Why did you think you couldn't just tell me that?"

"Anne doesn't want you to be upset with her. She says you're very good at it."

"I am not upset." Why would he be? Did he come across as *that* sensitive? "I like playing the cello. I do not particularly care to preform, but I enjoy music."

Slipping her arm through his, Sage leaned against his shoulder and nodded.

"What is this really about?"

"I told you the truth. It's about the stories. About getting to know my grandfather before he dies. Maybe even understanding why he did what he did. But every time I try, I hit a wall. I want to know why he has an old cello up here. Does he play?" She pushed away from him, striding toward a covered piece of furniture shoved toward the back of the roof. "I want to know who used this gorgeous thing. How did it get way out here on the prairie? Why did it get shoved up here and forgotten?" She tugged on the dust cloth, and it slipped away, revealing a large, heavily framed freestanding mirror. Her voice built in fervor as she continued, picking her way across the room until she came to a lower draped furnishing. "And this . . ." Her words broke for a moment. She ripped the cloth from it and glared at the revealed cradle.

Suspended on a stand so that it would rock, the cradle was made of dark wood, with a series of round spindles and solid ends. When Sage rested her hand on one long side, a creaking protest moaned into the space as it begrudgingly swayed.

Sage winced as she looked back at Grant. There was fiery pain in those eyes that usually laughed. "Was this my grandfather's? When Gramps hauled it up here, did he feel any remorse for rejecting his own son? Or is it like they say, out of sight, out of mind?"

Grant's heart pinched at the unmasked pain. "Sage." He picked his way toward her.

Sage shook her head. "I don't want your pity, Grant. I want your help. You promised me a favor back when you asked me to go to the wedding with you. This is it. I'm calling it in. I want to know the truth."

Stopping on the other side of the cradle, Grant studied her. "How would me playing that old cello help you find the truth?"

Her shoulders sagged, and her gaze drifted toward that item behind Grant. "Maybe it would open the lock."

"You mean Gramps?"

"Yeah. I mean music can do that, right? It's emotional—and so often tied to memories."

"What if it provokes his anger?"

Biting her bottom lip, she shrugged. "It would be better than his stubborn silence."

She's alone . . . so incredibly lonely. The insight struck Grant with clarity—and he wondered why it had taken so long for him to recognize the truth of it. He'd admired her drive to live joyfully, but for some reason it hadn't occurred to him to look for something beneath that drive that fueled the need of it.

A very un-Grant-ish oversight.

His out-of-character moment wasn't going to end there. Turning back toward the cello, still in its resting place on the floor, he felt his muscles tense. Even so, he proceeded. "I do not know if it is playable, Sage. As I said, it looks old, and the strings need to be replaced."

"But if it is?" A spark of hope tinged her soft reply.

Grant sighed. He did not like infringing on others' wishes. "Playing someone else's instrument is . . ." *a violation.* Almost to the degree of being with another man's woman. An honorable gentleman did not do such things.

Grant did not do such things.

But Sage likely would not understand that. And even if she did, she likely wouldn't care. She wanted answers. She wanted the truth. Her desperation for it was palpable.

And Grant could not blame her. She had lived her entire life under a shadow of abandonment and faithlessness. That sort of burden begged for leeway when it came to proper measures.

More though, he had something like a soul-driven need to see her happy. No, to see her at peace.

The realization was like a strike of match. Like the murky darkness had been pierced, and he saw her clearly. Past her unique charm. Even past his deep attraction to her.

He saw the divine appointment. And he remembered the prayer he'd penned at the beginning of all of this. *Let it be for good.*

Sage needed redemption.

She needed to have the past reconciled. Her tetherlessness mended. And her very soul redeemed.

She needed a real hero.

That was entirely beyond him, and the weight of it made him shudder. For so long the most persistent cry of his heart had been for God to see him—to let him *know* and *feel* that God saw him. That he mattered, and his life had purpose. But now . . .

Dear God, save her.

While he silently prayed for her soul, Sage picked her way over and between the scattered furniture and boxes until she reached the box containing the cello. There she knelt, and with a ginger hold, she lifted the instrument from its resting place.

The velvet lining, made crispy by time, neglect, and dust, crackled when the wooden piece was resurrected. Grant's heart stuttered and then galloped at the sight of the cello rising, and he moved to Sage's side. She passed it by the neck into his hands, and a sense of reverence filled him as his palm touched the cold tone wood.

A slip of white fluttered from the back, returning to the velvet of the box below. Sage eyed Grant for a breath, one brow arched in curiosity, and then she reached for the slim piece of paper that had been hidden from view.

It appeared to be a thin white typing paper, folded in half. Sage unfolded it, and her eyes scanned the black ink penned within.

Her expression morphed from excited curiosity to cold fury, and then she moved to rise.

"Sage?" Grant gripped her wrist, halting her retreat.

She trembled beneath his hold, and her mouth flatlined.

"What is it?"

With a small wobble in her chin, she passed the handwritten note to him. The script was hasty and yet neat—the sort that a well-practiced hand could produce in a hurry, and the page contained only one line.

I will never forgive you.

When he looked back at her, Sage was glaring at the floor, cold fury in her eyes.

No doubt, in her mind she saw her grandfather.

CHAPTER TWENTY

"GRANDFATHER!" SAGE'S JAW HURT from clenching it. "Just tell me. Don't you want the truth to finally be said?"

The man sitting across from her, trying with everything in his elderly strength to ignore her ongoing string of demanding inquiries, flickered his attention from the TV to her.

Finally. At least he acknowledged she was there. More than he'd done since she'd stormed down ten minutes before, the old note between her fingers and her mind thrashing wildly.

"You had no business being in the attic." Gramps spoke with measured anger. "I told you to stay out of it."

"When you die, I'll go through it all anyway." That was callous. But why was he being so unreasonable? Was his pride so great that he couldn't own his poor choices even now, some sixty years later?

Wasn't he at all sorry? Yes. Yes, he was. Everything about this locked-up-tight life screamed regret. Why couldn't he just say it out loud?

Gramps flinched but then steadied his hard look on her. "Then you can wait until I'm in my grave."

"You must have had a reason, Gramps." Sage swallowed, lowering herself onto the coffee table. "You're not the heartless man I've been told."

A new emotion flickered across his face, and though it contained remorse, it wasn't what she had expected. It wasn't guilt. It was . . . pain.

Guilt could be painful though. Even so, something in her soul warned there was more to this story than she'd known, than she could guess.

"Was Clara unfaithful?" she whispered.

Gramps looked away from her, landing his focus on the window. His watery eyes misted. "Don't talk about the past, girl." The same words he had spat at her before. But this time there was no fire behind them. Only brokenness.

"Please, Gramps." Sage leaned forward, touching his leg. "I want to understand."

Shutting his eyes, he shook his head.

With that, Sage felt the door to their conversation—heaven help her, possibly to this hard-fought relationship—firmly close.

Gramps shut her out.

The real curse of her family—the inability to trust. To connect. To love.

Unwilling to cry, Sage blinked her world into focus and stood. Looking toward the kitchen, she found Grant waiting for her in the doorway, his expression sad. Sage bit her bottom lip and demanded the roiling emotions get back where they belonged. She'd lost way too much control over them in the past hour.

No more. She'd spent too many years schooling her heart, keeping it in check, to have it fall to pieces now. The only thing she allowed to flow freely was happiness. If she couldn't feel that, she locked herself away to feel nothing.

That was the safest strategy for a person like her. Cursed with faithlessness and ruination.

Swallowing, Sage resecured that resolve to steel herself as she passed Grant on her way into the kitchen. "Did you say there was food?"

"Sage."

"I'll dish Gramps a plate, and then you and I can take ours out back."

"Sage." He came after her, his steps slow and deliberate.

She shook her head. "If he doesn't want to talk about it, then I don't need to hear about it."

"But—"

She held up a hand. "Dinner, Grant."

His concern held on her in the silent beats that passed between them. Then he resigned with a slight nod. "Supper. That's what the evening meal is called around here."

"Very well, supper. I'm hungry." An outright lie. She had no appetite at all.

But Sage was a performer. She could play out this scene. Turning to the stove, she lifted the lid to the Dutch oven Grant had brought, pulled down three plates, and served the helpings. Grant took one of the plates, added a fork and a napkin, and without a word took it to Gramps. From her spot at the stove, she could hear his murmured voice, but discerned no reply form the stubborn old man.

Fine. Just . . . fine. She would let it go. Move on. Enjoy Grant's kindness, the uniquely gentlemanly man he was.

Brushing up the sort of face she felt would go best with this supper scene, Sage lifted both plates and turned to meet Grant with a smile. He met her with a long look, gathered two more forks and napkins, and then led the way toward the backyard.

Once they were seated in the wooden chairs she'd retrieved from the blasted attic, Sage passed Grant a plate. Their eyes met again.

"This looks delicious."

"No masks, Sage."

Self-preservation screamed to ignore his quiet demand. To keep him at arm's length and to remain hidden behind her happy-about-life character.

But those gentle brown eyes . . . probing, inviting. Safe.

Could anyone be safe, truly?

Sage didn't have an honest answer to that. But though it was dangerous to admit, she knew what she wished for it to be.

"I need to know why he did it," she said. "I need to understand, because maybe if I understood, I wouldn't have to be the way I am. Maybe I wouldn't have to keep searching so relentlessly for joy, and I could just *be* happy. I wouldn't feel like I am on the precipice of an ongoing family curse with every relationship I've ever edged close to. If I could reconcile the past, maybe then I wouldn't feel bound to it. I don't want to live in resentment. I don't want to despise people I've barely known. I just want to . . . to be free."

She felt breathless and terrified having all of that out. But there it was, and what would he do with it?

The leaves rustled in the gentle evening breeze, and the soft slosh of the slow-moving river at their backs filled the growing space of quiet that followed. Grant sat thoughtful but not disapproving.

"Sage." Grant finally spoke quietly against the gentle evening, after she had thoroughly cast her despair at his feet. "Have you considered that this longing for answers that is driving you may well be a need for something else?"

"No. What else is there? You said yourself that truth is important. I want the truth."

"That is so, but what if the truth you seek is a Father, not a confession?"

Though that suggestion fit instantly into place, Sage pushed against its absurdity. "I can't have a father, and I've never had a desire to know the man who never wanted me. Nor do I see Gramps as a—"

"I know that." He shocked her with his interruption. He wasn't the interrupting type. "But you have a gaping void in your life. The longing to fill it is the fuel that keeps you going. Running." For a breath, he looked as if weighing whether or not to say what came next. "You are lonely, Sage Greene. And you don't like it."

Sage swallowed the truth of it. "Everyone feels lonely sometimes. Don't you feel it too?"

He nodded. "I do. But I think it is not the same."

"Why? Because you are a man?"

"No. Because even in the loneliest moments of my life—times when I have felt keenly my dad's rejection, or when I feel panicked by the chaos of a crowd in which I do not fit, or when I realized that Brenna was never going to love me as she did Craig—even then I knew a refuge. I have an anchor that holds me fast. I know One who *knows* me, and His care and concern for my life has sustained me."

Such passion in a man's voice . . . Sage had never experienced it. Even if Grant had professed undying love for her soul, Sage was not sure he could move her more deeply. He was right. She ached to know that kind of stability.

But it seemed as realistic as the romances she narrated. Such things were works of fiction.

"You mean God?" The idea was painful and provoking. But also breathlessly tantalizing.

Grant nodded.

"I'm not sure about Him."

"That is clear. Perhaps because you do not know Him."

The God I know is the author of joy and peace . . . So then, Grant and Miss Jane knew the same God? Or at least they believed they did.

Normally Sage would have laughed such a discussion off and moved on to lighter things. Things that did not stir up more unanswered questions. Wonderings such as, why was God so bad at His job of giving joy and peace to miserable people such as herself?

That evening, however, Sage could not simply wave the driving queries away.

Into her silence, Grant stood. Tugging her hands, he pulled her to her feet, and then he tucked her into a safe embrace. His hold was tender but firm. "Sage, I wish I could be the hero in your story—even if you don't think you need one. But the truth is, even if you can't see it now, you *do* need one. You need a Savior, the lover of your soul. His name is Jesus, and He is love. The very love I know you wish you could believe in. He is everything, and you will never be satisfied without Him."

He is everything . . . That was quite a statement.

What if it was true?

What if she did believe? In love? In the possibility of a faithful man—one such as Grant?

In this God—this Jesus—who had given Grant peace, who had been his refuge in a world that was not always kind?

Sage pressed into the shelter of Grant's arms while the possibilities danced around her heart. Never before had she come so close to believing . . .

So very close.

• • • • • • • • • • •

Sage woke up with a persistent headache and her heart sore from all of the twisting it had gone through in the past twenty-four hours.

She'd caved. Grant had gently but firmly commanded her to remove the mask of *all is well*, and she had caved. It had been terrifying and . . . comforting. No one knew how much she had longed to find something stable in her heritage. She'd never shared with anyone how much she hated the legacy of slashed relationships that she had been planted in.

But now Grant did.

He had listened quietly. Attentively. Compassionately.

And Sage's heart had unfurled like the wings of a freshly hatched monarch. Fragile and timid but with a driving instinct to reach for the sun. And during the time that Grant had been there, his quiet, unintrusive strength felt like the soothing warmth her uncocooned heart needed.

Night had come. Grant had gone home, and Sage replayed her vulnerability in the silent solitude of her room.

Not safe! Not safe! Not safe . . . Her thoughts thrashed relentlessly.

Whether the meaning was aimed at Grant or at herself (likely the latter, she had nearly decided), it ushered in the fear that had her scurrying back within the safety of her protective cove.

She had shared too much.

Even so, the drive to know the truth of the past and to somehow reconcile it with the elderly, crusty but somehow still endearing old man she called Gramps fueled her purpose. For the first time in years, the fear didn't send her flying as fast as her long billowing skirts would allow. She found that she could set aside the breach in her keep-everything-friendly-and-happy resolve when it came to Grant Hillman.

But she could not put away the need to uncover the whole story Gramps was determined to take to his grave.

Her determination to not allow that doubled. But she needed an ally. Someone besides Grant.

At the image of an elderly woman's face—one who was as prone to grinning as Gramps was to scowling—Sage's riled emotions settled.

Ah yes. Miss Jane. Why had she not considered it before?

Miss Jane was the right temperament—the woman was determined and friendly and knew everyone in Big Prairie. More importantly, she was approximately the right age.

Very possibly an eyewitness.

Flinging back the light covers on her bed, Sage swiveled and planted her feet on the chilly wood floor. She had a plan. And it didn't involve falling apart in Grant's arms.

Or standing at the edge of her heart, staring at something vast and terrifying.

Ignoring the bothersome nudge of regret at that, Sage applied the full strength of her resolve and topped it off with a smile at herself in the mirror across the room.

Take off the mask.

She ignored the prodding in her mind—which sounded a whole lot like Grant's soft, rich voice—and scurried about her small room to pull on her favorite floor-length broom skirt and light blue scoop-neck T-shirt before she trotted downstairs.

The moment her feet touched the kitchen floor and she inhaled, she froze. The coffee was already made. A small spark of light hope flickered in her chest. She poured herself a mug and wandered into Gramps's room.

"Morning," she said.

He grunted.

"Must be feeling better."

"Still alive," he muttered.

"I'm glad."

"That so?"

His words pricked guilt. Sighing, Sage sat on the coffee table. "Gramps, what I said yesterday . . ."

His eyes, rather clear this morning, found hers and held. A truce settled into the silence. "You were mad."

"Yes."

"Me too," he admitted quietly.

"I wish I knew why."

He held quiet for several heartbeats, taking up his mug to drink his coffee. Then, with a soft thunk, he set his mug on the side table to his right. "I want to offer a deal."

"A deal?"

"Yes. A compromise."

"About . . ."

"About your snooping," he snapped, though Sage hardly believed he was truly grumpy about it. Not when he'd been all soft and grandfatherly just a breath before.

In that moment she felt a sense of privilege. Gramps had let her into his world, his life. His heart. How many had he allowed that over the years? Miss Jane maybe, and that was basically it, from what she could tell.

She crossed her legs and sipped her coffee. "I'm listening."

"You can go through all the stuff—I won't bark at you about it anymore."

"That's a promising start. And in exchange, I continue to perform my stories for you?" She winked.

A twitch at the corners of his mouth very nearly gave way. But he tucked that grin in tight, squinted at her, and shook his head. "Your theatrics are no bonus, girl." Yet again there was zero conviction behind his snark. "The deal is this: you can look to your heart's content, but don't ask me about Clara."

She felt her victory fade as her shoulders drooped. "But—"

"I mean it, Sage. No prodding about her. At all."

Gramps *never* called her by her given name. That alone told her he was resolutely, unmovably, and in all other terms serious. Which didn't help her a whole lot.

"What about James?"

Gramps flinched, looked down at his lap, and shook his head. Sadness filled his tone when he responded. "Hardly knew the boy."

"You never saw him after . . ."

"No."

If she had actually seen her own father at all in her lifetime, she might have found that part unbelievable. But from her experience, it was entirely possible.

Resentment bulged in her gut. Men. Men who made babies and didn't love them. Didn't even want to see them.

Sage knew her glare pinned on Gramps was harsh, but she did nothing to tame it. He looked up, silently meeting the resentment she lasered his way and answered back with wordless sorrow.

"Why?"

"He didn't want to know me."

"Did you ever reach out to him?"

"Once."

"And?"

He shook his head. That was all.

Sage pondered that. If her own father had reached out to her now, would she respond? Would she want to know him?

Maybe by way of curiosity—after all, she had wanted to know this man sitting across from her. But emotionally? No. No, she didn't feel that she did. Not unless there was a reason offered for his abandonment. His rejection.

"That's the deal," Gramps said quietly but firmly.

"Can't you just tell me why—"

"That's the deal." He repeated each word slower. With low finality.

Fine then. At least they wouldn't bicker about her forays into the attic.

"What about the cello?"

"What about it?"

"Did you play?"

"Yes."

"Do you want it down here so you can play it again?"

"No."

That was it? A simple no? Ugh.

"Grant plays."

"So I've heard."

"He says it's a beautiful instrument."

"Then give it to him."

Sage sat back and blinked. "Truly?"

At long last, a ghost of a smile won against that stubborn frown on Gramps's face. He held an almost kind look on Sage and then waved her off. "Go on now. You're blocking the TV."

Snorting a small laugh, Sage stood. She paused in a moment of indecision and then crossed the ugly gold carpet until she was standing beside him. With a surprised expression, Gramps looked up. She bent and placed a kiss on his thin hair. "You're a softy, Gramps."

He grunted. Sage believed that was a laugh. And it sent a wave of warmth straight into her soul.

CHAPTER TWENTY–ONE

GRANT COULD NOT HAVE been more shocked. Especially after the last talk they'd had. Sage hadn't argued with him when he'd shared that God had been his refuge and anchor. But her expression had spoken her heart.

She had no idea what he was talking about.

That had been crushing, and Grant felt entirely unsteady about what to do next.

He and Sage had met by divine appointment, he felt certain of that. Just as certain as the attraction he felt for her. And the growing tenderness he had for her. And those last two things made this entire situation supremely complicated. So much so that he had spent most of the past night awake and in prayer.

Could this be God's answer?

Likely gawking, Grant looked across his shoulder at the redhead who had slipped into the seat beside his sometime during the pastor's opening prayer. Sage chewed on her bottom lip, and her normally exuberant expression was pensive.

"Good morning," he leaned to whisper.

She nodded.

"Are you okay?" he asked quietly.

Another nod. Her hands burrowed into her skirts, fisting and unfisting. Tension radiated from her whole body.

Grant had no idea what had driven her there, but clearly she felt uncomfortable. A feeling he was well familiar with. He moved his open Bible from his hands to rest on his thigh and then reached for her closest hand, though it was tangled in the fabric of her skirt. At his gentle squeeze of her fingers, she looked up at him.

No mask. Just a sweet, lost woman looking for something solid and steady. A home.

They weren't so different after all.

He gave her an encouraging smile, pointed to where Pastor was reading from 1 John, and kept his hand protectively over hers. And prayed.

Grant missed all of what was said in the sermon that day. Because he could only think to pray for Sage Greene's wandering soul.

••••••••••

"I'm glad to hear it, Lane." Miss Jane tipped her head to look at the young man she had been helping. "My Daisy Jane is equal to your stubbornness. One of you certainly needs to blink though."

The man—Lane?—cleared his throat. "Yes, ma'am. But I just need—"

"An address. Of course." Miss Jane waved at him, a silent command to stay where he was.

Sage watched with curiosity as the man's neck darkened from a summer-sun tan to a tomato red. Oh, this looked to be the middle of a good story. The kind Sage loved to sink into.

How about that? A romance right there in real life . . .

Yeah, well, by the looks of it, something had gone wrong, because this Romeo was apparently searching for his flown-the-joint Juliet, and he needed an *address* to find her. If that didn't scream *another broken relationship*, she didn't know what.

Well, other than a little entertaining to watch. And that right there was the thing of it. Sage was all for watching such drama. Reading it. Even acting it out as a vocal artist. But living it?

Those things did not end well. She had never once seen a romantic relationship stop at happily ever after and not slam into a painful brick wall of betrayal and breakup, hearts in smithereens.

No thank you.

"Here you go, young man." Miss Jane returned to the counter with a slip of paper in hand. She began to pass it toward the waiting suitor but then held off, paper in midair. "Don't make me regret this."

Lane rubbed his chest while his gaze zeroed in around his boots, but then he dared to look up. Right into Miss Jane's eyes. "I swear, Miss Jane—I love her."

Miss Jane's brows rose in mild challenge. "More than words, Lane Carson. More than words."

After an audible swallow, that steady look holding fast, this Mr. Lane Carson nodded that handsome head. "I promise."

Miss Jane passed the slip of paper. Lane took it, and the exchange ended with him turning for the exit.

For a moment Sage stood transfixed, distracted by the desire to know what went on there.

"Ah, Sage Greene. It was nice to see you in church the other day." Miss Jane wiped her hands on the neatly tied waist of her apron and planted them on her hips. She motioned toward one of the four tables in her small establishment. "Sit down, how about, and I'll get you some lunch."

Sage didn't want to talk about church. She didn't know what to think about church, and she wasn't even sure what had driven her to go.

No, she knew what had fueled that strange act. It had been Miss Jane's intrusive comments. And Grant's passionate claims. And her own instability—the one Sage worked terribly hard to keep under control.

But none of that matter to Sage's purpose that day. "I didn't come to eat."

Miss Jane, who had scurried to the glass case containing salads and sandwiches, stopped short of opening it. "Oh?"

"No. I came to get answers."

She stood straight. "That sounds serious. Perhaps we can indulge in something cool and sweet while we see if we can't find any of those. Tea? Lemonade?"

The mention of lemonade immediately summoned the memory of Grant standing oh so close to her in the doorway of her kitchen, telling her he'd pick a raspberry lemonade for a treat . . . Why did that memory made her stomach summersault in the most pulse-skipping, delightful way?

Oh, she knew. It was the way his voice had reached her ears, all low and soft and intimate. And the way his eyes had caressed her face, his intense stare ending on her lips. And the way she'd felt his body hover closer, as if the magnetism between them was irresistible.

Wow, her imagination was something.

Touching her forehead with two fingers—was it hot in there or what?—Sage righted her derailed thoughts back on the here, present, and real tracks. "Lemonade sounds lovely. Thank you."

Miss Jane dipped one firm nod, slipped into the back—likely her kitchen—and reappeared with two tall glasses of frosty lemonades. After setting one in front of Sage, she plopped the other on the opposite side of the small table and settled herself onto a chair. "Now. What are the questions we are puzzling out?"

"My gramps."

"He does seem to be a conundrum, doesn't he?" Miss Jane chuckled. "But he's not really that complicated."

"Have you known him long?"

"Since I was a girl. He was my older brother's friend."

"Did you know him well?"

"Back then? No, not really. My older brother was several years older than me, and I was adopted when he was near a teen. Though he was never unkind to me, we were never close."

Sage felt her shoulders cave. "Oh."

"I've come to know Harold better as an adult."

"Why was that?"

"He needed a friend."

"Before or after he married my great-grandmother?"

"After Clara left Big Prairie."

Sage waited, watching for a sign of discomfort or guilt, because for some reason she sensed that Miss Jane's offer of friendship to her grandfather was perhaps more than simple *friendship*.

Miss Jane met Sage's stare with a look of challenge. "Well, are you going to ask?"

If she was going to be so blunt about it, then . . . "Were you the reason they split?"

"No." She didn't flinch. "Harold was ever faithful to his vows. As I said, I got to know him better after Clara left."

"If he was faithful, why did he divorce her?"

Miss Jane's lips flattened. The look was severe and so out of place on this jolly woman's face that it set Sage backward in her chair. But the woman said nothing.

"That's what I came to ask you."

"That's not a story I can tell."

"Why?"

"Because he wouldn't want me to."

"Why?" Impatience made the word harsh.

Again, Miss Jane's lips pinned together into a line, but this time sorrow filtered through what had been a chilled stare a moment before. Miss Jane shook her head. "It is simply not a story he wanted told."

"But it's been *years*. And everyone has their own idea. Some say he was a drunk, and she left him. Some say he was intolerable. Some say he simply didn't want Clara or his child."

"Been asking around town, hmm?"

A touch of shame filtered heat into her cheeks. "No."

"Then?"

"These are what have been told to me by my mother—and her mother."

"And Clara? Was this what she told?"

Sage shrugged. "I would guess. I didn't know her well—she suffered from dementia and died when I was young. Frankly, she was a cold, bitter woman, and my mother didn't really like her. I doubt we would have ever been close, even if she'd lived until I'd grown up."

Miss Jane nodded. Folding her hands in her lap, she allowed her attention to drift toward the window. After a long span, she spoke, though she continued to look away. "Why did you come to Big Prairie to stay with a man you'd never met and about whom you had only been told awful things?"

Ah, back to the beginning of all this mystery. "He was leaving his house and property to us—to my mother and me. I wanted to know why he would do that when he hadn't cared about his wife and son—who turned out to be a truly wretched man, likely thanks to his father's rejection. I wanted to see what Harold had to say for himself. What he would do if I confronted him."

"And?"

"And he let me move into his house and pester the daylights out of him."

Miss Jane chuckled softly. "I am guessing you no longer believe what you were told. Not one hundred percent." Her gaze came back and planted on Sage's face again. "Else you would not ask me."

Sage swallowed, running her finger along the side of the perspiring glass in front of her. "I . . . I don't know. That's why I ask. Gramps is a grump—he's a gruff old man who claims that he just wants to be left alone. But he's not only that. And he's definitely not a drunk."

"No, he is not that. Though he has imbibed too much in the past, it was never a habit."

"He's . . . gentle, under the spiny armor. And protective." Sage squinted at Miss Jane. "And sometimes he can even smile, though he tries hard not to."

A full grin broke free on Miss Jane's face. "Isn't that a fun game to play?"

A sense of shared conspiracy tugged at Sage's heart. Perhaps Miss Jane would prove to be an ally. "Why the contradiction? And all the secrecy?"

Miss Jane sobered again. With a sigh, she shook her head. "You should ask Harold."

"I have. Repeatedly. Clara is a forbidden topic. At this point, she is the only thing that truly makes him angry with me."

"Then that is all I can tell you."

That was unacceptable, plain and simple. Sage was not going to leave this mystery—and whatever legacy she'd inherited—to *that is all*. Though most couldn't understand, to Sage it felt like her life, her future was at stake. "Miss Jane, if you know something about it—"

"It is not my story to tell, Sage."

"But—" Defeat pressed in Sage's chest, quickly followed by irritation. "It was a lifetime ago. And surely you know that by keeping his secret, you make yourself look guilty."

"You are welcome to think what you wish, my dear girl."

Miss Jane's lack of indignation was like ice water on Sage's fierce anger. Of course Miss Jane had done nothing wrong. The woman was only honoring the confidence of a friend. It made Sage a lousy person to make such unqualified accusations.

But for heaven's sake, why all this concealment?

"Did you say your great-grandmother said she was divorced?" With a timid look, and a voice to match, Miss Jane ventured back into the topic.

"Yes—that was what I was told."

After a thoughtful pause, Miss Jane dipped one firm nod. "Then I would advise you to check the records."

"Records?"

"Marriages. Births. Divorces. Deaths. They all are kept on public record."

"Are you saying—"

"I'm not saying anything. Public records are just that—public. That is all."

"Oh."

Another long, stiff pause stretched between them. Then with a smack of her palms on her legs, Miss Jane stood up. "Do you know what I just thought of?"

"What?"

"Grant Hillman."

Sage furrowed her brow at the woman. "Did you?"

"I do believe he likes lemonade. He'll splurge on one on occasion, if I remember correctly."

"Uh . . ."

With a stretched smile and a dropped lid over one sparkling blue eye, Miss Jane rubbed her hands together. She bent close and whispered, "I remember these things correctly on most occasions."

Sage couldn't help but laugh. "Raspberry lemonade, you are correct."

"Aha." She reached to cup Sage's cheek. "I knew you would know."

"How did you know that?"

After a gentle pat of Sage's face, Miss Jane spun away. "It's a gift, I think. And I haven't missed yet."

· · · · ● · ● · · · ·

Grant looked at the tall plastic cup of lemonade stretched out toward him. His heart gave a little leap of delight, and he lifted his study to the small woman who had brought it to his office.

"I know, I know." Sage smirked as she pressed the cup into his hand and then leaned a shoulder into his. "You don't like surprises. But I didn't show up unannounced. I called first. And you did say you liked this."

Ah, Sage . . . She was exactly the right sort of surprise. He gripped the drink and lifted it. "I do like this." He paused, wondering if he should dare . . . Yes. Yes he should. And would. He wrapped one arm around her and tugged her in close. "And this."

Sage placed a palm against his chest and burrowed against him willingly, causing that delight to dance. Maybe her worldview was shifting. Maybe she hadn't believed in love because she'd never experienced it—she'd never witnessed what it truly was.

Love?

He'd thought himself in love before. That had not ended well.

No, but it had not ended terribly, had it? He had been disappointed, had felt the sharp sting of feeling unwanted again—a tender wound that he had lived with all of his life. But the truth had been that even in that, as he had sat with his achy heart and disappointed hopes, there had been a blessing of sorts.

God had sat there with him. His tender presence, though not immediately felt at the time, had never wavered. *You saw it all—and never did You leave me alone.*

What a revelation! One that stretched past even his breakup with Brenna. It reached into his boyhood and touched the loneliness and painful realization that he was not, nor would he ever be, what his father had wished for. Even then Grant had not been left alone.

The clarity of what he had claimed the evening before became stunning. God saw, and He cared. He had been Grant's refuge in the loneliness, a shelter in the hurt. And not only that, the path of Grant's life bore evidence of God's tender care.

He had seen fit to bring them back to Big Prairie in Grant's early teen years. Here in this little town, God had given Grant the understanding and subtle protection of his cousin Clay. And He had sent Grant and Clay both to the yearly summer Bible school program at the community church, and there He had presented the greatest gift of all.

He had shown Grant the Redeemer. In a small classroom of that country church, Grant had met Jesus and asked Him to be his Savior.

God is good, Grant. No matter how lonely you feel or how disappointing life can be, cling to this truth: God is good.

Words of a Sunday school teacher, given to him when he was about thirteen. Spoken, unknowingly by that teacher, to a young man who did in fact feel rejected and lonely. Those words had been like a prophetic lifeline, a truth Grant would need to hang on to for the journey. Because much of it had been hard and lonely. Disappointing.

But not all of it.

There had been the gift of music—something that made sense to Grant's soul when people certainly had not. There had been quiet sunrises that created painted skies, the beauty of which soothed the smaller disappointments. There had been the satisfaction of working with kids like Trenton, who needed his unique way of seeing life and people, and witnessing some breakthroughs in their worlds.

And now there was this. Sage tucked close to his heart, surprising him with his favorite treat and making the music in his heart play with joy.

And there she remained, quiet and still. Did she feel this too? Grant looked at her, studying what he could see of her face through the draped curls of that lovely red hair. He couldn't make out her expression, but something seemed off. After placing the drink on his desk, he stroked the length of those locks, savoring the softness of it beneath his fingers, and then tucked it away from her face.

Brow furrowed, lips tight and unsmiling confirmed it. Something was not right.

"Sage?"

He felt her soft sigh right before she pulled away, looking up at him with the painted version of her bright smile. "Guess what?"

Grant wanted to tug on her elbow and bring her back where she had felt safe enough not to put on that pesky mask. However, as he watched her eyes pleading for him to let her process whatever it was she needed to process, he restrained the impulse. "Another surprise?"

"Of sorts. I think you'll like this one too." That grin gentled into something more sincere. "Gramps gave me permission to go through the things in the attic. And . . ."

"And?" He lifted a brow, feeling his own lips quirk a smile.

"And he has given the cello to you."

He froze, stunned. "He what?"

"He said to give you the cello."

Shaking his head, Grant crossed his arms. "Sage, I will not claim such an heirloom. Why on earth would you have asked that of him?"

She scowled. "I didn't. I mentioned that you said the instrument appeared to be a good one. He said to give it to you. That's all."

"Sage."

"Grant." She huffed and shook her head. "Don't you make my day cloudy too. It was a nice thing for Gramps to do. And a surprise. It made me happy. Almost as happy as his giving me permission to go through all that old stuff. Why do you men have to be so blasted stubborn about things?"

"Your day has been cloudy?"

Her eyes pinched as she pinned a furrowed brow his direction. "Are you changing the subject?"

"No. You said your day has been cloudy."

"I also said that the cello in the attic is yours. You haven't accepted it yet."

"But—"

With a single hand held up at him, she shook her head. "No. Not until you say thank you."

"I do not—"

She crossed her arms and took one long step that put her firmly in his space. "Thank. You."

Grant stared down into those fiery eyes, feeling his stubbornness dissolve. This woman . . . He exhaled slowly and did not bother to discipline the fingers that strayed to touch her hair. "Thank you."

At his touch her eyes slid shut. He cupped her cheek, letting his thumb glide over the charming smattering of freckles that gathered along her cheekbone.

Sage pressed her face into his hand, and then he felt the warm thrill of her touch at his elbow. Delicate and electrifying, her fingers slowly traced a trail up his forearm to his wrist, and there she held on.

"Sage." Her name was barely audible from his lips as he leaned closer. He breathed her in, all warm sunshine and bright lemons. "Thank you." With the barest contact, his nose brushed her forehead, drifting slowly down the side of her nose.

She sighed, the warmth of her escaping breath teasing gooseflesh along his neck. There was nothing for it. No trace of stoic self-discipline driven by the fear that he'd be rejected. He knew only the demand to find her lips and test them.

And he was not disappointed.

· · • • • • • • • · ·

Sage shivered as he pulled away. She didn't want the crack of space between them. Her heart raced, sweet adrenaline coursing through her body, numbing the warning in her mind.

But Grant had slowly, reluctantly ended their kisses, and though his hands still cradled her head, he had pried enough distance between her thudding heart and his that her thoughts surfaced.

What was she doing? That had crossed the line between *closest of friends* to *someone's going to get hurt* real fast.

And the truth was, Sage wasn't ready to cross back.

But she wasn't the kind of girl who believed in this sort of thing. In romance. In . . . love?

That was a far leap. One kiss and somehow the word *love* seeped into her thoughts? That was some kind of kiss.

Yes. Yes it was. And she preferred the sweet, hazy warmth of it to this stiff and chilly warning that was crowding out all the good stuff. With both hands at his shoulders, Sage held on to Grant as she chased his retreat.

His lips took hers one more time, though far less passionately than before, and then he held her away from him.

"I have wanted to kiss you since our picnic." His steady look seemed to peel back the layers of the masks she wore. The *smile bright* one. The playful one. And now the *let's kiss and not worry about the implications* one.

Sage did not like someone—a man—so easily seeing though her defenses. She was uncomfortable with how close he was creeping near her heart. She went for a coy grin. "We don't have to stop just yet."

Rather than a low chuckle and an eager reentry, as she had hoped, Grant's eyes grew distant, and his lips flattened. "Yes we do."

"Why?"

His silence and unwavering look said *I think you know why.*

And she did. Grant was not some man who opened his life and heart up to a woman flippantly. He wasn't the type of guy who kissed a girl the way he'd just kissed her and have it mean little to nothing.

She was playing a dangerous game, and it was his heart on the line. She knew better.

As heat flared in her cheeks, she stepped back. His hands fell away, and she looked at the ground. The long stretch of silence made the distance between them feel like miles rather than mere inches.

"Tell me what I should know," he said at long last.

I'll shatter your heart because that's who I am. That is the legacy of my heritage.

He didn't mean for her to confess that. Or perhaps he did, but she wasn't that brave. So instead she reached back to their pre-kiss conversation.

"Gramps offered me a deal. I could pick through his things as long as I don't ask about Great-Grandma Clara."

A lifted brow was his only response.

"I don't like that deal, but he's stubborn. So I went and talked to Miss Jane. There must be a reason she's his only friend, you know? But she is nearly equal to his stubbornness, although she did advise me to look into the public records."

"What for?"

"She didn't say much, but it seems like Miss Jane thinks my grandmother lied about being divorced."

Three lines carved into Grant's forehead. "Why would your grand-mother lie about that?"

"I don't know. But I feel desperate to find out."

For a long moment, Grant silently appraised her. Then, "Why is this so important, Sage?"

She had no idea where it came from, but a strong surge of emotion burst within her chest. "I already told you. Because it's part of me. Who I am."

"What do you mean, who you are?"

Sage blinked and stepped back. "Never mind." She knew what he was fishing for. He was summoning back the things that had poured between them the night before.

"Tell me."

She couldn't. The truth was that she *was* lonely. But his simplistic solu-tion wouldn't fix it. Sage felt certain that she bore a family curse—but who could say that out loud? It was simply easier to say that she didn't believe in romance, in love. That was a much easier pill to swallow than what she really believed. That she had a heritage of unfaithfulness and rejection, and unless she solved the mystery, she was stuck with it.

She was cursed. Cursed to never know love, even if it was real.

Except, maybe . . .

Standing there, with Grant's concerned attention fastened on her and the memory of his kisses still tingling on her lips, the importance of dis-covering the truth doubled.

She squeezed her eyes shut. *Show me the truth.*

Sage wasn't certain, but that sure seemed like a prayer.

Chapter Twenty-Two

"I'll help. If it is that important, then let me help you."

Sage glanced up at the man sitting across from her at the large, heavy wooden table in the basement of the county courthouse, a pull of gratitude making it ever more difficult for her to separate herself from him emotionally. That, and yesterday's kiss.

Never mind it.

She refocused on what they were doing. According to the clerk, they would need to look through old banker boxes full of records. The county hadn't digitized everything yet, and the clerk's initial digital search had come up with only a marriage record for Harold and Clara Teller—she didn't have all day to play sleuth for Sage.

So they would have to do some manual digging for themselves to find the divorce record. And Grandpa James's birth certificate.

"It's got to be here somewhere . . ." Sage muttered.

"Maybe it was filed somewhere else? Another county or state? You said your great-grandmother had lived in California and Colorado?" Grant paused his search through the box marked *January–June 1957*.

It had seemed unlikely that they'd find it in that box, since according to the marriage record, Gramps had married Clara on March 7, 1957. Even so, they had decided to try from the beginning of 1957 and work forward from there.

"*He* divorced her." Sage emphasized the point of it. "*He* has never left Big Prairie. It's got to be here. And so does James's birth . . ." She huffed out a sigh. How could it be this hard?

She looked at the method they were dealing with. And sighed again. Cardboard boxes full of brittle, faded yellow folders? This couldn't be reliable.

"We'll find something, Sage." Grant's gentle voice soothed her frustration.

She sent him a halfhearted grin. "Thank you for helping."

In a way that only Grant Hillman could, he held her with a look that made her heart fill with longing. For him. To hear him say what his eyes told her.

He loves me.

She was such a selfish woman. Worse than she'd ever imagined. Why did she continue with this reckless wish when she knew it would smash into a wall of heartache and regret? He didn't deserve it. He was far too good a man for a girl like her. If she was a different girl from a different heritage, she would thank her lucky stars to have caught the heart of such a man.

Stupid family curse!

A fierce urge to yell out that very thing and to beg for some sort of exorcism of such a sad evil nearly tore from her throat. Instead Sage planted an elbow on the table and rested her head in her hands. Behind her shut eyes, she had a vision so lovely and sweet, she nearly sobbed.

Her seated next to Grant in that quaint little church. Her hand held securely in his, and his open Bible on his knee, positioned so that she could see too.

Love is of God . . .

Such a bizarre picture. Besides the one time she'd sneaked in and sat beside Grant, she had never been to church. Had never seen a reason to go.

How could one visit paint itself in her mind? How could one tiny line from such a big book have engraved itself in her memory? How could one man dig in so deeply in her heart?

She was a bird. Free to flit and roam as she pleased. Fly whenever the mood struck.

Such were her mantra claims. Be that as it may, she didn't feel like roaming anymore, and she most certainly didn't feel free.

"Sage?" Grant waited until she sat up and glanced at him. "Are you all right?"

"Fine." She grinned. The kind he'd call a mask, and he would be right. She nodded toward the box with the hope of distracting him from her lie. "How far have you made it?"

Grant frowned but didn't press. "Almost through June. Then I'll start on the next box."

Sage nodded and busied herself with her box—January–June 1958. They rifled through folders and records in silence.

"Hold on . . ."

At Grant's quiet words, Sage looked up. "Found something?"

"Perhaps." A pair of lines drew between his brows.

"Divorce?"

"No. Birth, but . . ." He stood, pinching a paper in between his fingers as he came around the table toward her. "Was James a middle name?"

"I don't think—" She cut herself short when the paper he held drifted into her view.

Henry James Teller, born August 28, 1957. The form bore a stamp that read *amended.*

Sage shook her head. "That can't be him."

"Why?"

"March to August? That's—"

"Maybe she was pregnant before they were married."

It was possible. It happened. Though more commonly now than in 1957, right? Especially in a small town like Big Prairie.

Her heart backed away from the possibility that this was the birth record of her grandfather, though she couldn't understand why. "Grandpa's name was James. That's all I've ever heard. And if not James, why would they name him Henry rather than Harold?"

"Maybe Henry was a family name."

"I've never heard of it."

Grant rubbed his jawline, his look thoughtful. "I think we should keep it out, just in case. And I'm going to ask the clerk if she has any digital records of Harold's parents or other family. It might be that there's a Henry in there, and then we'll know this is the guy."

Sage nodded but didn't put a lot of hope in that. Or maybe she didn't want it to be the case. Again, she couldn't quite say why. But if Grandpa had a different name and there was a Henry involved, it seemed like that would have been mentioned somewhere.

Then again, they were dysfunctional, so who really knew?

She returned to her own records search, looking for a birth certificate for James Teller, likely in the early part of 1958—a respectable time lapse from marriage to birth—and a divorce filing for some time after the baby had been born.

Her search had gone into March of '58 when Grant came back.

"Well?" Looking up, she found his expression cautious. She lifted her brows. "Do we know a Henry Teller?"

Grant nodded.

"And?"

"Henry Teller was Harold's younger brother."

· · · · ●· ●· · · ·

The implications seemed clear to Grant, but he kept them to himself. After a full afternoon of searching—during which Sage was unusually reserved—she sat quietly beside him in his Altima as he drove her back to the Teller place. He wasn't sure what she was so afraid of with all this, but he had a sense that whatever she found might rock her beliefs.

He hoped for it, at least.

"Will you ask Gramps about Henry?" Grant asked as they pulled into the drive. The sun still had two hours before it would bid them good night. Across the prairie to his left, rays of light scattered bright gold against the ripening grain of the fields. Onto the trees that danced and shimmered in the breeze next to the river ahead and to his right, it sent flecks of brilliant white leaping off the green leaves.

It would be a lovely evening for a walk. If Sage was up for one.

Perhaps he would take her hand. If he held it gently, securely—just right—would she feel the current of his heart for her? Would she feel safe at his side and let go of her long-held claim that she didn't believe in love?

He needed her to believe in love. Because he loved her. In the single day that had spanned between their kiss and this moment, Grant had become convinced. He absolutely loved Sage Greene, and he wanted more than anything he'd ever longed for in his life for her to love him back.

"I promised I wouldn't talk about Clara. It was part of the deal." Sage sounded defeated.

Her flat demeanor made Grant terribly sad. She was a bubbly, joyful person. Why did this pull her down so far?

Grant parked near the front porch and unbuckled. He twisted in his seat to face her. "But this is Henry, not Clara."

She pulled in a long breath and released it slowly. "I'm pretty sure he'll be grumpy about it, and this morning he wasn't feeling well again. I don't want to push it. I think I'll be better off searching through the attic. He has a million things up there."

"You didn't mention that he was not feeling well again."

"Sorry."

The need to touch her had him tracing the soft curls at her temples with the tips of his fingers. "Sage, you are exhausted."

"I didn't sleep well last night."

"Why?"

For a held breath, she gazed back at him, her mouth unsmiling, her eyes tortured. "You."

"Because . . . because I kissed you?"

"Yes. And I kissed you."

"And that makes you upset and not sleep?" He hadn't slept well either. Prayer and hope, and the lingering thrill of her soft lips against his, had kept him awake. But he wasn't upset about it.

Not upset, but . . . uncertain how to proceed from there.

Reaching across the space of the car, she ran her hand over his cheek and down his jawline. "I warned you, Grant," she whispered.

He caught her hand before it fell back to her lap. "Whatever it is that is torturing you, I wish you would just tell me."

"I did tell you. From the beginning I told you. I don't believe in romance. I don't believe in love."

"I remember."

Wiggling her hand free, she sighed. "We were supposed to be friends, Grant. *Friends.*"

"We are friends. But I can't let that be all. I've tried, and I cannot do it. Sage, I—"

She winced. "Don't." Crossing her arms, she tucked herself away, huddling close to the passenger door. "Stop there and don't say it." Shaking her head, she refused to meet his eyes. "I don't believe in love. It doesn't last. It isn't real."

With a cupped hand, Grant nudged her chin until she met his gaze. "Sage, what you are saying and what I see in your eyes are not the same thing. Tell me what is really under that claim."

Lifting her face free of his touch, she reached to open the car door. "It's getting late. I should go check on Gramps."

"It's seven o'clock."

"Right. He'll be hungry, I'm sure." Sage slipped from the seat and stood next to his car.

Grant got out as well, but she stalled him with an upheld hand. "Let's call it a day. Please?"

He didn't want to. What he ached for in that moment was to pull her into his arms and hold her until whatever this fear was that kept her locked away let her go. Until she would admit that she was lonely and longed for *something* to fill her soul. And then he would tell her again that the God he knew had a love that could.

And that when she was ready, he had a space in his heart for her.

But Grant remained planted beside the Altima while she disappeared into the house.

He guessed there would be no sleeping tonight either. For either of them.

• • • • • • • • • • •

Gramps's cough had returned. Deep, violent, and persistent. Sage battled panic as she simmered soup on the stove. She should not have left him on his own so much over the past few days. He hadn't been ready, wasn't well enough.

"I should have stayed home today," she told him when she delivered a small bowl of soup.

Though his movements were weak, he shook his head and clasped her fingers. "Thank you," he rasped.

"For the soup? It is far too late. Like I said, I should have stayed—"

"Thank you."

She stopped babbling and looked at the weary eyes that held hers. They shimmered. The hand that had clasped hers, all bony and weak, squeezed.

"I don't know why you came to me. But thank you. You are . . . a touch of redemption."

Stinging heat filled her eyes. Why would Gramps talk like this? He wasn't sentimental. Soft.

"You look like her. Did you know that?"

"Clara?"

He nodded.

"I've been told a few times. Perhaps it's the wild, stubborn red hair."

"I liked her hair."

"Did—" Sage hesitated. This broke his iron rule. How soon would this calm spell end? "Did you love her?"

Gramps shut his eyes. A tear leaked from the corner of one, and he nodded his head.

"I don't understand," Sage whispered.

His Adam's apple bobbed twice before he blinked his eyes open. "There's a box."

"What kind of box?"

"It will tell you what you want to know."

"Where is it?"

"Buried. Just east of your garden, under the big cottonwood."

A tear escaped her eyelid, cutting a trail down one cheek. "You're scaring me, Gramps."

"All stories come to an end at some point, Sage. You're a story-teller—you know that."

"But—" But when she told a story, the end was happy. Everything was neatly tied up, and the future looked clear and bright.

Which was the reason she knew it was all fiction. Real life didn't go that way.

Something deeply unsettling filled her heart. It was a spanning void. An ache too big to be filled by any sort of transient story, but one that demanded satisfaction.

Eternal emptiness . . .

The thought made her want to curl up in a ball and weep. For Gramps. For herself. What could possibly fill such a gaping need?

His name is Jesus . . .

Gramps coughed again before he continued. "Mine will finally close. And when it does, I want you to say *the end* over it." His focus on her narrowed, his watery eyes clearing. "I mean that, Sage. Speak it out loud, and remember it. My story is done. Clara's is done. Our tale is not to bleed into your life. You get to live however you choose."

Brows gathered tight, Sage stared at him. "I don't know what all of that means."

"And don't gossip." His voice came sharp and insistent on that. "Promise me, Sage. Right now—swear it."

"Gossip about what?"

"Make the promise. It is everything to me. The reason I have lived this way. So swear it."

"Gramps, you're really scaring me." Not to mention confusing her.

"Girl," he barked and then fell into a coughing spasm.

She tucked his hand in tight and pulled it to her chest. "I promise. Whatever secrets you have, I'll keep."

A few more coughs sputtered from his chest, and then he exhaled, as if relieved. He shut his eyes, lying back into the chair, as if done.

"Gramps." Sage's voice wobbled. "Don't go yet. I don't know you . . ." Her chest shuddered as the chilled sense of being robbed of something precious spread within.

A small smile captured the wrinkles of his face. "You have blessed me, girl. Know that." He pressed one more squeeze to her fingers and then let go.

Sage waited for more. He drifted to sleep, his countenance peaceful. All she wanted to do was sob.

Preferably with Grant's steady arms holding her tight. Would that fill the gap in her soul?

CHAPTER TWENTY-THREE

GRANT REREAD THE TEXT that had come through about one in the morning.

please say we are friends

I desperately need you to be my friend

Sitting on the edge of his bed, dressed in his running clothes and shoes ready to be put on, Grant leaned forward, pressing his elbows into his legs and his head against the heels of his palms. He knew he'd not deny her. How could he?

But . . .

Dear God, I'm in deep. But the thing is, she's a mess—the kind that only You can unravel. And I'm a mess—the kind that keeps desperately hoping You'll fix me.

He blew out a ragged breath, sat up, and typed out a text.

We need to talk, Sage. But know that I am your friend. Could he really do that, remain Sage's *friend* when he loved her this way?

Love was not love if it could not sacrifice, was it?

Greater love has no man than this, that he would give himself up for another. Jesus died to demonstrate His love. Love that was not returned in the same measure. Love that had even been denied.

Sage was not asking Grant to die for her but to be her friend.

Help me . . . As he felt his desperate prayer reach heavenward, a stunning and challenging thought pierced back.

What if God was showing Himself to Sage through Grant? That was heavy. But God did such things, didn't He? The possibility felt daunting.

Lord, don't let me fail You.

He stood and stretched, and while he did, the phone in his hand chimed with a new text.

gramps told me of a box buried out back

he said it would answer my questions

will you come help me find it

Alarm shot through him. That did not sound like Harold Teller at all. *Is your Gramps okay?*

no but he is still with us this morning

I can call Anne . . . Grant shot back.

I have already

she is stopping by soon

but the box Grant

I want to find it before

In the back of his mind, it occurred to him how her lack of punctuation and choppy texts did not bother him. He barely noticed it anymore. No, that was not right. He noticed, but only to the extent that it made him think *This is Sage. My opposite, but only in ways that don't really matter . . .*

And that was something to ponder.

But not right then. Grant refocused on her request and on the day before him, and then he sent her a reply.

I have two clients scheduled today and a short video conference I must attend. I should be done by two. Can you wait until then?

She made him wait for several minutes, which seemed like a mean little act of torture. Finally, one word lit his screen.

yes

Dumb as it was, and not at all fitting for the moment, reading it made him more bold and more certain than ever.

He wanted all of her yeses.

· · • • • • ♦ • · · ·

Gramps was slipping away quickly, a truth Sage had already known but was confirmed by Anne's evaluation.

"I can see what I can do about getting hospice care set up." Anne squeezed Sage's hand.

"Doesn't that require a doctor, and insurance, and paperwork?" Sage asked. "I don't even know where to begin with any of it, and he won't see a doctor. You know he won't."

Anne nodded, but her expression was set with determination. "Let me talk to some people and see what we can do. Sometimes small towns can be a real asset." She then tugged Sage close and wrapped her in a hug. "And if I get Miss Jane involved . . ."

Despite the weight of grief in Sage's heart, that comment made her chuckle. Miss Jane was a force that could topple mountains.

Sage stepped back. "What do I do in the meantime?"

"You've done exactly as you should, Sage. Keep him comfortable. And honor him." Admiration filled Anne's gaze. "That is the kindest thing you can do."

Sage nodded and Anne left, allowing her to ponder the odd twist of this pursuit she had set upon. She had come here with the claim that she wanted to know the patriarch of her dysfunctional family. The one who had started the curse. In her mind, she had settled that she would find him exactly as had been told—a mean, selfish drunk who did not deserve an ounce of her pity. Even if he was leaving his earthly property to her mother and herself.

They could take that inheritance and never once feel sorry about never knowing the man.

That had been her surface reason.

But perhaps underneath the blustery claims, she had hoped for something different. For this.

What was this?

Crossing her arms, Sage leaned back against the doorframe between the kitchen and parlor, her watch settled on the old man sleeping in the recliner.

This was . . . What did Gramps call it last night?

A touch of redemption.

She didn't even know what that was exactly.

But she did know that the man Gramps really was and the monster she'd been told were not the same. She was certain that the story Great-Grandma Clara had told was only one side of the truth, and maybe not even really the truth at all.

I want to know the truth.

As she watched the old man struggle to breathe, his sallow skin revealing every blue vein running corridors though his body, a tear leaked from one eye.

The heart in her chest tremored and warmed and ached and grew all at once. The feeling was deep and strong and scary and lovely. It rushed in and soothed, but in the next breath it sliced and divided. The enormity of the emotion made her quiver even before the word was named in her mind.

Love.

This was love. And it was real. So big it was terrifying. So consuming it hurt. And yet . . . yet . . .

What?

Sage shook her head, her thoughts a collision of randomness. This pain hurt. Losing Gramps cut deep. But she was incredibly grateful to know the real man and shockingly relieved to discover that what she had been told was not the truth at all.

And beneath this great discovery lay something more. Like the edges of something greater and more potent sitting beneath this layer. Something foundational and necessary . . .

And too much for her to consider right now.

Swiping the wet trail alongside her nose, Sage strode into the parlor and took Gramps's hand. "I have some work to do upstairs," she whispered. "But I'll come back soon to check on you."

A shallow breath and a twitch of his rough fingers against hers was his only response.

She was glad to be done with the narrating she had been working on. Now she needed to edit and master the audio before she sent it for proof. That required a different sort of attention—and one that did not delve into her emotions the way telling a story could. A relief, because her rocked soul could not manage much more.

Several hours later, after making decent progress on the audio and checking on Gramps every thirty minutes, Grant texted.

I finished early and thought I would head your way. Should I bring something? Anything?

Though it was nonsensical, Sage could feel the gentle touch of his fingers near her temple while she read. Shutting her eyes, she sensed the warmth and weight of his stare on her from the previous night. And that feeling bulged in her heart again. Big. Warm. Inviting.

Terrifying.

Love.

Breathing became difficult. It was one thing to love Gramps. Perhaps because he was not long for this world, which was a sad indictment of her heart. Even so . . .

She could not let Grant love her.

I am a bird, wild and flighty. I come and go as I please, and nothing will clip my wings.

The proclamation brought her no comfort. But for Grant's sake, she clung to it.

Chapter Twenty-Four

They had pocked four holes into the ground without success. But Sage's determination had not wavered, so Grant firmed his grip on the handle of the spade and plunged the sharp head into a section of untouched ground. The sandy silt, held together by a mat of native grasses and wildflowers, gave under the weight of his foot against the shovel. He rocked the head back and lifted, disturbing six inches of soil. So a new hole began. As with the others, he dug two feet by two feet and then down. Unlike the others, at a depth of just over a foot, the tip of the spade clunked against something other than dirt.

"There is something here," he said.

Sage had been working on her knees to refill and pack the fruitless holes they'd already dug. She scrambled to her feet. "What is it?"

Grant knelt and ran a hand over whatever he had hit. Cold metal winked at him in the late-afternoon sun. "A box."

In an instant Sage was there, dirty fingers clawing at the dirt still entombing her quarry.

With a hand to her shoulder, Grant stood. "Let me get around it and loosen the dirt."

She sat back and allowed him to work. Once he got beneath the item, which looked to be an old rectangular bread box, he pried it free. Sage retrieved the treasure and wiped the soil away.

Not a bread box, but a metal saltine cracker tin.

She tried prying the lid free, but rust held it stubbornly shut.

"The shed." Popping up from her seat on the ground, she hurried toward the eight-by-eight shack at the back of the property. The building leaned to the right and looked as if it could come down at any moment.

But that, like almost everything else, was not going to stop Sage Greene.

Grant leaned the shovel against the big cottonwood standing at the edge of the yard and followed Sage. She flung the door open and rushed within the dark building, clearly not worried about its structural integrity and evidently already familiar with what was within.

Shockingly, the inside was tidy. Tools hung up along the wall, a blank spot open for the shovel Sage had given him. A bench ran the length of the shed at the back, with a dozen large, old tin cans. Grant supposed there was an assortment of nuts, bolts, screws, nails, and the like within those containers. Above them, a dark-brown pegboard supported hand tools—among them a hammer. Sage gripped that tool, and using the bench as support, tapped the rim of the lid. Dirt and rust and rotted metal flaked from the can.

It took several turns around the can, but at last the lid pried free. "Got it!" Sage looked up at Grant, a wild gleam in her eyes that was not quite thrill but rather nearer to something like desperation, and they both turned to go outside.

The bright sun made them blink. Sage finished taking off the tin lid and reached into the can. She pulled out a folded letter-sized manilla envelope. The front outer part bore Harold's name and address. The upper left hand of that read *Clara Teller estate.*

"She had an estate?" Sage mumbled.

"Likely, if you know of none such, that is simply legal terms for a lawyer to distribute final wishes."

"I didn't know she even had a lawyer."

"Perhaps this was left in a lockbox at a bank or something. They would have mailed it upon death maybe?"

"Maybe." Sage turned the envelope and opened the back flap. "It's a bunch of letters mostly." She withdrew a thin handful of them, holding them up like a deck of cards.

"Who from?"

Sage flipped through them. "They're all from H. Teller. Harold Teller."

"Hmm . . ." While a spring of warning and doubt bubbled from his gut, Grant shifted so that he stood behind her and could read over her shoulder.

Sage reshuffled the small stack so that the one that had been on top could be read first. That one she opened.

March 1957

My Dearest Clara,

My beautiful girl. You know my destiny can't be bound in this little lifeless town. I am not a regular man who was meant to toil in mundane things. You also know that I cannot become what I feel is my birthright if I am tied down as a family man.

You have torn me in two, and I must choose.

I know you will do what is best for us both. As will I.

I am going. The time is now, while I am young. I can feel the call of destiny, and I must go. Be happy for me, my sweet.

—H

"He left her?" Sage's brow furrowed. "Could not have been for long. They were married in March. Or perhaps this was sent after they were married?"

She opened the next letter, and they both read.

April 1957

My Dearest Clara,

You cannot imagine how big and glorious life is beyond the confines of Big Prairie. It is, as I imagined, everything at your fingertips. My dreams are

*right here, waiting for my claim. Wait and see, my dear girl. Wait and see .
. .*

But there is this one thing, a thorn that pricks at my full happiness.

I lie in bed at night, and the memory of you haunts me. Your breath mingling with mine. Your touch against my skin. I remember every shiver. Every moan. And the craving is a painful echo.

Tell me you think on those sacred moments too. Say that you have not, you will not, forget.

You are my obsession, and I must have you again.

—H

"Whoa, Gramps." Sage glanced back at Grant.

He wished she had not. Heat smothered his face.

Sage's brows bounced. "He was a little steamy, the Romeo!"

Grant did not join in her small amusement. Instead he swallowed against the pit of growing anxiety. This was not at all as Sage imagined, he was sure.

May 1957

My Dearest Clara,

I feel like the stars are within reach. These hills lift me up, and anything is possible. The night sky above me dances with starlight. There is energy and beauty here, so different from our dusty plains. So much promise. Though I hated your tears, I know now that this was the right choice for me. Adventure is my insatiable need, and the success I know I am capable of fuels me onward. I cannot deny it any more than I could deny breath to my body.

But you are still my desire.

When I close my eyes, I see yours. So green and full of mischief and set aflame with passion. For me, I hope. Still, always for me. Say you feel it too, my darling. Tell me it will always be so.

Miles cannot douse this passion we share. Nor can time tame it.

I will make something of myself. If the Duke from Iowa can, so can I. I will send for you. You will love the life I will make for us.

Wait for me, my beautiful one. We will be together again soon.

—H

"Who is *the Duke*?" Sage asked.

Grant reached for one of the envelopes in the stack and ran his thumb over the return address. *Hollywood, California.* "I would guess John Wayne."

"John Wayne? As in the actor?"

Grant nodded.

"He was from Iowa?"

"Yes."

Once again, her brows furrowed. Only deeper and without the hint of amusement she'd worn before. "This isn't—"

Making sense. Grant finished her sentence silently. No, it didn't make sense, not for Harold. And she was finally beginning to see the truth, even if she was fighting against it.

Sage quickly opened the next letter.

June 1957

Your silence slays me, Clara. Do not punish me this way. I did not desert you. And I only asked that you see to what was best for us both. Only you know this heart of mine. I must pursue the life I am destined to live. It could not be there. Not on the farm. Not to simply relive my father's life. I would never be satisfied with such a paltry, ordinary existence.

Come to me now, my beautiful girl. Forgive me the mistake of leaving you behind, my darling. Forgive, and fly to me now. What is in the past is behind us now. Let us embrace what can be.

Come, my love. Heal this crack in my soul.

Come to me, my beautiful one. We can build this life together, you and me and no one else. We will chart our own path, carve our own happiness, and no one will take if from us.

Come quickly to me, my darling, else I drown in this ocean of longing.

—H

Though this letter was the most poetic one yet, and surely so full of romance it made the dramatic part of her heart swoon, this time Sage made no comment, though she did glance up at him again. No doubt she could see the flush of his face at reading such intimacies.

Grant had little doubt that *H*'s intent was met with success. But he doubted very much the story was fitting right in Sage's mind. While she seemed lost in the high romance of it all, Grant braced for the crash he felt certain was coming.

Sage paused before she dug into the next letter, a hearty sigh escaping from her lungs. "I wonder what happened? He seems so in love with her. Why would he divorce her only a year later?"

"There's no record of a divorce, Sage."

"There must be somewhere. We just haven't found it yet."

"Sage."

She blinked up at him.

He tapped the left top corner of an envelope. "These are from Holly-wood."

"I know that, Grant. I can read too."

"I don't know a whole lot about Harold, but I do know that he has never left Big Prairie."

"No. You don't know that. Even if that's what everyone says. You don't know."

"Sage." Grant felt certain of his next claim. "Harold did not write these letters."

Rather than responding to him, Sage opened the next envelope.

Grant stopped her from reading it with a hand over hers. "Why are you fighting the truth so hard? These are not from Harold."

Tightening her jaw, Sage glared up at him for a moment. Then she pushed his interfering hand away and unfolded the next page.

Clara,

My brother? You married my brother?

How deep the betrayal! Did I not spread open my bed to you? Did I not offer the bounty of my glorious future? I asked but two things of you. You did neither. And now I am left to imagine you in my brother's home. In his arms. In his bed.

You have carved out my very soul. And left me cold and empty.

You are dead to me, woman.

Dead.

Sage gasped as she finished the letter. Then she let her hand drop to her side. "Henry."

Finally. Grant nodded. "I believe so." He could not understand the level of devastation this summoned from her. She liked Harold. Should it not be a relief to find out that he was not the horrible, faithless man she had heard him to be?

"Why would Clara have married Harold if it was Henry who loved her?"

Ah, so she was still not following entirely. Swallowing, Grant slid the stack of letters from her limp hand and shuffled the first back to the top. He read silently until he found the part that had confirmed his suspicions from before. That, he read aloud.

"'You also know that I cannot become what I feel is my birthright if I am tied down as a family man.'

"'You have torn me in two, and I must choose. I know you will do what is best for us both.'" He looked at Sage, feeling a mix of sympathy for her, pity for Harold and Clara, and strong resentment toward the man who had penned these false claims of love. "She was pregnant, Sage."

"But—"

"*Henry* James Teller. Born in August 1957. Your grandpa James was Henry's child."

Sage blinked. As she bit her bottom lip, she nodded. Her sad gaze shifted, and she stared toward the river, her expression all remembered sorrow. "'Your great-grandfather was a worthless man. He made promises he never kept. He was selfish and cruel.' All these things I was told." Her eyes flickered back to Grant. "And I believed them, and they were true. But not of Harold. Henry was the man." Her eyes widened, as if the story was coming into focus. "But why would Harold marry a girl who carried his brother's child?"

Grant shrugged. "Perhaps for honor's sake. Henry apparently left her alone and pregnant. He clearly expected her to *take care* of the problem. If Clara chose to have the baby instead . . ."

"Would you do such a thing?" Sage's rushed question seemed desperate. "Take a woman as your wife, claim her child as your own, knowing it was not?" Sage studied him with so much openness—entirely unmasked. As if his answer would determine what she would believe.

About Harold?

About himself?

Or perhaps even about God?

Do You see me? Do You care? Questions Grant had himself asked the King of Heaven. But he'd asked them believing with his whole heart that God was good and gracious and that, yes, He did see, He did care. Because Grant knew the God of the Bible.

Sage did not. She only knew what she'd been told by those who, for whatever reason, chose to believe the lies that Satan was so good at sowing. That God could not be trusted. That He was fickle and driven by power lust and selfish caprice.

She had not tasted and seen that the Lord is good. Not yet.

But she had believed the worst of Harold too. And now she was finding out the stories she'd been fed had been lies.

Lies could be overcome with truth.

Grant could not help but stare into those searching eyes. His heart was lost to her, and there was no hope for it coming back. He wanted to love her the rest of his days. He wanted her to let him and to love him back.

But first she needed to know Love was real. He was powerful *and* good.

Grant forced himself to consider what she had asked. Would he marry a woman who carried another man's child? A brother's, who was apparently selfish and worthless—a Casanova if ever there was one. Would he take Sage under those circumstances?

It would be hard. Harder than living with his father's disappointment. Harder than feeling like an eternal outsider.

But to love . . .

"Yes," he breathed.

Lifting her empty hand, Sage cupped his jaw. "I believe you would." Eyelids fluttering, she stepped back from him, letting her touch fall away. "You are . . . what I thought did not exist. What I never looked for, because I did not believe in. You and apparently Gramps." There, her eyes misted until the cloud of moisture gathered and slipped from one corner of her eyes.

She shook her head. "Only he is not my grandfather."

That crushed her. For a girl who did not believe in love, Sage Greene loved a whole lot. Maybe she didn't even realize it yet, but she loved.

She loved that grumpy, locked-up old man who had not been the evil he'd been named.

And she loved this awkward, uncompromisingly boring man. Grant felt sure she did, even if she wasn't ready to admit it.

Perhaps she just needed more time. And a few nudges.

Grant reached for her hand. "He claims you as his granddaughter. Just as he claimed James as his own son. He would not leave his property to you and your mother if that wasn't so. And he certainly would not have allowed you to stay here if that was not so. Though perhaps not by blood, by choice you are *Harold's* granddaughter."

Her shoulders sagged, as if his words gave her relief, and Grant was glad.

"That still leaves the mystery unsolved though." Sage slipped her hand free of his and searched through the big manilla envelope. "Why did Clara take James and leave? Why did she write to Harold that she would never forgive him?"

"I do not know." Grant leaned close enough to peek into the envelope. "Is there anything else?"

"Nothing." She dropped the letters back into the bigger envelope and searched within the old tin. "Nothing else in here either."

"Can you ask him?"

She shook her head. "I don't want him to relive this. It seems it wrecked him enough for one lifetime. Maybe he did send her away. Maybe he discovered these and . . ." Taking her bottom lip in her teeth again, she looked back at the house. "Would you stay with him and let me borrow your car?"

"Sure." Grant stuffed his hands into his pockets. What if Sage was right and Harold had sent Clara and James away after all? With all his heart, Grant hoped that was not the truth. "Can I ask why?"

She didn't look back at him but instead strode toward the house. "I need to talk to Miss Jane."

Grant hated it when he could not predict, let alone control, an outcome. But this tale . . . He could do nothing.

But he could pray for Sage as she went. He could ask the good God he knew to grip her heart, show her truth about Himself, no matter what had really happened in the past.

As she went, he did just that. And wondered why it took until right then to do so.

Chapter Twenty-Five

"Can I get you a tea or a lemonade?" Miss Jane's bright smile was as it had always been, welcoming, though something in her blue eyes held caution. As if she could sense this visit from Sage had an ominous purpose.

"No thank you." Sage strode straight to the counter and braced her palms on the butcher-block counter. "Miss Jane, I need answers. Not vague ones."

Drawing a breath, Miss Jane shook her head. "Sage, my girl, I have told you what I can, but I won't dishonor my friend by—"

Sage lifted the envelope in her left hand and placed it on the counter. "I found this. Gramps told me where it was and that it would answer my questions."

Brow furrowed, Miss Jane ran a finger along the edge of the flap. "What is it?"

"Letters. To my great-grandmother. From *H*, who sent them from Hollywood, California."

Miss Jane shut her eyes and swallowed.

"They're from Henry, aren't they?" Sage asked.

Nodding, Miss Jane motioned for Sage to follow her, and then she walked stiffly toward the back of the little shop.

Sage found the room to be a small space. The back wall held a door and a row of pegs for coats and aprons. Along one wall sat an old church pew—or half of one—with room enough for two.

Miss Jane lowered onto one side and patted the wood space left over. "Sit, Sage."

Sage did so but wasted no time in prodding. "Henry was my great-grandfather, wasn't he?"

"If we're talking strict biology, then yes. Henry was little James's father. But Harold would not stand for anyone to say so. Even after Clara was gone, he would not stand for anyone to talk shamefully about her or her son. He claimed them both as his and demanded that everyone in Big Prairie accept it as fact."

Sage could picture that. Harold was an absolute mule when he chose to be. Was this why he withdrew from town, from life though? That it was too much to constantly fight the rumors?

As a girl who ran from anything that neared hard or uncomfortable, Sage could relate.

"Did he make her leave?" Sage barely whispered the question. She no longer wanted to believe it was so. She couldn't imagine that of Gramps—of Harold . . . no, *Gramps*—anymore. He was not that man. *Please, let him not ever have been that man.*

She wasn't sure why she was asking God for anything, let alone to possibly rewrite a history that was already carved in stone.

"No."

Relief sagged through her at Miss Jane's firm response.

"He found a note from her in place of where he'd hidden the letters"—Miss Jane tapped on the envelope now sitting between them—"these letters, I assume."

"He hid them from her?"

Miss Jane turned her face away. "Yes. That is what he told me. He hid them because she was his wife and they were making progress. She was warming to him. He hoped that she would realize that Henry would never be a faithful man, that he would always be chasing rainbows, and he had hoped that she would come to love him, Harold, instead. But—"

"But she found them."

Lips pressed into a sad line, Miss Jane nodded. "She found them, and within a day she was packed up, and she and the baby were gone."

"What happened with Henry?"

"Near as I can tell, he never warmed to James, and his passion for Clara died not long after she reached him in California." Miss Jane sighed, and her focus fell to her hands. "But I don't know the details of any of that, really. All I truly know is that she left and never came back, though if she had, Harold would have taken her."

That pathetic tale wove sorrow in Sage's heart. Her grandmother had truly lived a sad life—but *she* had chosen it.

And what of this kind, gentle woman next to her? Miss Jane—who had never married. Who knew more of this story than anyone else in town. How was she connected to all this?

The ache on the woman's face hinted the truth. "You loved him," Sage said.

After sucking in a long breath, Miss Jane's gaze focused on something—or nothing—in the distance, and her blue eyes misted with unshed tears. "I did." A weighted pause extended for several heartbeats. "Even more so after he confided in me what had happened. That was a few years after Clara left. But—"

"But he was still married."

She nodded.

"He broke *your* heart, and yet you have remained kind to him."

"Harold did not mean to hurt me." Miss Jane gripped Sage's hand. "I pursued friendship with him, at first because I felt so terrible for him. It was me who . . . It was not his fault. He chose to remain faithful to his vows.

As long as Clara did not file for divorce, he was going to remain married to her. There is something honorable in that, and I will not fault him for it."

"He chose to seep in bitterness."

Face tipping toward her lap, Miss Jane's eyes, full of sadness, though Sage suspected that was not for herself, briefly touched hers and then locked on to the table. "Disappointment wore on him. He is not the man he once was." Her face looked at Sage again. "You would have liked him before everything went sideways. Actually, he was a lot like Grant. Serious but kind. Quiet, contemplative, responsible. And as I said, kind."

"Clara broke him."

A long sigh sagged through her chest, and Miss Jane shook her head. "Your great-grandmother had her own heartaches. They were both broken souls."

"You once told me that we all are broken souls."

She nodded.

"But you, Miss Jane? You remain kind, though your heart was hurt. Your eyes still laugh. And you still offer kindness to Harold, though he became a bitter and angry old man."

"We each choose what to do with pain, Sage. Every one of us has a choice."

"But how? This . . . it blows my mind. You loved a man who could have loved you back. You could have been happy together if he could have only let go of the past. But he didn't. Yet you remain . . . How?"

Miss Jane smoothed her denim overalls, her thin, sinewy hands showing a lifetime of work. For a long moment, she studied Sage, as if she was willing her to hear—to understand. Then she tipped her head sideways. "I believe that God will redeem every broken part of our stories. Perhaps not fully in this life, though I have been given so many beautiful friendships, so many joyful moments well past my little drama with Harold. I don't take those lovely gifts for granted. But ultimately Jesus has given us a glimpse into the future, into eternity. And He has promised to wipe away every tear. There will be no more sorrow or pain. He will mend every heartache, every disappointment, every tragedy. For those whose names are written in His book of life, He will give exactly that: life. Abundantly."

Miss Jane recaptured Sage's hand. "There is always joy to be found in this life, Sage. And you are so very gifted at finding it. I hope you always do so—and you lift gratitude for that. But there is life beyond this. And I believe that when the believers in Christ are delivered to His eternal kingdom, the things that made us weep in this world will fade. They won't matter anymore. Every moment of pain will be redeemed, and we will be left with only joy."

Sage's mind swam in the depth of such possibilities. On one hand, Miss Jane's eternal hope seemed too lofty to be taken seriously.

But on the other . . .

"So you live with hope, and that makes it easier to choose joy?"

"Yes."

"It seems like a far-off thing."

"Indeed. But take it from an old woman—time speeds away. The older you get, the faster it goes, and suddenly you will be like me, eighty-some-thing years old and wondering how it all went by so quickly."

· · · · ● · ● · · ·

Grant sat in his silent, empty house, the old cello box open at his feet. Outside, the moonless night was clear, allowing every star its best opportunity for brilliance against the blackest night. It occurred to him that some might say this night was the darkest of the summer. Some, however, would claim that it was the most dazzling.

It depended on what one put his focus.

Or, perhaps, one could say both were true at the same time.

Running a hand over the century-old instrument, Grant decided that both could be true. And so he could feel deep sadness and a well of gratitude at once too.

Harold had become an unlikely friend. One who, that late afternoon while Grant had sat with him, had issued a warning meant as kindness. As fortitude.

"You love her." Using a garbled, rusty voice, Harold had startled Grant.

He had looked to be sleeping, and Grant had not been entirely sure the man knew who sat with him, if anyone at all.

Standing from the far side of the couch, Grant moved to be nearer. He lowered onto the table in front of the recliner. "Your granddaughter?"

"Yes."

"I do."

"She is likely to run."

"I realize that. That's all she's ever known, ever seen in her life."

Harold winced, then nodded. "Will you love her anyway?"

Grant could not imagine *not* loving Sage. He also, however, did not want to imagine the knife that would cut if Sage did as predicted.

"You loved Clara, though she ran," Grant said, rather than answering Harold's question.

He inhaled sharply, then coughed. "For a long time. And then . . . then I let it turn sour."

"You never divorced her."

Shaking his head, his eyes held a shame that Grant did not understand. "I hoped she would come back. When she didn't . . ."

"You were angry."

"Yes."

"I can understand that."

"I couldn't make her love me."

"Maybe she was too ashamed to come back."

A long stretch of silence followed. Harold's breathing became raspier, and he shut his eyes. Grant supposed he had dozed off again.

"People say I'm cruel."

Again, Harold's weak voice startled Grant.

"People talk about things they don't know."

"They say you're odd."

"That is true. And I am."

"Does it bother you?"

"That I am different?"

Through half-closed eyes, Harold held Grant in his gaze.

Grant clasped his hands together and nodded. "Sometimes."

"I see a good man," Harold said.

A sudden, unexpected urge to cry caused a lump to bulge in Grant's throat. He found Harold's gaze and held it. "So do I, sir."

A tear leaked from one corner of Harold's eye and slipped down the side of his face. "Not always. I wish I had been."

"I would wager you had your reasons."

"Even so . . ." He exhaled, the breath ragged. "Sage is not her great-grandmother."

Back to Sage again. Grant waited.

"She is not me either." Rolling his head, Harold pinned another meaningful look on Grant. "You make sure she knows that."

Grant was uncertain he would be able to convince Sage of anything, but he nodded anyway. "What should I do if she runs?"

The long sigh seemed sad. "Let her go." He shook his head. "I never should have hid the letters . . ."

"From Sage?"

"From Clara."

"But she was your wife . . ."

Harold shut his eyes. Though he waited, hoping this was another small break in the conversation, Harold did not speak again. Sage had come back not long after, more upset than she had been before. Though the sporadic conversation stayed near the front of his mind, he turned his attention to her.

She held him at arm's length.

"What did you find out?" he had asked quietly.

"That you were right. Henry is my grandfather."

"I did not say that. I said Harold claimed you."

She shook her head, her face tilted toward the ground. "I come from messy, selfish people."

He gripped her shoulder with one hand. "Sage—"

She moved away. "I'll get the cello. He wants you to have it."

"But—"

Sage did not stop but made her way up the stairs. Grant didn't follow but stood with his mind scrambling. What could he do? What could he say? She was already leaving. He could feel her pulling away.

Returning with the big box in her arms—and he should have followed her to help her lug that thing down, if his mind hadn't been so muddled— Sage had passed it to him. Then she'd risen up on her toes, pressed a fleeting kiss to his cheek, and whispered good night.

That was his blackness. The darkness of the night was her shielding her heart from him.

But it hurt her to do it. He could feel her reluctance. Though it was misguided, it was her care for him that held her back.

And there was something lovely in that, wasn't there? A twinkling of hope, like those brilliant little stars up there in the black night sky.

Grant held on to that thought as he positioned the cello between his legs. Using his bow, he drew it across the fresh strings he'd just replaced, and a strong, low b resonated from the body. The note sang true, and Grant moved his fingers into a d minor scale. Satisfied that the notes were pure, he went back to the b and moved into the first eight bars of "The Gale."

The haunting melody filled his home. His mind. His heart. The music moved him, as it usually did, and he played the rest of the song from memory. Grant let himself get lost in the music, lifting this offering of hope and sorrow as worship. First, through the whole of "The Gale," then on to Karl Jenkins's "Benedictus." Both songs were an offering of his soul. A prayer played rather than spoken, because the notes were more complete than any words he knew.

He came to the end, and his heart strummed. There was still ache. For Harold and for Sage. And for the looming possibility that he would lose both. But there was something else as well. Something holy and sacred that reached deeper.

God had heard this wordless prayer and had given a silent answer. One that gripped his heart more surely than anything he had felt thus far in his life. Grant had been seen, and he was held.

Held secure by the goodness of God, come what may. That was enough. It was more than enough.

· · · · · · · · · ·

The end had come quietly, sometime in the night.

Anne promised that Gramps had slipped with minimal pain into the other side. Sage was unsure what the other side was exactly. Except that it meant that the man she called Gramps—though he actually was not—had died.

She cried.

So many tears, and the irony of it was not lost to her. She had come here to make him sorry. Sorry that he had rejected his family, remorseful that he had passed on this legacy of faithless, selfish men. And now she cried at her loss.

Harold had been a good man. One wrongly spoken of. A man whose goodness had been trampled on. And she had barely known him.

Grief was a dark cloud filling her mind. All she could think was to make it stop. Make it stop hurting. Make the darkness go away. Nothing did. Not Miss Jane's gentle hand, her grandmotherly hugs. Not Anne's continued kindness. And not Grant's strong, steady presence.

Mostly, not that at all.

Sage wanted to find happy again. That had been her life's goal, to live happy. And she had been fairly good at it. Mostly by keeping the potential sadness clear. Grant had moved into her heart without her consent.

That felt too dangerous. Look how Harold's life had turned out. And Clara's. And even dear Miss Jane's.

Such sad, sad tales.

A week after they buried Gramps, Grant came to the farmhouse where Sage was now entirely alone. He had done so every day since Gramps's final day. And he brought her food. They ate in relative silence—he did not seem to mind her lack of words. But when he took her hand to lead her outside to where they would likely cut down the footpath to the river, cross over the makeshift bridge of logs he had made, and walk the path where he had been running the day they met, Sage pulled back.

"No walk this evening?" he asked without censure.

"No." She wriggled her hand free. Rolling her lips together, she dug around in her heart for courage. What she found was mostly resolve—she was unsure if that was the same thing. "I'm leaving, Grant."

His steady stare did not waver. Those dark eyes didn't flicker with surprise. But he did shake his head, the movement slow and intentional. "You do not have to do this."

"Yes, I do."

Stepping nearer, Grant seemed to surround her, and she was tempted to take comfort in his blocking presence. "I love you, Sage."

Panic beat wildly in her chest. "I warned you."

With the back of his fingers, he traced the stream of her tears—the first she became aware of them. How long had she allowed them freedom?

"Even birds have homes," he whispered. "And running isn't freedom."

Her hand shook as she gripped his wrist and then nudged away his tender touch. "You don't want a girl like me, Grant."

"I never even knew a girl like you walked this earth. But had I known, I would have searched for you."

"We are opposites." She could not look away. "That never works. You said so."

Again he shook his head, and one corner of his mouth hinted at a wispy smile. "We're not so different. We both long to be known. To see good. To love and be loved back."

Sage exhaled and forced her eyes from his. If she kept staring into those penetrating, hypnotic depths, she would never get through this. Goodness, he was a hard man to leave. Why did he have to be all calm and steady, logic and kindness? Couldn't he get mad? Tell her she was being stupid and stubborn? Then she could get mad back at him and storm out and feel justified.

His hand found her face again, his thumb gently lifting her chin. "He said you would do this."

"Who? Gramps?"

Grant nodded.

"And did he say to make me stay?"

"No. He said to let you go."

"That didn't work out so well for him. Or for Clara." She heard herself . . . and wondered if that was Grant's hope. But . . . but . . .

She couldn't think straight. So much of her wanted to stay, to cling to this man who had proclaimed *love* for her. But love was fictional. Wasn't it? And she had a family curse. Didn't she?

She didn't believe . . . *but I want to.*

Sage squeezed her eyes shut against the spinning thoughts. "It didn't work out so well for him."

What was she saying? Was she challenging him to *make* her stay? And what would she do if he did?

Grant closed the space between them, the warmth of his body a blanket to hers, and then he pressed a kiss to one closed eyelid. Then the other. "You're not them." His breath fanned across her cheek as he whispered. "He said to tell you that. You're not your grandma Clara. And you're not him. You get to live your life however you choose." That warm breath on her skin was sealed by another kiss, this one on her cheekbone.

Then he pulled away.

A chill sank in where his warmth had been.

"You can choose not to believe in love, Sage. It won't change the truth."

She swiped away a fresh stream of tears. "What truth is that?"

"That I love you." He covered his heart with one palm. "And whether you run or you stay, I'm not going to stop."

CHAPTER TWENTY-SIX

SAGE WOKE UP WITH a sore back. Hide-a-beds were awful.

But that was all Mom had available in this new trailer house she'd moved into. Ray, her latest boyfriend, had claimed the second bedroom as his "trophy room." The entire eight-by-eight-foot space had been plastered with bowling balls, plastic trophies, and medals hung on thick black lanyards.

Sage had no idea how Mom met these guys. Or why she took them in. Her best guess was loneliness, but at that point Sage had enough emotional issues of her own. She had no brain or heart space to spare to pick through her mother's issues. She simply needed a place to land while she got her head on straight and while she searched for another freelance job.

Dressed in her high-waist yoga pants and a formfitting tank, Sage finished a cup of morning spiced tea and flipped on the television. With a few quick flicks of the remote, she found her favorite YouTube channel for Pilates and took her position. Ten minutes of good, targeted stretching should work out the knots she'd gained through the night.

When she neared the end of the video, her mom came through the front door. "Hi, hippie," she chirped. "There's mail for you."

Pressing into the final move, meant to stretch her lower back muscles, Sage glanced at her mom. She wasn't an overtly tender woman. But she did care about Sage. She wanted Sage to be happy, whatever that looked like. She did love her.

See there. Love. Like Harold loved you. And . . .

She shut that line of thinking down. Her heart was too raw and confused to toy with it. Besides, on the six-hour drive bus trip from Big Prairie to northern Colorado, where Mom was living now, she had sorted that out. Parental love and grandparental love wasn't the same thing as romance. So her claim was still valid—*romantic love* was not real.

That felt as steady as a house of cards.

Blowing out a long, cleansing breath as the instructor commanded, Sage left her spot in front of that awful couch and walked to where Mom had slapped down the mail.

The envelope addressed to her was from the same law office that had sent the original notification that had started this whole messy story. "Mom, it's from Kinder and Son."

"Saw that."

"Why is it for me?"

"Open it and see."

This felt . . . ominous. Sage eyed Mom with a bucketful of caution dumping in her gut. Then she ripped the flap and pulled the letter free. Scanning the paragraphs gave her enough information to know things had changed.

Harold had changed his will. She had no idea when. Or how he'd managed to do it without her knowing. But—

"What does old Kinder and Son have to say?" Mom put her half-finished bowl of cereal next to the sink and came to stand beside Sage.

Sage wasn't sure how this was going to go down, but she passed the official notice to her mother. Silently, Mom read it through, then passed it back.

"Good work, Sage."

She had no idea how to take that. "Mom, I didn't ask him to do that."

"I didn't think you did."

"This is not why I went there." Panic set in. Mom was showing no real reaction to this. But certainly she was upset, wasn't she? How could she not be?

"Look, Sage, I didn't know the man. Never wanted anything to do with him. I made that clear to you. But if you managed to make peace with him and he wants you to have his stuff, I'm not going to be mad about it."

"But . . . but he originally was going to leave it to you."

She spread her arms wide and turned a small circle. "Why would I want his crappy farmhouse when I have all this?"

Oh, but the guilt that loosed. "Mom—"

Mom finished her slow spin and then looked at Sage. Then she smiled. Like, a real, sincere smile. "I'm not mad, Sage. Why would I be mad that finally some man took responsibility for his procreation? Even if it is a few generations late, at least he did. And he's taking care of you. That's a relief to me, if we're honest. Now you don't have to wander around like I did. Now at least you have a place to land or something to sell and get yourself started. You don't have to live like me."

Sage considered correcting her mother about Harold being responsible for this line of *procreation*, but it felt like a diversion at the moment. The point at hand was that Harold had given Sage his house and property, not her mother. "But you could have sold it. It could be your nest egg."

Mom snorted. "Right. So I could then hand it over to the likes of Ray, like I've done too many other times before."

She knew these guys were taking her? "Mom."

Mom shrugged. "It's the life I've chosen. I don't love it, but I got you out of it, so there's a bright spot."

"But why do you take up with men like him?"

Opening the fridge, Mom grabbed a diet soda, popped the top, and took a swig. "He fills the void. For now."

"What about . . ." Did she dare even ask? Compulsion had the words on her tongue before she was sure. "What about love?"

"I'll take what I can get. This is as close as I'm ever going to come."

"But you think that love is real? Like, romantic love? The kind that lasts?"

"I'm sure it is." Mom wandered the short distance from the kitchen to the living room and plopped onto the couch. "It's like gold. I'm sure it's real, and people find it out there in those mines. But not many. It's a rare thing, and I know I'm not that lucky. So I'll take the cheap look-alikes when they come my way, enjoy them until they rust, and then move on."

Sage followed her and lowered onto the floor, sitting with her legs crisscrossed. Her mother's almost flippant attitude about something so precious made her want to cry. Which was weird. Why should she want to cry about something she didn't even believe in?

"What if you found it? The real thing, I mean?" Sage knew she sounded breathy and desperate. She felt breathy and desperate.

Mom sipped her drink, eyeing Sage. When she put her soda down, a soft near grin tugged at her mouth. "I'm guessing my answer to that doesn't really matter, Sage."

"What do you mean?"

"Because I would thank my lucky stars and hold on to that pure gold with both of my grubby little hands and all of my puny might. But what I would do isn't what matters here."

"Why not?"

"Because it's not really me we're talking about, is it?"

Sage leaned back on her hands, a little shocked that her mom had so much insight. They didn't open up to each other much. Her relationship with her mother was pretty much like her relationship with everyone else—basically friendly but surface level. This seemed extraordinary.

She wasn't sure how to answer or how much to open her heart. Or, truly, even if she could.

Mom leaned down from her spot on the couch and gripped Sage's hand. "My hippie girl, I know all you've seen from me is wandering around. Flitting like a homeless bird. But if you've got a treasure, keep it. If you're lucky enough to have found something as rare and precious as real love, hold on to it."

Finally looking up, Sage had to blink her mother into focus. "I didn't know you wanted that for me."

"Of course I want better for you, Sage. I love you."

It seemed a tragedy that this moment was so rare that it existed entirely set apart in her memory. A tragedy, and yet a gift. Sage sniffed and took her mom's hand. "Thanks, Mom."

A squeeze of her fingers was Mom's silent response.

"Can I ask you one more thing?"

"Since were sitting here being sappy, sure."

Sage chuckled. "It's about Great-Grandma Clara. Did she leave anything behind?"

"Getting greedy now?"

"No." Shaking her head, Sage laughed. "No, not like money. Like letters or journals. Or just anything that would tell me something about her life."

Mom's brows pulled together. "Why are you so interested in these old people?"

"Their history could determine my future."

"Well, that's silly. Only if you let it." Mom pushed to her feet and walked toward Ray's trophy room. "But if you need something to pacify your curiosity . . ." She disappeared for several minutes, leaving Sage with the sounds of the rickety closet opening, boxes shuffling, and papers rifling. Then she came back with a thin book and a small stack of envelopes. "There you are."

"What's in them?"

Mom shrugged. "Grandma Clara was a sharp, bitter woman who never had a good thing to say about anyone. Everything was always terrible, and that was always someone else's fault. If you want to know the truth, it was a relief when she died. I was never curious about her life, so I didn't read her stuff. Could be a journal. Could be a book of grocery lists or something. I have no idea."

As Sage closed her fingers around the book and envelopes, her heart rate stuttered. It felt like her future was written in these pages.

She was terrified to read what it said.

· · · · ● · ● · · · ·

Journal entry September 1979

James is gone.

The boy is just like his father. Selfish and a deserter. He refused to listen to me about the drinking. Refused to hear me about the women he chases. And the final straw—he called me a pathetic woman who deserved the life she got.

He is right about that. I could have had such a different life. Harold would have given me better. If only Henry had never written to me. I could have been happy with Harold. I would have learned to love him. I was learning so, before I found those blasted letters.

Why did Harold let me go? He could have fought for me. He could have stopped me from leaving somehow.

I wish he had tried harder. James would have had a father. A good father. Maybe he would have turned out to be a good man. Now, he is a drunk. A philanderer.

He is just like Henry.

That is my curse. Men who are just like Henry.

•• • • •• • • • ••

Sitting on a plaid blanket on the rocky shore of the Poudre River, Sage shut the journal and huffed. She had read ten other entries, all of them pretty much exactly like that last one. Clara had been, like Sage's mother had said, a bitter, sharp woman who was a perennial victim of everyone and everything.

The weather had caused her back to ache, and that was why she did not go to work, which was why the horrible boss fired her, and now she had no job again. Cursed weather.

The sun had given her a burn because it was brighter than she had expected, and she stayed out longer than she wanted because the ridiculous neighbor kept talking, and that was why she got a sunburn, and the sunburn kept her up, so she obviously need a drink or two or three, and the alcohol was clearly stronger than what was labeled, so that was why she was hungover, and that gave the next horrible boss an excuse to fire her. Cursed sun.

James had refused his dinner the night before, and so that had made him extra crabby in the morning, and so the ten-year-old boy had thrown his oatmeal all over the floor, and she had to clean that up instead of making sure he got ready for school, and so that was why he was late, and that made the horrible principal keep him after and also call a meeting with her because this had happened at least a dozen times, and her new boss was tired of her getting phone calls from school, and so that was why this horrible person fired her. Cursed oatmeal.

On and on it went. Everything was always horrible and cursed. And never her own fault.

Sage found herself thanking the stars on Harold's behalf that Clara had never gone back to him. How could one live with such a person?

How did one become such a person?

No, the more pertinent question was, how did one *not* become such a person?

Taking up a stone, she turned it round in her palm. The cool granite was smooth against her skin. Sage examined it, running her thumb over the gray that winked at her with a thousand tiny mineral sparkles. Looking around her, she compared that smooth stone to other broken pieces scattered alongside the flowing water. Some were large, some small. Some smooth, like the one in her hand. Others, freshly broken from a bigger stone, were jagged and rough.

Those freshly broken ones, they would stay jagged and rough. Unless the water picked it up and rolled it. Those sharp pieces would wear away under the current and pressure of the moving water, being knocked against other stones until finally the sharp edges smoothed.

An interesting parallel to think about. Except stones had no choice, whether they submitted to the water's course. People . . .

People got to choose how to live. What to believe. How to handle life's ups and downs.

Clara had chosen spiny bitterness. Harold had too for a time, though he did let the current of time wear away his anger.

Miss Jane had chosen to love no matter what. And Grant had promised the same.

Mother had chosen to settle for cheap imitations.

And Sage . . .

"I get to choose," she whispered to the stone in her hand. "I get to choose how I live. What I believe. Who I become."

And what would she choose?

She rolled the stone around in her palm. The chill had dissipated, the granite taking on the heat from her hand. Standing up, she walked herself to the edge of the river and picked out a rough-edged stone. Holding the two up, one in each hand, she examined them both. Then she closed her hands around both, drew back the fist enclosing the jagged one, and tossed it into the water.

"You," she said to the smooth rock still in her hand. "I choose you."

With that she gathered her great-grandmother's journal, the letter Harold had sent her not long after she'd left, declaring that she could always come home, and the other letter from Henry expressing that he was a free spirit and could not commit to a life with her, let alone with her and a child, and snatched up the blanket.

This was her life. And she'd been offered a treasure in it.

It was time to go home.

CHAPTER TWENTY-SEVEN

"YOU DIDN'T TELL ME all of it." Sage strode into Miss Jane's shop. She had waited for the last of the patrons to leave before she'd made her entrance.

Miss Jane blinked. "I told you Harold remained faithful. That is the truth. That is all of it."

"But . . ." Sage stammered through whirling thoughts. She hadn't entirely thought this visit through. Actually, she had barely thought it through at all. Coming back to Big Prairie had been an impulsive thing to do.

Wasn't everything Sage ever did impulsive?

"Grant said you'd gone." Miss Jane sighed, then she laid a compassionate hand over Sage's. "You've been to your mother's and you found Clara's things, didn't you?"

Sage nodded. "She . . . she was miserable. Every entry of her journal held the sting of bitterness. Every person, every job, every thing was named a curse. She died alone. Her grandchildren didn't like her."

"I am sorry to hear it, Sage."

"You didn't know?"

"As I told you, Clara never came back to Big Prairie. Once she left to chase after Henry, she never stepped foot back in this little town. To be honest, most forgot her."

"Most. But not you. Not Harold."

"No. Not Harold."

Sage rolled a fist while frustration balled through her. "All she had to do was come back. *He* was here, waiting for her. *He* would have taken her back, forgiven her, and given her a home. A life. And love."

Through the edges of her consciousness, she was aware of how profound it was for Sage Greene to proclaim such a thing—all she knew was how intolerably frustrating her great-grandma Clara's story was. A tale that could have been beautiful—and that maybe would have changed how Sage herself had been raised and then saw life—was instead pathetically tragic. Unnecessarily hopeless.

Grandma Clara was just a jagged rock. She had died, still a broken, sharp thing.

"Hmm . . ." The sinewy hand that had covered Sage's firmed a tighter grip around her fingers. "I think that you have found quite a parable."

"A parable?" The edges of frustration still clung to Sage's voice.

"Indeed—a story, in this case, a very sad story, that holds a larger, much more important truth within."

Pulling her hand away, Sage drew back. "I know what a parable is, Miss Jane."

"Very good."

"Are you saying my story is the same—might be the same? That Grant is Harold and I am Clara? That he will love me until he dies, even though I've broken his heart?" Sage had already considered the possibility—and it had given her physical pain. She didn't want that life—not for herself and certainly not for Grant.

Which was one of the reasons she'd come back. Miss Jane didn't need to twist that knife.

How did Miss Jane know what had happened between Grant and Sage anyway?

"No, that wasn't what I was going for. I don't know exactly what has gone between you two. Grant would be the last person on earth to tell something that is private."

Oh. Of course that was true.

"And I'm not a seer," Miss Jane continued, "so I can't tell the future—but I imagine that if Grant loves you, it is with his whole heart. But that, my dear girl, is not what I was thinking about at all. I was pointing to something on an eternal scale."

"Eternal, as in . . . God? I'm still not sure I believe in God."

Also not entirely the case. Sage had found in the last few weeks that she was becoming more and more convinced that she had mislabeled a God she did not know as *not good*.

Because Grant's God was good. Grant's God did good. Grant had said so. He'd said that God had been his refuge and his strength. If Grant could be the man he was . . . kind and steady and gentle . . . and if he could love Sage even if she refused him the one thing he wanted most—her love—and he could be these amazing things because God gave him the strength to do so, then Grant was right and Sage was wrong.

Grant's God was real, and the one Sage claimed not to like was fiction.

Miss Jane laughed. She laughed! "He doesn't need you to believe in Him to make Him real."

A statement that seemed awfully familiar.

Feeling handily put into her place, Sage had nothing to say to that, and she turned away, ready to retreat.

Why was she in such a huff about this? None of Grandma Clara's story was this woman's fault. And it wasn't Miss Jane's fault that Sage had run when she should have stayed and she'd broken a good man's heart and now she had to figure out how to face him.

That was the rub. She couldn't figure out how to face Grant. She desperately needed to. And it wasn't like she believed he'd tell her she'd had her chance and be gone. Even if she deserved it.

Except for, what if he did?

"May I point out to you that you have declared in the past that you didn't believe in love—the kind that lasts?" Gentle as ever, Miss Jane nailed her again.

Oh! Another dead-center blow to the heart!

What if, after everything, she found out that she had been right all along, though now she desperately wanted to be wrong? What if the end of this only proved to her that lasting, romantic love was not real? That she had been duped?

That might crush her soul.

Sage remained pinned in her place. "Perhaps I meant the happily-ever-after kind. The kind that never faces anything bad, after the one black moment in the story. Everything beyond is rosy and lovely. Perhaps I meant that."

"No, I don't think that's what you meant. You meant the kind of love that remains faithful come what may. That loves when it's hard. When it hurts. When it is undeserved. You didn't believe that was possible. Isn't that true?"

It had been true. Such a devotion, Sage had firmly concluded, was beyond the human heart.

"But now?" Miss Jane pushed.

Now there was Great-Grandfather Harold, who remained faithful to vows he'd made to a woman who had never treasured his heart, never appreciated what he'd offered, and had died a miserable, lonely person rather than running to his love.

His enduring love.

Who loved like that for their whole life?

Gramps had, that was who.

And Grant . . . Grant would.

"Love is real, Sage. It's not just something wild and imaginative we invented to sell books. There really is love like that, and it has an ultimate source."

"Why would you conclude that?"

"Because something that profound, that beyond our natural scope, cannot possibly come from nothing."

It was like the final piece of the puzzle that had been Sage's heart fell into place. She could no longer deny there was a God, and she could no longer claim that He was bad at His job. And now this.

In her mind, she saw it again. Her, sitting next to Grant Hillman in church, reading the open Bible spread on his knee. But this time, the most significant thing about that image was not her hand held securely in his.

It was the words that she read.

Love is of God.

She believed them.

CHAPTER TWENTY-EIGHT

BROWN CRUNCHY LEAVES LITTERED the river's shoreline, and the trees that gathered on its banks reached with yellowing leafed branches toward the sunny sky. A soft morning breeze stirred the tall grasses, setting their full seed heads into a dance that moved alongside the narrow path beside the water.

Anxiety pulled in her gut like a cord being knotted. *God, help me to be courageous.*

This praying thing was still new, so she hoped the quick-sent message wasn't offensive to the Redeemer who had called her His own. Miss Jane would say He was always listening, always ready to hear her heart.

So very much like Grant.

It had been quite a week. One where she had spent evenings with Miss Jane, peppering her with questions about God while they opened up Miss Jane's Bible and Sage discovered such treasures within. Gems like, *God so loved the world, that he sent His one and only Son so that whoever would believe would not perish, but have eternal life.* And *God demonstrates His own love in this: while we were yet sinners Christ died for us.*

And the one Sage had glimpsed that Sunday in Grant's Bible: *Beloved, let us love one another. For love is of God.*

Miss Jane had been careful to help Sage understand that wasn't necessarily talking about romantic love but the willingness to love beyond emotion. It was instructing followers of Jesus to practice love, which meant forgiving, being gracious, encouraging one another, and offering kindness even when it is not deserved.

"But God also makes romantic love possible? The kind that endures and is faithful?" Sage had asked.

"I believe so," Miss Jane said. "Since He is the first author of romance. All good things come from Him." She then proceeded to show her a verse in James that said exactly that.

Good things . . . Good men. Like Grant Hillman. A gift from God. *Meant for me?* Sage couldn't help but hope so.

As she thought on that man, the last time they'd been face to face pressed into her mind. Those intense brown eyes focused on her, the heartache of her rejection sheening them . . . The squeeze of her heart took her breath away.

With a long, controlled exhale, Sage attempted to dispel the fear and ache that came with the memory of that poignant moment.

She had loved him then—and she'd known it. And he had too.

With shaky fingers, she tucked her red curls behind her ear and turned to look down the path.

Would he come this way that day? Grant was a man of routines, not likely to change them on a whim. Having Sage reject his offered heart, walking away from his steady love, certainly was not a whim.

If he didn't come that way that morning, she would have to dig deep for the bravery to go to his house. Sage wasn't sure she had that sort of fortitude. There, by the river near the ramshackle house left to her by Gramps, she felt a little bit of strength at least. It had been the place of their beginning—surely Grant wouldn't forget that.

How could he? She had been at her most ridiculous that day, and he'd been utterly baffled by her. It had been adorable.

Maybe in this setting he would let that memory override the last one they shared. The one where she'd ruined everything—tossed away the best gift of her life because she was so tied up by fear. The one where he had told her that running wasn't freedom, and she'd done it anyway.

Oh, she desperately hoped he'd think on the beginning of their story rather than the end.

A gathering of grackles left their perches in the branches upriver, their sudden departure a noisy business of fluttering and squawking. As they became a peppering of black in the sky, a steady rhythm of muted footfalls touched Sage's hearing.

Her pulse skittered and raced. Rolling her fingers into tight fists, she squeezed her eyes shut and listened as the soft pounding on the trail drew nearer. With a sharp inhale and a hope that the fresh late-summer air would somehow bolster her heart, Sage stood up from the log she'd been waiting on, straightened her cream-colored knitted hat, and turned to watch the bend of the trail.

And there he was. Dressed in his black joggers and a white running shirt, Grant ran around the elbow of the path, entering her view. It took a moment for him to spot her, but the second he did, his run came to an abrupt halt.

Standing as if frozen, Grant's breath came and went with rapid puffs as he stared wide-eyed. Sage was certain that though he'd been the one running, her heart rate exceeded his by double. Suddenly, she didn't know what to do or say.

Hadn't she thought this through? She was going to tell him all the things she'd kept from him, let him have full exposure to her heart. That she loved him but she was scared. That she wanted to know his God—and actually, He was now hers too, but she was new at this and felt like a small child toppling around as she went.

And she hoped that it wasn't too late . . .

But she hadn't really banked on his silent, standoffish stare. For some reason she had imagined he would still hold her with that tender look of understanding, even after she'd broken his heart. Perhaps because he had promised it would be so.

Sage wasn't sure what to do with this chilled distance he held on her instead.

She licked her lips and found that smile she always had ready. "I thought about jumping from the bank, just to see how far you would go to be a hero, but I wasn't sure you would run by here today." Her default of seeking his bemusement kicked in, and she wandered into the distance that separated them and then stopped an arm's length away.

Rather than giving her that baffled-but-intrigued look she'd found so endearing, Grant pressed his lips into a firm line as his look hardened.

No masks. Not with me. His words had been gentle and inviting that evening. But as she heard them echo in her memory in that moment, they sounded frustrated.

Grant rubbed at his brow—likely to catch the sweat glistening there before it could run into his eyes—and looked toward the ground. "You know I would come in after you, if you needed it. But I would rather not be a game to you." With a quick glance at her—one that was sharp and loaded—Grant stepped back and then turned away.

"Grant." Sage moved forward, quickly covering the trail between them.

He stopped his retreat but didn't turn to look at her. In the pause, his head bowed again, and his shoulders sagged. "Are we to be friends, Sage? I need to know where I stand."

Oh how she had broken this gentle, kind man. The truth of it knifed her heart all over again. Why? Why had she done such a thing?

"I was scared," she whispered.

His chin came around as he looked over his shoulder.

Sage filled her lungs with shuddered breath. "I lived my whole life believing that love was a myth. That it couldn't be real and that whatever people thought it was couldn't last. I was certain that the aftermath would be destructive. It was all I've ever witnessed."

Grant turned to face her again, his silent gaze steady and unreadable. But just as he'd promised weeks before, he was listening.

"I didn't know what faithfulness looked like or even that it could be real."

His penetrating look shifted from her face toward the old farmhouse up on the opposite bank and then came back again. Slowly he shook his head. "That is not true."

Heat stung her eyes, and she bit her bottom lip. After a long, agonizing silence, she nodded. "You're right." She glanced back to the place where Gramps had lived out his years, remaining faithful to a woman who had so brazenly and stupidly rejected his love.

All she had to do was come back. He would have taken her in, given her a home and a future. And his love.

Emotion quivered through her entire body. Sage fought to control it. "I don't want to be Clara, Grant. And I certainly don't want you to be Harold."

"I do not want that story for you either, Sage." Warm tenderness filtered through his voice, though he still remained out of her reach. "But that does not mean that I want you to settle."

She shook her head. "That was never the issue—never what I thought. You are the most extraordinary person I've ever known. And your heart was the safest place I've ever been. I . . . I want that back."

The struggle between hurt and longing played in Grant's expression.

"Grant, I love you." Sage edged nearer still, until the warmth of his breath mingled with hers and she could finally touch him. It was a tentative touch, her fingertips against the place where his heart hammered.

His eyes slipped shut, and his Adam's apple bobbed in a visible swallow. She dared closer still. "I want you to be my home."

In one sweeping motion, he had her against his chest, his embrace powerful and yet somehow gentle. "Tell me again," he whispered in her ear.

"I love you, Grant Hillman." She leaned back to gaze into his wonderful brown eyes. She smiled a teasing grin, though it made him frown. "After all, I have found that you are not a villain."

For a beat, he stared at her, befuddled. Then his attention wandered toward the river, and a laugh cracked through that serious frown. "I had hoped to be your hero." His chest moved with laughter as his lips found hers.

She pushed her fingers into his hair. "And so you are—though I wasn't even looking for a hero. But you are my favorite one." She kissed him again. "My forever one."

EPILOGUE

SAGE SAT AT HIS side, her finger tracing the words in the Bible spread upon his leg. By her intense profile, she was inhaling the text, and watching her expression shot wonder through his veins.

God, You have done it!

He had given Grant everything. It wasn't enough that He sustained Grant's life, extended salvation to his soul, and provided for his daily needs. No, not enough for his generous God, because here sat this woman—the one who had captivated Grant's heart and mind from the very moment they'd met—leaning into him. Reading his Bible. Seeking and loving his God.

Grant thought back several months to the day he'd been running beside the river, agonizing over the wedding he had not wanted to attend and asking God if He still saw him.

Yes. God saw. He saw, and it mattered, and He had a plan. And it was good.

Now to Him who is able to do more than we can ask or imagine . . .

Grant inhaled a sustaining breath as the verse of praise scrolled through his heart.

. . . to Him be all glory and praise!

Sage sat back, finished with her reading, and shot Grant that joyful grin he so loved. "Ready?"

"If you are." He closed the book on his thigh, tucked it into the crook of his right arm, and took her hand with his left. "What shall we do for lunch?"

"I have a picnic planned."

Ah, a picnic. Just like the beginning. That would be perfect . . . "In a field? The wheat is harvested and the corn is tall, but—"

"Not a field. Not in your cousin's truck. Beside the river."

Another good option. Grant nodded.

"I have it all planned, so stop working it out in your head."

He looked down at her and tried to scowl. "What do you think I'm working out in my head?"

"Who knows? The perfect food. What to drink. The exact spot to sit that would give the premium amount of sun and shade?"

His brows knit. Never mind that she was not far from the truth. "I must be quite a cumbersome man for you."

"No." Her eyes sparkled with delight. "You are so much fun to tease, though."

"Ah. Yes. I do know that is your favorite thing to do with me."

"One of them." She winked and then bounced up to her toes to peck his cheek. "Not my *most* favorite though."

Heat flared up the back of his neck. Sage Greene never, ever tired of making him blush. He couldn't say that he tired of her doing so either though.

They reached his Altima, and after she was seated in the passenger side, he shut her door and walked around to the driver's side. In short order they pulled away from the church. The drive to the farmhouse was quiet, but comfortably so. Once they hit the dirt road, Sage slipped her hand into his.

"You were right. Did I tell you that?"

"Hmm . . . probably. But it never hurts to say it again. What was I right about?"

"I didn't know God."

His heart lifted, and he felt joy fill him clear up to his hairline. Grant couldn't think of words, so he simply lifted her hand and pressed a kiss to her knuckles.

They reached the farmhouse, and he parked in his usual spot. Out front, five strides to the front steps—the pair of which he'd had replaced the very day Sage had announced she was moving into Gramps's place for good. The new wood planks stuck out boldly next to the weather-beaten and timeworn planks of the front porch.

Grant took in the rest of the house. There was a lot of work to do. Then he turned his gaze back to Sage.

First things first.

"Wait here. I'll be right back." She didn't wait for him to respond but disappeared into the house, her light-green skirt billowing at her legs and her red curls bouncing against her shoulders.

Grant wondered why he was waiting rather than helping. But she was gone only long enough for him to open the screen door and step inside the house. She strode toward him with a blanket draped over her arm and a basket clasped in both hands.

"I told you to wait." She tried to frown. Her gleaming eyes didn't allow the facade.

"Let me help." Grant took the basket from her and held the door open until she passed through.

Sage led the way around back. At a glance, Grant could see the red of the ripening tomatoes waiting for her attention. Likely, they'd do some that afternoon. Sage had found a recipe for a taco soup that she liked, and she had busied herself canning the base for it with her garden produce. He had enjoyed helping her in the evenings. It felt blissfully domestic—like the beginning of the forever he longed for.

Following her lead, they picked their way down the steep trail that led from the overlook to the river below. Once at the narrow shore, Sage stopped to kick off her shoes and gather her long skirt in one hand.

"You did not prepare me for this." Grant lifted a brow.

"Take your shoes and socks off and roll up your khakis."

He looked at her with what he thought would be disapproval. "I made a bridge."

"It's not very stable. The mud will dry." She took the basket from his hands. "I promise you'll live."

"What's on the other side that will make wet, muddy toes worth it for me?"

Sage sauntered into the water, keeping to the shallows that rimmed her swimming hole. Two feet into the river, she looked over her shoulder, her expression a sly challenge. "Come find out, why don't you?"

The little red-haired vixen. Only she could do this—summon him into a chilly river with his nice clothes on, willing to follow her whimsical heart, though it meant abandoning his stiff ways. Sage, and Sage alone, drew him out this way.

Heart tripping over itself, Grant could not discipline the grin that slipped onto his mouth. He did as bid—careful to untie his shoes, place his socks neatly within each one, and fold his pant legs up so that they matched precisely. Sage uttered no complaint at the time it took as she waited in the middle of the river. She had released her skirts, and the hem swirled around her knees at the command of the gentle-flowing water.

She was his opposite. But not in all things. Much to his delight, they had discovered they wanted the same things. Joy. Stability. Home.

Love.

And they had those things. Together.

Grant reached into his pocket, wrapping his fingers around the thing that must not be lost. Satisfied all was well, he withdrew his hand and followed Sage into the water. And then out onto the opposite bank and to a fallen tree. She set down her basket and spread out the blanket.

It was a good picnic. She had made a favorite of his—pecan chicken salad on multigrain bread. And raspberry lemonade.

He did love raspberry lemonade. It tasted divine on her lips. He would have been content to indulge in that sweet treat all afternoon, but she pulled away after a time.

Her attention drifted across the river and up the rise and landed on the farmhouse. "It needs work."

Following her gaze, Grant looked at the old place. "The house?"

"Yes. A lot of it. But I have ideas." Her chin moved, and then her eyes were back on him. "We can do it. Although, Miss Jane gave me the name of a woman—Sarah Sharpe Chapman. She owns a company called Restorations by the Carpenter's Daughter. She and her husband work together. I think we could afford to hire out, and I'd like to see what she would do if—"

Grant didn't hear much past *We can do it* in all of that. The heart in his chest pounded, and his breath caught. "We?" He squeezed the word out around the bulge in his throat.

Sage stopped babbling, her smile growing wide as she reached to frame his face. "Ah, so you did catch that part."

He blinked.

"You would be willing to sell your house, wouldn't you?"

His mouth fell open. "Are you—"

"But only after we're married. Which, my sweet overplanning-type man, will need to be sooner rather than later. Maybe right here beside the river. Under a canopy of fall leaves, and just our closest friends. Anne and Clayton and Miss Jane . . . It would be lovely, don't you think?"

"Sage." Grant could not make his heart stop galloping, and he could not stop gaping at her.

Once again Sage stopped her stream of words. But her smile faded, and her fingers skimmed down his jawline until they fell away. "Usually I delight in befuddling you, Grant, but I have to say this is not the reaction I hoped for."

"Are you . . . proposing to me?"

She bit her bottom lip, and her eyes grew wary. Then she nodded. "I thought you would be happy. Or . . . not horrified."

A sudden burst of laughter relieved the tension in his chest.

Sage scowled. "Why is that funny?"

"I am supposed to propose to you."

"That's not a real rule."

"But look." He leaned to the side and dug the small box from his pocket. After opening the velvet black top, he held it out to her. "I was going to. Today."

The furrow of her brow smoothed, and delight replaced the put-out expression of her eyes. "You were?"

"Yes."

She laughed. "I beat you to it."

"I have the ring."

"Huh." Her smirk was adorably kissable. "You still haven't asked. Or answered, come to think of it."

Grant leaned forward, nipping that almost pouty bottom lip. "I will if you will."

"Marry me?"

"If you'll marry me."

"I think that's how it works," she whispered.

"Then that's a yes?"

Her smile was pure delight, and the way her eyes danced . . . *better than lemonade on her lips.* Maybe.

"Yes." She laughed.

With both arms, Grant hauled her in close.

It was a tie. The lemonade on her lips. And the way she looked at him with love lighting her gaze. A beautiful, wonderful tie.

And the best part? He would get to enjoy both for the rest of his life.

THE END

We meet again at the end of another story. I'm not sure I'm ready to say goodbye to Big Prairie and the wonderful friends I've made there! I hope that you have enjoyed the small town and the people that make it special. Would you do me the honor of leaving a review? I would be so grateful.

Some of you may have recognized the name of the woman who Miss Jane recommended for the farm house restoration. Sarah Sharpe was and remains a dear character to me, and her story is special. If you haven't read it, let me recommend you meet her and Jesse Chapman in The Carpenter's Daughter.

Thank you for giving me your time and trusting me with your imagination. I consider it a great honor!

Until we meet in the next story,

Jen